My name is John Charles Poe, and I am the descendant (via the bar sinister) of the immortal Edgar Allan Poe. Family lore has it that at the age of eighteen, while he was in the army, Edgar Allan fell passionately in love with a woman named Laura Crowley when he was stationed near her home. Laura gave birth to his illegitimate son, Montgomery Crowley, who founded this town of Crowley Creek and was also my ancestor. The details are all in the casket documents, which each of us Poes must read in our turn. Great-grandfather changed his name from Alexander Crowley to Alexander Poe when he inherited the casket and read, among other things, the heartrending tale of my ancestress Laura. My father told me the story, but I don't think I understood its significance for our family until I inherited the casket.

# RETURN TO THE
# HOUSE OF USHER

## ROBERT POE

**TOR®**

A TOM DOHERTY ASSOCIATES BOOK
NEW YORK

This is a work of fiction. All the characters and events portrayed in this book are either products of the author's imagination or are used fictitiously.

RETURN TO THE HOUSE OF USHER

A Tor Book
Published by Tom Doherty Associates, Inc.
175 Fifth Avenue
New York, NY 10010

Tor Books on the World Wide Web:
http://www.tor.com

Tor® is a registered trademark of Tom Doherty Associates, Inc.

ISBN: 0-812-54931-7
Library of Congress Card Catalog Number: 96-18270

First edition: October 1996
First mass market edition: October 1997

Printed in the United States of America

0  9  8  7  6  5  4  3  2  1

This work is dedicated to all the women who made it possible:

To Ms. Arpke and Ms. Aycock,
who never believed in me;
To Diane and Veronica,
who always believed in me; and
To Susan Crawford and Ellen Godfrey,
who believed in themselves.

# ACKNOWLEDGMENTS

I would like to acknowledge those who supported and encouraged me throughout the creation of this book: Natalia Aponte and all the folks at Tor Books, Petty Officers George Krisanda and Matt Dunlap and the crew of USS *Kauffman*, Marty and Collette Lawson, and especially Jeff Freundlich, Hillary and Lorian Hemingway, and all the people at the Hemingway Days Literary Convention and Writers' Workshop, 1993, in Key West, Florida.

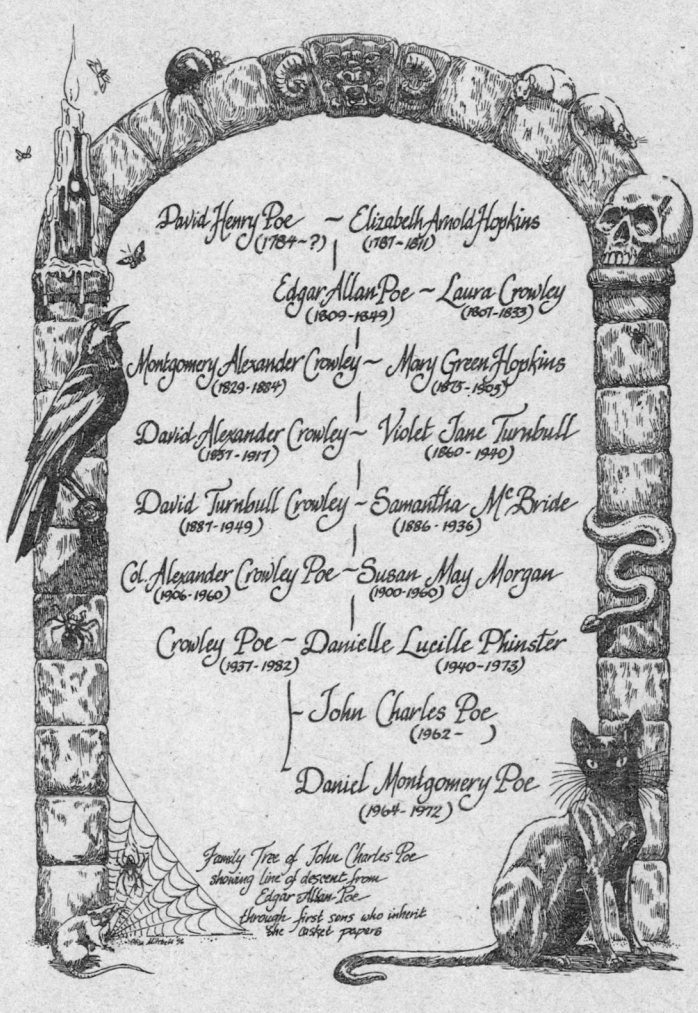

David Henry Poe ─ Elizabeth Arnold Hopkins
(1784-?)                    (1787-1811)

Edgar Allan Poe ─ Laura Crowley
(1809-1849)           (1807-1833)

Montgomery Alexander Crowley ─ Mary Green Hopkins
(1829-1884)                              (1815-1905)

David Alexander Crowley ─ Violet Jane Turnbull
(1857-1917)                       (1860-1940)

David Turnbull Crowley ─ Samantha McBride
(1887-1949)                       (1886-1936)

Col. Alexander Crowley Poe ─ Susan May Morgan
(1906-1960)                           (1900-1960)

Crowley Poe ─ Danielle Lucille Phinster
(1937-1982)              (1940-1973)

John Charles Poe
(1962-    )

Daniel Montgomery Poe
(1964-1972)

Family Tree of John Charles Poe
showing line of descent from
Edgar Allan Poe
through first sons who inherit
the casket papers

# RETURN TO THE
# HOUSE OF USHER

# ONE

The old house is too full of the past. My father is everywhere in it, particularly in the library where I now sit, drinking whiskey and listening to the November wind. Maybe if I changed things in this room I could put his ghost to rest, but somehow I haven't done so. Just one more thing I should do. That habit of not doing what I am supposed to, even when I know better, used to trigger one of my father's favorite reproaches: "It's not that you don't know what is right, John, it is that you don't have the strength of character to do it."

He may have had a point, but now, after a few glasses of Blanton's single barrel bourbon, the idea occurs to me that my father was no better. In fact, he was guilty of just what he blamed me for. He, too, left this library as he found it when he inherited Crowley House from *his* father, though I know it depressed him as it does me. The rows of books with their leather bindings, blotched here and there with mold—probably no one has read them for seventy, eighty, a hundred years, if ever. Luckily, it's so dim in here, you can barely see the books or the faded tapestries. The house needs rewiring. As I drink and reflect, the lights flicker with every gust of wind.

It must have been just the same when father sat here, worrying, not knowing what to do, getting himself slowly drunk trying to understand the peculiar choices he had made. I imagine they had their reasons for their destructive relationship with the old demon rum: my father, Crowley Poe, and my grandfather, Alexander Crowley Poe.

One thing I know now; a lot of the explanations for the morose temperament of the Poe men can be found in that damned casket.

I wish I had never seen the cursed thing.

It was not long after I made what I now think might have been a serious error—reading the documents in the casket— that I got the call from my old friend, Roderick Usher. The call that was the beginning of the painful and mysterious events I now so desperately want to understand.


My name is John Charles Poe, and I am the descendant (via the bar sinister) of the immortal Edgar Allan Poe. Family lore has it that at the age of eighteen, while he was in the army, Edgar Allan fell passionately in love with a woman named Laura Crowley when he was stationed near her home. Laura gave birth to his illegitimate son, Montgomery Crowley, who founded this town of Crowley Creek and was also my ancestor. The details are all in the casket documents, which each of us Poes must read in our turn. Great-grandfather changed his name from Alexander Crowley to Alexander Poe when he inherited the casket and read, among other things, the heartrending tale of my ancestress Laura. My father told me the story, but I don't think I understood its significance for our family until I inherited the casket.

No man in the family has read those papers without being changed. I know I should detach myself from the sense of corruption that emanates from those secret papers, and simply say that the documents in the casket shed a new light on some of Edgar Allan Poe's stories. But the truth is, the casket documents gave me a feeling of lingering horror. It is a feeling that seems to have haunted all of the Poe men. Each of us thinks we will break free of it, but so far no one has destroyed the casket papers or changed the library—so I think we are all trapped in some way by the past that the papers reveal.

Maybe father was right: weakness runs in our family. After all, old Edgar was not exactly an example of upright living.

But I am getting off track. On my thirtieth birthday, in this town of Crowley Creek (population 15,000), south of Richmond, Virginia, I was, in my turn, given the casket by that pain-in-the-ass lawyer Ambrose Prynne and then, within a week, by some eerie coincidence, received that fateful call from my old college friend Roderick Usher.

And, despite how it sounds when I talk about the casket papers, the truth is that I am a rational modern man, with a degree in English Literature from the University of Virginia. I live in this town of Crowley Creek, where I grew up, trying to make a success of my job as roving town reporter for the *Crowley Sentinel* (proprietor: Mrs. Fanny Boynton). I don't believe that the dead haunt the living (despite much evidence to the contrary in the story I am about to tell) or that the mysterious death of Madeleine Usher has any explanation except a natural one. Yet there remain, to this day, dark nights when unanswered questions trouble me deeply, and only good whiskey helps see me through until dawn.

It all began when I received that unsettling phone call from Roderick Usher. The phone rang just as I opened the refrigerator in the kitchen to see if I could sneak out some of the cornbread Mrs. Slack had saved to stuff the turkey for dinner. It had gone nicely stale and I considered eating it with some of her blackberry jam. Rod's call interrupted my meditations on this serious culinary subject.

"John? Is that you? It's Rod, Roderick Usher?"

His voice had the gentle, tremulous sound I remembered from our school days, when we had roomed together at the University of Virginia. Whenever he got that note in his voice, I understood that he was suffering. I knew that Roderick had a kind of sensitivity that would have been appropriate in an artist or a musician—in both of which fields he had extraordinary talent. But his temperament did not suit a man whose family had decided he would pursue a medical career. No doubt about it, despite my father's frequent snide comments to the contrary, I managed to be a model of sanity compared with Rod. Still, I understood him in a way no one else did, so it is not surprising that I was his only friend.

But the truth was that Rod did not feel much need for friends. He was a solitary person and his sister, Madeleine, with whom he had a deep bond, seemed to supply whatever he lacked. Once he graduated, got his medical degree, and set up the Usher House Sanatorium, with Madeleine as chief psychiatrist and neurologist, we drifted apart. Even though Usher House was only seven miles outside Crowley Creek, until that afternoon, I had not heard from Rod in five years.

"Rod Usher!" I said, surprised and pleased. "Hey, it's great to hear your voice. It's been way too long. How y'all doin' out there? How is Madeleine? How's business?"

"John, I need to see you."

Now I realized that his voice sounded peculiar—even for him. Febrile, nervous, frightened perhaps? I couldn't quite put my finger on it. "Great idea," I said. "How about tomorrow? I can't today, I'm working on a hot story for the old witch Boynton—whether Shelton's coffee shop is endangered by the town's teenage peril— and as usual, my job hangs by a thread so I don't want to blow it."

"No, John. I need to see you now, today."

From anyone else, I might have resented that commanding, insistent tone, but Rod Usher had the right to talk to me however he wanted. I will never forget how Rod stood by me when I completely fell to pieces after my father's death. Although not the first time I had tried to find my way out of life's problems in the bottle, it was by far the worst. Maybe I wanted to prove Dad's low opinion of me true, but right then nothing seemed to matter except that downward spiral toward oblivion. Rod Usher cleaned up after me, dragged me out of the bars, sat by me and talked me through. Rod put up with more abuse, more disappointment, more irresponsible behavior than anyone needs to do in this life. I let him down over and over and yet he was always there for me. He never judged me, he never told me what to do, he just stood by, doing what he could. In the end, his friendship led to me realize there was a certain goodness in life that made it worth enduring the pain. And when I was ready to climb back into the land of the living, he acted as if he had done nothing, then used all his family's pull to see that the university gave me a second chance.

"Hey, Rod—of course I'll come," I said. "But can't it wait until tomorrow morning? Otherwise, you'll have to promise to protect me if Ma Boynton comes after me with a tire iron."

He laughed.

I didn't like the sound of that laugh. It had an hysterical edge to it. I closed the refrigerator on the cornbread and looked out the window. A dreary November day. Sodden brown oak leaves blew across the lawn and piled up under the shadowy trunks of the trees in moldering, somber heaps.

"John," he said. "Please believe me. I'm in real trouble and there's no one else I can turn to."

"What about Madeleine?" I said. "Can't she help?" The wind was fierce. I didn't relish the thought of driving out to the House of Usher in this weather. But that wasn't why I was stalling. The problem was Boynton. She would blow a gasket if I left the office for the afternoon. She held to the opinion that I was an irresponsible dilettante and she seemed to latch onto the flimsiest evidence as proof positive. She knew I had an interview at Shelton's at three and would believe her worst suspicions of me confirmed if I didn't keep it. There were reasons I needed to keep my job, and they were important to me.

"Madeleine is part of what I want to talk to you about." His words seemed to fade away for a moment. I heard some kind of noise on the line, like whispering voices, and I could just barely hear him under the rushing sound. I pressed the receiver harder against my ear.

"John. Please. You're the only one I can turn to."

So of course I said I'd leave for Usher House right away, even though I had one of those flashes of intuition that experience has taught me never to disregard. This one told me that going out to visit Rod at Usher House could lead to something very dark, something that I did not want to know.

The clouds hung oppressively low and the failing afternoon seemed to be closing in on Usher House as I drove up. Perhaps it was the weather, perhaps the memory of my ancestor's story, "The Fall of the House of Usher," but I don't think so; I think even the most insensitive person would have felt the peculiar, gloomy atmosphere of the place.

How dreary it seemed, a great barracks of a house rebuilt on the property just where the original mansion had stood. I could see that same tarn, or pond, that E.A. described in his story, a black sheet of water that reflected the stone walls of of the nineteenth-century house and glistened with a peculiar silvery sheen. The pond must be polluted, I thought, as I slammed the car door and walked along the water's edge toward the house. A mist of glimmering phosphorescence rose from the water. It filled the damp autumn air with a smell like the stench of something very old rotting beneath the surface. And on that surface I could see the faint inverted image of Usher House, shimmering, distorted.

The house itself, built of huge, irregular chunks of limestone, seemed to be covered with a gray-green lichen or moss that gave it a peculiar furry look I found disturbing. The small windows looked down on me like dull opaque eyes as I walked up the gravel drive from the visitor parking.

I had last been there on the occasion of its opening, five years before, on Independence Day. It had looked nothing like this, I was sure. I remembered smooth green lawns gleaming in the afternoon sunlight; red, blue, and opalescent white balloons bobbing in the warm breeze; lovely women in summer dresses and big straw hats and gentlemen in white linen suits. Madeleine and Rod Usher had been splendid hosts and our doughty mayor, Jackson Lee Winsome, had cut the ribbon on "our newest and proudest institution," welcoming the opening of the Sanatorium and praising the Ushers for their business contribution to Crowley Creek. I had thought Madeleine particularly beautiful as she gracefully accepted the mayor's platitudes. Her smooth blond hair drawn back in a chignon under a large-brimmed midnight-blue hat with a deep purple flower on it, shadowed those strange dark-brown eyes of hers, eyes that looked as if she knew your deepest, darkest secrets but would be too kind to ever reproach you with them.

The rumor in town was that, after an excellent start, the Sanatorium was struggling. The rich patients paid their way, and the place was always full, but the Ushers took on too many charity cases, which burdened the institution. The town honored them for it. As long as anyone could remember, the Ushers had been one of the most philanthropic families in the county, if not in the state. And after all, should things get tough, Madeleine and Rod could always dig into their pockets to tide the place over—or so they said around town.

But it didn't look as if they had done much digging recently. The institution had an air of decrepitude. The tall, heavy oak doors needed a coat of varnish, and the brass studs that pierced it in a pattern depicting the family crest were tarnished with verdigris. A tired-looking old black man sat behind the reception desk as I entered. The reception area was dim. Only a little light came in through the small windows, shaded by heavy, almost opaque gray silk curtains streaked with fine crimson lines. The deep red leather chairs were stained and the magazines appeared to have been gathering dust since the last war.

I gave my name, and the old fellow nodded and gestured that I should follow him. He pushed a button on a console at his desk. A large door concealed in the blackened paneling of the wall behind the reception desk opened, revealing a dark corridor.

Like my own house, the lighting at Usher House seemed to have been added in the twenties and poorly updated. What appeared to be old gas jets, now electrified and placed at intervals high on the walls, cast a feeble light on this corridor, which looked to be a servants' interior passageway.

We have these serving passages at Crowley House too, so I ought to be used to them, but this one felt damp and oppressive and took so many curves and twists that I soon became completely disoriented and realized I could never have found my way without my guide. Here and there I saw other, narrower passages, flights of stairs, and shadowy alcoves. Everywhere I looked I saw worrying signs of deterioration and structural weakness.

After walking for what seemed a very long time, we approached a large door, which my guide opened.

The room I entered had probably been designed as the original grand salon of Usher House. Large and chilling, its high ceilings seemed almost invisible in the dimness. Small windows just below the ornate plaster cornice allowed in only a few rays of daylight. A single lamp cast a feeble gleam, leaving the rest of the room in shadow. It looked like the last place one would spend a blustery November afternoon. Here and there in the gloom I could make out piles of books, various stringed instruments, and musical scores. Everything seemed disorderly and neglected.

As I entered, Rod got up from a sofa on which he had been lying, came rapidly and silently toward me, and embraced me—something he had never done before. He held me for a moment and then drew back so I could see his face.

I was shocked. He seemed to have aged a lifetime since I saw him last, perfectly groomed and smiling in his white linen suit at the opening ceremonies of Usher House. Roderick had always been a strikingly handsome man. A high forehead, thin, sensual lips, and fine blonde hair that fell in a lock over his eyes meant that, where women were concerned, Roderick could take his pick. He had been so withdrawn, however, that I could not remember his ever taking advantage of his opportunities.

But now I could barely recognize him. He had let his hair grow; fine and silky and streaked with gray, it fluttered unkempt and wild around his face. He looked very pale, his expression extraordinarily inconstant. He had smiled at me when I entered the room, but then the smile quivered and vanished, his face growing almost vacant, his eyes glazing over. All this I took in at first glance, because as soon as he saw me he began to talk in that same high, nervous voice that had so affected me when I heard it on the telephone.

"Thank God, John, thank God you've come. You are the only one who could possibly understand. Come in, sit down, you look chilled. Let me get you something hot to drink. You'd rather have a whiskey? Of course." He poured one from a crystal decanter on a side table. "Forgive me if I don't join you. I don't dare touch it anymore."

I accepted gratefully.

He pointed to the sofa where he had been lying, and I sat down. The stiff velvet was worn and seemed to hold a chill, which penetrated my bones. The whiskey, as it went down, tasted most welcome. "Frankly, old buddy," I said as he sat, or rather collapsed, at the other end of the sofa, "I hope you don't mind my telling you that you don't look well. In fact, you look like hell."

He smiled, but only for an instant, his lips so tense the smile looked more like a rictus. "It's so good to see you, John Charles. You are just what I need." He leaned forward toward me, staring at me. "You are just what I need to save me . . . save me . . ." his voice tailed off and he fell back into the corner of the sofa.

I took a big swallow of the whiskey. Roderick had only the best; some had been in the family cellars for generations. This had to be one of the older bottles. "Save you from what?"

"I am sick, old friend, sick in the mind."

"Sick? What's the matter? What does your doctor say?"

He gestured dismissively. "Have you read the old story by Edgar Allan Poe, 'Fall of the House of Usher'?"

"Of course." When I knew Roderick, I had not yet had the ill fortune to have read the casket papers, to know dark things about the past of both his family and mine. But whatever the past's secrets, I thought, surely they could have no relevance for poor Roderick's current troubles.

"Do you know that there is much truth in that story? That an ancestress of mine did die and they buried her in a basement crypt in a house on this property, as is told in that story, and that the brother of that ancestress went mad shortly after and that during the great earth tremor of 1839 the mansion that stood on this property cracked and fell into ruins?"

"So I've heard," I said, letting my scepticism show in my voice.

"It's true, John Charles. We should never have built another house on the same cursed foundations! Never! All the horrors stem from that!"

"Wait a minute there, Rod. What horrors? What is it that's got you so upset?"

He stood and began to walk back and forth, his face shifting, as if several men inhabited his skin. An eerie sight.

"My namesake, Roderick Usher, who lived in the first half of the eighteen hundreds . . . he had it . . . his father had it . . ."

"Had what?"

"Madeleine has been researching it, but . . ."

I felt frustrated. "Researching what? What are you talking about?"

"That's why he went mad, you know. In the old story, 'The Fall of the House of Usher,' my ancestor said it himself. He knew that the house had given him some kind of a disease and that the disease caused hallucinations. *He* thought it might be the tarn or the moss . . . I've wondered if there isn't something hereditary . . . but it's horrible . . . I feel it coming on, taking my life, my sanity . . . it's getting harder and harder to resist." He sat down, ran his hands through his hair as if to neaten it, then straightened his spine, like a soldier coming to attention. "I must not give in to it. . . ." Then he wilted, slumping back against the cushions. "But John, it's getting so I don't know what's real and what I'm imagining. I'm afraid . . ."

"What are you afraid of, Rod?"

He shook his head. "You'd never believe me. You'd think I was mad."

"Don't worry about that," I said, "Of course you're crazy. Only a crazy person would have put up with me when I went around the bend when we were at school together."

For the first time he smiled a real smile. "Thank you, John Charles," he said softly.

"After all," I said, taking another deep swallow of his excellent whiskey, "isn't craziness what we have in common? That's probably why you asked me over—I'm the craziest person you know. You can tell me whatever you have on your mind. It will be okay with me."

He smiled again at my joking tone when I spoke of our mutual madness, and I knew that he understood what I really meant. There was a deep link between us, after all. We both sensed things that others did not; we lived with these feelings. Whiskey helped me, but what did Roderick, so controlled as he was, do for relief? For a moment I saw in that confused and tormented face the familiar face of my old college companion. He sat up, fixed his eyes upon me, and spoke calmly.

"Here is what I feel, John Charles. Here is what I know. I know Madeleine is dying, though she says she is in perfect health. I know that patients here at Usher House, who are dead, certified dead and buried, are walking our halls and grounds at night. And I know that these ideas are—as Edgar Allan Poe wrote—'deplorable folly.' Because they cannot be true. I have a sense that something in this house is driving me slowly mad, that inside me the madman and the sane man are locked in battle, and that I am helpless, I can't do anything to stop it!"

"You say you know these ideas aren't true?" I said, watching his face.

"Of course, they're ridiculous," he said, avoiding my eyes. His mouth twitched. "So why do I believe them?" His voice slid upward in a wail. "Why does it all seem so *real*?"

"Look Rod," I said. "Calm down. This is not 1839. We have doctors who can treat this kind of mental problem. You need to get help. You're a doctor, Madeleine's a doctor, a psychiatrist. You both have to know there's a medical solution somewhere."

He returned my gaze, and I felt rising up in me a peculiar sensation, yet one I recognized; an intuition that something was going to happen that I had to prevent. Something very bad.

"Madeleine has tried to help, of course she has. We have tried everything: therapists, medication, even alternative medicine. But no matter what we do, it makes no difference. Nothing affects the increasing sense of dread, of fear." He got up and began to pace back and forth. "No one believes me. But I know it. I just know it is the house—something in this place is causing this disease. It destroyed my namesake and it is going to destroy me!"

I looked at him and suddenly I felt the feeling he described. It seemed, in that moment, to pass from him to me and I felt as if I were drowning in it. I became aware of the wind, which had been increasing all day so that now it gusted strongly, causing the old house to groan, its mossy stones exhaling that same dense odor of decay I scented when I first approached.

I had to get hold of myself. I could not allow him to infect me. That would not help my friend. With an effort, I repressed and mastered the sensation his words aroused.

"This is ridiculous, it's utter nonsense," I said sharply. "I will help you separate fact from delusion. We will work at this until we figure it out. I am not going to let you destroy yourself."

A smile that I did not understand crossed his face and he sat down, leaning back on the sofa with a sigh I took to be relief.

"Thank you, John Charles," he said. "Thank you."

# TWO

Two weeks earlier, I had inherited the casket papers.

It was a beautiful fall afternoon, and I was sitting in my office at the *Crowley Sentinel*, pretending to work. There had been a sensational car crash that week involving our mayor, Jackson Lee Winsome, and the town's sexiest woman, Marilyn Larue. Both blamed the other, and I was looking forward to interviewing Marilyn at length, hopefully over a drink at The Old Forge. When the call came in, I was studying State Trooper Dupree's peculiar drawing of the accident. Arrows and cryptic notations made the thing look like a medieval stellar map. My concentration—such as it was—was interrupted by the telephone.

Actually, "office" is a misnomer. I share a large room in the storefront premises of the *Crowley Sentinel* with the entire *Sentinel* staff: the other reporter, the secretary/accountant, the two ad salespeople, and the typesetter. Only Mrs.

Boynton has her own office, in the back. From the front window I can watch the kids coming from Thomas Jefferson public school on their way to Shelton's. They drop the brown-bag lunches packed so carefully by their mothers into the big, black municipal trash can right in front of our window, and then emerge from Shelton's a few minutes later with bags of greasy french fries.

It was a beautiful, crisp late fall day, with the last autumn leaves drifting into the gutters and the sun sparkling off the cars parked along Central Avenue. "It's for you," Mrs. Boynton said, coming out of her office and pointing at the telephone in a way that suggested that she was surprised I had received a call. *I* was surprised she had picked up the call. Sometimes I had the impression the old biddy snooped into my affairs; I couldn't imagine what about them would interest her.

"Hello, is this John Charles Poe?"

I allowed that it was.

"We have scheduled an appointment with Ambrose Prynne at three this afternoon. Can you attend, sir?"

I was obviously speaking to a secretary. Old Ambrose Prynne had been my father's lawyer, Prynne's father had been my father's father's lawyer, and so on, back into the mists of time. As the secretary well knew, I would come. She knew, and I knew, that a call to me from Prynne was a sort of summons, no doubt regarding some tedious business relating to my legal responsibilities to spend my unearned inheritance keeping up that pestilential pile of a house I have also inherited. Sometimes I wonder if I would not have been better off as an orphan. Actually, I often wonder that. Surely I would have long since finished the great American novel I intend to write if family matters didn't take up so much time.

The offices of Prynne, Prynne and Prynne are where they have always been, in an elegant set of rooms above the Crowley Creek First National Bank. Prynne, Prynne and Prynne and the bank have some sort of incestuous relationship that would make a great investigative report for the *Sentinel*, if we printed such stories, which we don't. Mrs. Boynton doesn't believe in waking sleeping dogs, and she may be right. Crowley Creek is full of them, and once wakened, I am not sure if any of us could handle the hellish racket that would ensue.

Ambrose Prynne rose from his desk and greeted me most politely. "How do you do, John Charles. You are looking rather chipper today, if I may say so."

Prynne was a man in his early sixties, impeccably dressed, as always, in a navy blue lawyerlike suit, a tie with tiny redcoated hunters on horseback leaping over hedges upon it, his cuff links glinting gold. He had a graying Vandyke beard and looked uncannily like the oil portrait of his great-grandfather, which hung over the fireplace that dominated the large office. Hard, beady brown eyes peered from the portrait, and the same eyes studied me as I took my seat across from his large mahogany desk.

"Thank you, sir. You too are looking well."

We smiled at one another.

"You are thirty years old today, are you not John Charles?"

I wondered what business it was of his, but kept this thought to myself. "Yes, sir. That is correct. Have I inherited some more money? I thought I had gotten it all."

I shouldn't have been facetious, but old Prynne had made such a to-do about my inheritance that I couldn't resist.

He frowned. "Matter of fact, it *is* a sort of inheritance I want to discuss with you today, John Charles. But not money. You have indeed inherited all the assets that there are in the estate. Surely you are finding them sufficient?"

I admitted that he was right about that. The Crowleys, when they were not worrying about the Poe business, had made quite a fortune over the generations. I would be hard-pressed to get through it, and in fact had very little interest in doing so. Money, as anyone who has inherited it without doing anything to earn it can tell you, can be a damned curse.

Prynne cleared his throat. "No, John Charles. It is my duty to now inform you of another type of inheritance. An inheritance I trust you will guard carefully and whose secret you must swear to keep."

"What inheritance is that, sir?"

"Hold on a minute. Do I have your assurance that you will keep what I am about to tell you in the closest confidence?"

What a pompous prig the old fellow was. I had no intention of holding to any such blind promise. Secrets have powers, and one must think carefully about them. He may have thought my word was the word of a gentleman; if so, that was his problem.

I smiled blandly. "You can count on the Crowley family honor, sir." I failed to mention that as we had changed our name to Poe several generations ago, the Crowley honor may have been a good thing in itself, but was hardly relevant to John Charles Poe.

"Excellent. Excellent." He rose and walked over to a large oil portrait of another Prynne. This portrait, hanging over a side table on an inner wall, showed the Prynne in question on horseback, ready for the hunt. Someone was offering him a stirrup cup and he looked as if he needed it badly.

Prynne swung the painting aside to reveal an old-fashioned safe with a combination dial. He opened it and removed a most curious object, which he brought over to the desk and laid reverently before me.

"This, sir," said Prynne, "is the casket." His tone, when he uttered the word "casket," was full of portent.

"Is that so?" I said, staring at the thing. It was about three feet long, eighteen inches wide, made of oak, and strapped with brass. A large chased lock secured it. It appeared to be very old. It looked rather like a miniature coffin.

We both looked at it for a moment in silence.

"What is in it?"

"Papers, my dear John Charles, family papers. I myself have never opened it. It is for Crowley/Poe eyes only. But I understand that your illustrious ancestor, Edgar Allan Poe, placed his most secret papers in this casket, many relating to the true events behind his famous stories. He left instructions for his descendants to add their own secret family papers if they so wished, and for each to pass it to his oldest son, on that son's thirtieth birthday."

"It's all nonsense, sir. Why not break the chain now and go for a fresh start?"

He frowned. "You do not have that right, John Charles. Family responsibilities cannot be so easily avoided as you may think." He tapped portentously on the casket. "But I feel it my duty to say that I and my father, and his father before him, have noticed that each Poe (or Crowley) who inherited this casket seemed the worse for it. Whatever is in it, you must guard yourself against."

"As you say, sir. Is that all? I have an accident to investigate."

Prynne sniffed. I could see I had offended him by not taking the casket seriously. But I had had enough boring family stories to last a lifetime. Now some more musty papers had appeared, to add to a library full of old books, a house too big for me that needed servants to maintain, and who knew what other weird responsibilities to come? True, I felt a strange sensation when I looked at that casket, but that was probably just the result of Prynne's dark hints. Suddenly, I just wanted to be rid of Mr. Ambrose Prynne and of this past that seemed to always be there, whether I liked it or not.

"Thank you, sir," I said politely, picking up the casket. He walked me to the door and opened it. I hesitated, for it seemed he had something more he wanted to say. We looked at one another, and I realized that old Prynne was actually nervous.

He spoke very softly. "Take care, John Charles. You joke, but the casket has caused harm to your father and to all your forefathers. Whatever is in there seems to bring darkness into their lives. Take care, the world needs that blithe spirit of yours."

I was surprised. It almost seemed as if old Prynne cared about me. And what could he mean by "blithe spirit"? Surely I was one of the most depressive fellows on the face of the earth. The moment passed. His usual pompous expression reappeared. "Mark my words, John Charles. You hear me?"

"Yes, of course, sir," I said. We shook hands and I took the pestilential casket home and locked it up to read its contents later. Then I set out to interview the luscious Marilyn Larue.

* * *

That afternoon I met Edith Dunn for the first time. After returning from Crowley House, where I had locked the casket away, I spent an hour or so at the office continuing my clever representation of a man at work, and then headed over to The Cutting Edge, where Marilyn Larue worked as a hairstylist. She had agreed to meet me after work for a drink at The Old Forge, so I could do an in-depth interview about the accident. Marilyn was much too sharp to buy this transparent excuse, but she was a woman who liked a good time, and I had hinted that we might have one together as soon as our business was concluded. What I didn't know was whether or not her idea of a good time coincided with mine, and whether or not I would have the nerve to find out.

As soon as I opened the door to The Cutting Edge, the sound of hair dryers, Loretta Lynn, and loud women's voices assailed my ears. I caught sight of Marilyn standing at the back, putting the finishing touches on a neat, short, shining brown bob whose owner had her back turned to the door. Marilyn herself was a small, curvaceous blonde, whose ornate mop of curls would have made Dolly Parton stand up and take notice. I had always assumed her hair was a kind of professional advertisement. It had a sort of bedroom look that gave a man ideas. Marilyn caught sight of me in the mirror and waved me over.

"John Charles, darlin', I'm just about ready. Take a seat while I finish up on Edith here. Okay Edith?"

Edith nodded. An elegant-looking woman of an indeterminate age, her face seemed drawn and sad. She was looking into the mirror with an expression that seemed to suggest that whatever she saw there was not going to be sufficient to solve her current problems.

"Hey, wait a moment there, John, I just had an idea. I want you to meet Edith." Marilyn put down her can of hair spray. "Edith, this here is John Poe, he works at the *Crowley Sentinel*. John knows just about everyone in town. If there is a job anywhere, John is going to be the first to hear of it, right John?"

"Job?" It was hard to think of the woman I was being introduced to as someone looking for a job. She was dressed in a manner more sophisticated than one expected to see in Crowley Creek; white, cashmere turtleneck sweater, wide black trousers, and small gold earrings that looked like real eighteen carat. She wore little makeup and had made no attempt to hide the dark circles under her eyes. What I felt most, when I looked at her, was sadness. This woman had some trouble, no doubt of it.

"Yes, darlin'. Edith has just joined the ranks of us loved-em and lost-em divorcées. Mr. Dunn has taken off with his secretary and Edith has two teenage boys to support. She needs a job, it's as simple as that."

"That's a real shame," I said, upset at hearing this too familiar tale. "But won't your husband be obliged to help support the boys?"

Mrs. Dunn looked uncomfortable, and I realized that she did not have the habit of discussing her personal affairs with complete strangers. "I beg your pardon, ma'am," I said. "I didn't mean to intrude into your private troubles."

She smiled, and what a beautiful smile it was. Her whole face lit up in that instant and I just took to her. It happens sometimes like that. It wasn't a question of her being a woman and me a man, although that was there. I just liked her.

"That's all right," she said. "The fact is, there's no money, and Marilyn is right, I've got to find work. The problem is, a degree in American history doesn't qualify you for many jobs in Crowley Creek."

"No," I agreed, "it would hardly impress over at Shelton's, which, as far as I know is the only place hiring right now."

"They're always hiring at Shelton's," Marilyn said. "Turnover is hellish there. But Edith is too good for Shelton's. She's smart as a whip and she was just telling me that she can research just about any damn thing. Surely you could use a good researcher over at the *Sentinel?* You could print historical features, like they do in the Richmond State newspaper."

"Mrs. Boynton is not interested in historical features," I said, "but I surely will keep my ears open in case anything comes along." I felt bad because I was pretty certain there would not be any suitable jobs for Edith Dunn in Crowley Creek in the near future. It kind of makes my blood boil when a man takes off on a woman like that, after she's raised his kids and all. And it was not as if Edith Dunn had let herself go. For her age, she was a truly fine-looking woman.

We chatted while Marilyn put the finishing touches on Mrs. Dunn's coiffure, then we watched as she paid and left. "You've got to find her something, John Charles," Marilyn said, as she slipped on her coat. She smiled up at me the way Southern women do when they want something; and, in the way Southern men do, I immediately wanted to do it for her. "That woman deserves better than the miserable rotten life that she had with Dunn. She's hard working and she's no-body's fool. You find her something, you hear?"

I promised to do my best.

That was two weeks ago. Now, returning late from my visit to Roderick Usher, I decided the situation needed serious thought. The best place for serious thought on a dark No-vember evening, in a high windstorm, when you are chilled to the bone after driving miles in a Bronco with faulty heat-ing, has got to be your local watering spot. For that reason I drove directly to The Old Forge.

It was past midnight when I parked. I could see through the front window that the place looked almost empty. It was a week night, and there were only a few regulars sitting in the booths in the back discussing the fate of the town high school football team, or whatever.

Almost before I sat down at the bar, Tommy White had pulled out the bottle of Blanton's he kept behind the counter for me and had a nice full tumbler ready and waiting, along with a chaser of ice water. Tommy and I go way back. We puked up together after smoking our first snitched cigars when we were kids at Thomas Jefferson. Life has taken us in different directions, but old friends are old friends.

I looked around. The place was just how I liked it. The bar was empty except for me. The brass rail gleamed and right behind Tommy I could admire the row of trophies the town had won for the best floats at the county Independence Day parade. Everywhere you looked, brass objects hung from the walls. Tommy liked the "old forge" theme, and he had really gone to town with it. The place was old, all right. The floorboards were uneven and darkened with age; the paint along the cornices and on the tin ceiling was so thick the detail was lost. In between the brass horseshoes and farming implements and kitchen utensils hanging on the walls, Tommy had stuck up old-fashioned posters of famous Virginia patriots. In one, Patrick Henry clutches his heart as he intones "Give me liberty or give me death," and in another, Paul Revere rouses the citizens as he gallops through a storm-swept landscape. Of course, all this ambiance was to some extent undermined by the jukebox and the shelf of red-plastic ketchup and hot-sauce bottles, but I liked the effect.

Tommy knows most of the town secrets, including mine, and as far as I know he has never betrayed a confidence. So after I had warmed up a bit, I told him that there was trouble at Usher House and Roderick had asked for my help.

"Don't surprise me. Folks say that Mr. and Miss Usher have their problems over there," Tommy said, leaning on the bar.

"Business troubles? I thought the place was going great guns."

"Well, I guess in a way it is. They have lots of rich patients who pay through the nose. Miss Usher is supposed to be a famous head doctor. And Mr. Usher is an expert in old people's diseases. He was in here one time and showed me an article about the place in the *Washington Post*. Said he was a 'world-class expert in gerontology.' Old age disease. So I guess they know what they are doing all right. Problem is, those two have good hearts. They take in too many as can't pay their share. That's what I hear."

"Doesn't surprise me one bit. Roderick Usher was always a soft touch. Madeleine now, I can't say as I would have thought she'd let sentiment get the better of her business sense."

Tommy shook his head. "Lovely woman, Madeleine Usher. She'd do anything for her brother."

"It's ironic," I confided. "Here is her brother, having some kind of a nervous breakdown, and one of the best psychiatrists in the state is right there and seemingly can't do anything to help."

Tommy shook his head and comforted me by pouring another.

"Of course, psychiatrists can't treat their relatives," I said. "It's against their professional ethics."

"Sounds like common sense, too," Tommy said. He took out a rag and began to polish some lamp chimneys. We always had a few power outages every winter, and it looked as if Tommy wanted to be prepared. "Family is usually a big part of a person's problem."

I looked at him. Was he trying to tell me something about Madeleine Usher that I didn't know? I considered it as I sipped. No, I didn't think so. On the other hand, Tommy's comments about business problems at Usher House did throw a new light on Rod's condition. The pressures my old friend Usher was facing were obviously not just psychological. It was definitely a more-than-two-drink problem.

That's when I got my brainstorm. Of course, I guess it really wasn't such a sudden inspiration. Probably, I had been worrying over Edith Dunn's problem in the back of my mind ever since I met her. I knew from Marilyn that she hadn't found a job, though she had been trying hard. But at that moment, as I sipped at my Blanton's single barrel bourbon, it seemed somehow that fate had put on my road the very person who could most help me go down it.

No doubt about it, more often than not, the solutions to life's problems are there, waiting for us, and a few nips of the right stuff can make everything clear as crystal. Or so I thought at the time.

First thing next morning, I called Edith Dunn and asked her to meet me for a coffee at Shelton's explaining that I had an idea about a job. When I came in, she was already there, sitting very straight in the back booth, apparently oblivious to the regulars—most of Crowley Creek's business establishment—laughing and joking over their morning coffees and doughnuts. She wore a pale-gray suit with a white blouse and pearls. As I approached, she gave me a long, thoughtful look and I felt as if I had been given some kind of examination. She smiled, and I knew I had passed.

I sat down opposite her and ordered coffee.

"No doughnut for you this morning?" Edith said. She had lovely gray eyes, I noticed.

"No thanks, I had breakfast already. But go ahead and order for yourself. My treat."

"That's kind of you John Charles, but I gave up Shelton's doughnuts when I was thirteen."

"Probably why you're still alive to tell the tale." We both laughed. "Miz Dunn . . ."

"Edith."

"Edith, I'm working on a project and I need help. The project is not connected with my work at the *Sentinel*, and

Mrs. Boynton, my boss, keeps me on a short leash. I just don't have time to do the research. I was wondering if you . . . I mean . . ."

She gave me a sharp look, a look that seemed to see right through me. I persevered. "A research assistant . . . is what I need. Say twenty, thirty hours a week." I named a salary I thought fair. "You could use a room in that big house of mine as an office. Basically, you'd work on your own, but we'd meet most afternoons when I come home, so you could pass on what you'd found out during the day."

She looked down into her coffee. She was drinking it black, I noticed, and now she turned the cup in the saucer, lining the handle up exactly at right angles to her spoon. "I wonder . . ." she said very softly, so that I barely heard.

"You wonder what?"

She looked up at me, and I saw that same sadness in those gray eyes. "You're not doing this out of charity, are you, John Charles? Because if so, I want no part of it. I need a job all right, and people in town say you are a very kind person, but I can stand on my own two feet."

"Really, Edith, I need help," I said. I knew, looking at her, that it was true. And suddenly, I desperately wanted Edith Dunn to be on my side, by my side, as I delved deeper into the Usher mysteries. "Please."

We looked at one another and something, a kind of understanding, passed between us. Then she smiled. "John Charles," she said, "I accept."

I felt very happy as we worked through the details. I gave her an outline of the situation without divulging too much information about the casket papers. We decided that, while Edith organized an office at Crowley House, I would sniff around at the Usher's. Edith pointed out that the first step was to find out if the problems there were all in Roderick's head, or if there were more to it. I completely agreed. It looked as if my "Help Roderick Usher Project" might well be off to a good start.

So now, having promised Rod that I would help him, and having hired Edith, to research some background on Usher House and the Sanitorium, I figured the best thing would be for me to go out there and look around the place. It seemed pretty clear that there were two possibilities: one, Rod was seeing things that weren't there and needed a headshrinker (I intended to talk to Madeleine about that); the other, that something was going on at Usher's that had a rational explanation. Maybe if I looked around, asked some questions, I might find out what it was. It was obvious that Rod was in no condition to search out concrete causes behind the fears he had described. My idea was to do what I could without Rod's help. I didn't want to put any extra pressure on him if I could avoid it. He had looked and sounded so fragile that I thought it wouldn't take much to push him over the edge.

This time I went in the morning. I hoped to escape the spell the house had cast on me on my last visit. I intended to be logical and cold-minded. Sober too.

It was raining heavily as I drove into the visitor parking. Dark clouds had massed in the east and the rain splashed viciously into the tarn as I walked toward the house. Just as I passed the roiled and turbulent pond, I thought I saw someone on the other side. It seemed to be a little, old, white-haired man who was dodging around peculiarly, as if he didn't wish to be seen. Because of the rain, visibility was poor and I couldn't be certain. Why would an old man be walking around in this downpour?

I headed in his direction and he vanished from view. There were several large Blue Atlas cedar trees on the other side of the pond, their trunks and drooping branches casting shadows over the glade. Perhaps he had gone in there among the trees. The ground was mushy underfoot; moisture seeped into my shoes as I took off after him. I thought I saw him under the shadows. He dodged from tree to tree, then peered around and stared at me. I could make out a wisp of white beard, glasses misted with rain, and he seemed to be wearing a green garbage bag as a cloak. But perhaps I had imagined the whole thing; the light was so poor, he was so indistinct, and as I approached, he vanished altogether.

Under the cedar tree where I had thought I saw him, I studied the ground. Light depressions in the sodden turf suggested that someone had, indeed, stood there. Emerging from the glade, I looked around. The rain was fiercer now, and I could not see very far into the distance. Still, I have sharp eyes, and if there had been anyone to be seen, I think I would have seen him. What could have happened to the old man? Could he be standing behind one of the huge elm trees that dotted the grounds? There seemed no point in playing hide-and-seek with someone who didn't want to be seen.

Thoroughly soaked, I headed back for the house. Once inside, I reintroduced myself to the old fellow at the reception desk, who seemed at first not to remember me. I explained that I had come to pay a visit to Roger Boynton. This was the excuse I had cooked up in my mind on the way over. Roger Boynton was Ma Boynton's husband. He was the de jure owner of the *Crowley Sentinel*. He had never been serious about it, however, preferring to leave the actual running of the paper to Ma Boynton while he enjoyed the good life. But too many country club dinners, too much fine wine, too much Virginia hospitality of the best sort, had led old Boynton to gout, to stroke, and to the Sanatorium.

Still, he had had a good run. I remembered that Roger Boynton and my father had made significant inroads in the Crowley House cellar together; my father always said that old Boynton was one of the few in Crowley Creek who knew a good cognac from a great cognac.

A nurse now wheeled him out, and seeing me, he smiled on one side of his face and said something I took to be a greeting. "Would you like to visit with Mr. Boynton in the solarium?" the nurse asked. I nodded and then followed as she wheeled him down a broad corridor covered with a faded red Turkish carpet into a long room that had obviously once been a veranda, but was now glassed in. She positioned him next to an armchair facing out into a rain-soaked courtyard.

"It is good to see you, sir," I said. "How are you keeping?"

"Could be worse," he said. Now that I was closer, I understood his speech. For a few minutes we exchanged politenesses while I observed him. Once a rotund man with a high-colored face, a shiny bald head and genial blue eyes, he was now a small, shrunken fellow whose skin had an unhealthy waxy look. How sad it is to see what age can do to the heartiest and most fun-loving among us. Obviously I should take it as a warning. I hope I will, but past evidence suggests that it is not likely.

"How do you like Usher House?" I asked him. "It is said to be the finest place of its kind in the state."

"You a friend of Rod Usher's, that so?" he said, his words sounding as if his mouth was full of grits.

"Yes, sir, we went to college together. But I haven't seen much of him these last five years."

"Man has too good a heart. He should wake up and see what is going on around here."

"What is that, sir?"

His blue eyes looked at me. "You wouldn't believe me if I told you. You wouldn't believe it." His eyes begged me to say I *would* believe it.

"You can tell me. I have an open mind."

"Open mind, open mind," Boynton muttered. "Take more than that to believe what's going on around here. That's the trouble with being old. If you tell the young what's right before their eyes, they think you are mad as a hatter."

He seemed to have had some bad experiences with young people. "I wouldn't think that, sir. My father always said you had an unerring instinct for the best cognac—surely a sign of supreme intelligence."

He smiled. "John Charles, you are a good soul. Your father didn't do you justice, no, he didn't do you justice. Was convinced you would never amount to anything. Guess he couldn't stand the thought of you following in his footsteps." He laughed, but only with half his mouth.

"Well, I haven't amounted to anything yet, sir," I said. "What strange goings-on were you just referring to?"

"Strange goings-on. That's it all right."

"Such as?"

He hesitated. I said nothing. We looked at one another. One of his eyes was sharp, aware. The other seemed lost and confused. His good hand tightened on the arm of the wheelchair. "People, people walking who shouldn't be. That's all I'll say."

"What people?"

Suddenly he shouted, "I am NOT crazy! I saw them."

A nurse emerged from a doorway that led into a small office. She hurried over to Mr. Boynton. "Mr. Boynton, calm yourself. You mustn't get excited. No one is doubting you." She gave me an angry look.

"I wasn't doubting him," I said, "not for a moment."

"Mr. Boynton is recovering from a stroke. We don't want his blood pressure driven up."

"I understand," I told her. "I'll be careful." Somewhat reassured, she hovered for a moment, straightening the old man in the chair, where he had slipped sideways in his excitement, and smoothing the robe that covered his legs.

As soon as she left, I said, "I saw something odd. I saw someone in the garden, in the rain, who seemed to be hiding. An old man wrapped in a garbage bag."

Boynton leaned forward. "What did he look like?"

"About five-two, slight, small wisp of a beard, glasses."

"One of the ghosts," Boynton muttered, under his breath. I doubt he realized I heard him. When my father and I were hunting, and he one of the best in the county, I always heard our prey before he did.

"Pardon, sir?"

"One as shouldn't be walking . . . that's all I'll say. I've seen 'em too. I'm tired." He slipped sideways again. "Call the nurse."

Poor old Boynton. It was sad to see him like this. I watched as the nurse wheeled him away down the corridor, his head bobbing to one side. What had he meant by "one of the ghosts"? How reliable was he? Who was the old man I had seen in the rain? What was going on at Usher House anyway?

As I drove away, I realized I knew less now than I had before. If I were to help my friend, I would need to do better. Much, much better.

# THREE

*I draw to your attention how very frequently the first, or intuitive impressions have been the true ones. How unjust, that the imagination has not been ranked as supreme among the mental faculties. For this faculty brings man's soul to a glimpse of things supernal and eternal—to the very edge of the great secrets. How often has it come to pass that only by use of this faculty do I perceive the faint perfume of a deeper truth.*

*Now I confide in you, my unknown descendant. It was through the prescience of intuition that I perceived the truth about my oldest, dearest friend, Roderick Usher. I knew he was hiding a terrible secret from me, a secret so perverse and so evil that I dare not speak of it, even to you, who come after me and live in a better, cleaner time than our own.*

*Will you think it strange if I say that his House was a conspirator in the concealment of this dreadful truth? You must believe me for it is so.*

*Know this: on his death bed, Roderick Usher whispered these words to me: "I have sinned against God and Man and my sin has destroyed my sister, my House and my life. My family must make amends forever, to God and to the World we have wronged."*

*At that transcendent moment, when he paused on the boundary between this world and the nether darkness which awaited him, Roderick Usher clutched my hand and sought reassurance from me that his last Will and Testament would redeem him and cleanse the stain from his House. He swore to me that in his Will he had bound his descendants to certain acts of Mercy and Goodness forever. Might this hasten his passage from Hell to a more restful sojourn in Purgatory?*

*But alas, I fear that the curse has not been lifted as Roderick hoped. And it may well be that Roderick shall wander forever, without rest or solace, grieving and desolate, in the dark corridors of that Other Place.*

*For the Usher heirs have begun to rebuild an enormous house upon that tainted ground. Even should they keep to the terms of the Will, the Evil is too great to be contained— it has penetrated the soil itself and releases its pestilent vapor into the air to poison all who walk in that place. Thus, I enjoin upon you, my descendant, tread carefully should your path cross that of the Usher family, and their cursed House!*[1]

---

[1]This passage is taken in part from Edgar Allan Poe's letters and essays.

Edith lifted her head from the crumbling papers that lay before her on her desk, in her office at Crowley House. Pale sunlight streamed in through the windows, and Edith, in a soft, gauzy, gray and mauve blouse, long gray skirt, and gray suede boots was quite a welcome sight first thing in the morning. It gave me a good feeling to see her, poring over those yellowed sheets from Edgar Allan's casket, seated at her desk on which she had placed the computer she had selected and the flowering red begonia I had bought her. Against one wall, where once had been a cracked oak armoire, there now stood a shiny grey metal file cabinet.

"What do you make of these papers, John?" she said, taking off her reading glasses and rubbing her eyes. "It's hard to see how what your ancestor wrote in 1835 could have any relevance today."

A good point. But I understood only too well what old Edgar Allan meant by intuition, and mine told me to heed every word about the Ushers in the casket papers. Which was why—despite misgivings—I had given them to Edith, and now waited for her opinion. As for why I had held some of the papers back (in fact, hidden them from Edith), I had no idea. I told myself I had given her only those that could bear upon the Usher situation, but I had a feeling there was more to it than that.

"You don't look as if you agree with me," she said. "You think they have some relevance to what's happening now?"

"What you say makes sense," I admitted. "E.A. wrote this stuff a long time ago."

"Then what is troubling you, John Charles?"

How could I tell this calm, controlled, older woman that I just *knew* the papers were important to our investigation?

What could I say that she would believe, that wouldn't make me look a fool?

I changed the subject. "I think we need to investigate this will business," I said, without looking directly at Edith. "Could you do that? Could you check out the archives and see if there is any record of an Usher family will that could bind the family today?"

"Of course," she said. I saw from her expression that she knew I hadn't been frank with her, that she suspected I understood things about the casket papers I did not want to share with her. She might even know somehow that I was holding some of them out on her. Maybe she felt a little hurt, but she had made up her mind to be professional. "Is there anything else you'd like me to look into?"

"Yes. Tommy White tells me the Ushers have business problems. Could you check into their finances? If you have trouble getting information from the bank, let me know. I might be able to find you some help."

"I'll get right to it." She stood up and walked to the window. "I hope you will grow to trust me, John Charles," she said softly. "I would never betray a confidence; never."

Or laugh at it? I wanted to ask. But I didn't. I assured her that she had my complete respect.

When I left the house I turned back for a moment, and there she was, standing in the window, looking out into the garden, that same sad expression on her face that I had seen when we first met.

Crowley House is on the outskirts of the town of Crowley Creek. Because we have so much property, the house kind of stopped the town growth on the western side. Any sensible family would have sold it to the town for some municipal purpose by now, but then no one has ever accused the Poes (or the Crowleys before them) of being sensible.

I got in the Bronco and headed out of town toward Usher House. I had been brooding about my meeting last night with old Boynton and about my "sighting" of the fellow in the garden, and I thought it would be worthwhile to try to get some straight answers from Rod. As I drove, the quiet in the car felt suddenly oppressive and I flipped on the radio.

HURRICANE JEAN, THE SOUTHEAST'S MOST BIZARRE STORM IN OVER A HUNDRED YEARS, HAS LEFT THE BATTERED ISLAND OF HAITI AND TAKEN A ZIGZAG COURSE TOWARD NORTH CAROLINA'S OUTER BANKS. THE STORM HAS BEEN BLAMED FOR HUNDREDS OF DEATHS IN THE CARIBBEAN, WHERE WINDS REACHED SPEEDS OF OVER 120 MILES PER HOUR. AROUND THE EDGES OF THE STORM, HEAVY RAINS AND TORNADOES DAMAGED CROPS AND DESTROYED PROPERTY. HURRICANE WARNINGS HAVE BEEN ISSUED FOR CHARLESTON. . . .

I wondered if the hurricane would come our way. It didn't seem likely. The weather was very calm. A high ceiling of stratus clouds muted the light, bathing everything in a steely gray radiance.

The same calm reigned over Usher House as I pulled into the visitor parking lot. The grounds appeared deserted and I saw no sign of skulking old men among the trees.

Getting out of the car, I saw Madeleine Usher emerging from the shadows at the side of the house. She wore a long dark cloak with a hood and carried a wicker basket filled with white daisies. Catching sight of me, she changed direction and came toward me. As she approached, I saw that she did not look at all well. Her face had become very thin, her large brown eyes, shadowed by the hood of her cloak, were luminous and febrile. "John! How wonderful! Have you come to see Roderick? Your last visit did him so much good. You know you are always welcome here."

She took my arm and put it through hers, and we walked toward the house. "I've been gathering some flowers to put in his study. He hardly leaves it now, and it is so gloomy in there. I'm worried about him."

I asked if she could spare me a few minutes to discuss the state of Rod's health, and she readily agreed. Still holding my arm, almost too tightly, she led me through the dim anteroom, up a broad, curving staircase to a small office. There she took off her cloak, hung it on a bronzed hook, and set the basket of daisies on the deep windowsill. A thin beam of light came through the leaded panes of the window, falling on the daisies so that they glowed in the shadows.

Madeleine turned to study me. Apparently satisfied with what she saw, she directed me to a chair that faced her desk, a large, antique, cherry-wood partner's desk, covered with papers, medical journals, and old, rotting leather-bound volumes. On a side table was a computer and modem. She sat down, swiveled in her chair, and turned off the computer monitor. The luminous characters shivered for a moment on the screen, then faded and vanished. But before they did, I managed to read enough to see that she had been studying a medical report on her brother.

"How long has it been?" she said, smiling at me. "I don't

think I've seen you since the opening of the Sanatorium, on that sunny day when we thought we might truly be entering into a new and happier time for the Usher family. How promising everything looked then."

Like her brother, Madeleine had aged since I saw her last. Her blonde hair, streaked with silver, had lost its shine. Her beautiful skin, without makeup, looked dry, and there were hectic pink patches on her cheeks. Seeing me looking at her, she self-consciously smoothed back a lock of hair that had escaped from her chignon, and I saw that her hand had a tremor.

I could not hide my concern. "Madeleine, you don't look well. Roderick said he was worried about your health. Are you taking care of yourself?"

She frowned. "I have been fighting off the flu, that's all. This time of year there's always a few virulent strains going around. It's likely that the stress of worrying over Rod's health has lowered my resistance. But it's Rod we need to be concerned about, not me. What did you think when you saw him?" Her hands restlessly moved over the papers on her desk. They reminded me of white birds, seeming to flutter and to touch everything so lightly, as if afraid to come to rest.

"I'm worried too," I confessed. "The problem looks psychological to me. Can't you get him some help?"

"I too thought that was it at first," she said. "But every therapist and analyst I've sent him to is baffled. His symptoms don't match any known psychological disease etymology. And Rod won't cooperate with a proper psychoanalysis. He says that the cause of his illness is not in *his* past. I'm so worried. Maybe it's time to listen to Rod's diagnosis. After all, the patient can sometimes be his own best diagnostician."

"What does he think?"

"Well, sometimes he's not rational. He says it's a family curse—obviously that's part of his delusions. But when he's lucid, he says it might be something chemical, maybe even biological. Some toxin in the moss on the stone walls, or in the tarn, that he is allergic to."

"Is that possible?"

Madeleine got up and began to pace around the room. She was as tall and slender as her brother, but she moved with more control; there seemed more energy and purpose in her step. "Is it possible?" she repeated. "Who knows? I can find nothing in the medical journals that corresponds to Rod's symptoms . . . at least . . ." she paused, paled, and hurriedly opened a door I had not noticed in the paneling. I caught a glimpse of an antiseptic, white-tiled bathroom, and as the door shut behind her, I heard the sound of retching.

I heard running water, and a few minutes later she emerged. She had put on makeup, I saw, concealing her pallor under powder and lipstick. The effect, though attractive, was slightly garish.

"Are you all right?"

She gestured dismissively. "I told you, it is a touch of the flu. These sudden waves of nausea are a common symptom."

"Don't you think you should be in bed?"

She ignored the suggestion. "As I was saying, there is no disease paradigm in modern medical science to explain Rod's symptoms. But in these old nineteenth-century books, I do find descriptions of conditions similar to his . . . I need to study more before I can say for certain. And even if I should find a disease description that corresponds, they were so backward in those days, in their understanding of causes and cures, I am not sure it will do us any good." She came over to my chair and leaned on it, as if she were feeling suddenly weak. I could smell her perfume, and underneath, a scent I had smelled before, when visiting the very ill in hospital, the odor of the dissolution of the flesh. "We have to help him, John. He is so . . . so frightened."

"But what is he frightened of?"

She walked back behind her desk, sat down and stared at me. "He says he is frightened of chimeras, fantasies; he says . . ."

I felt a cold draft behind me, heard the sound of a door opening and turned to see Roderick Usher himself coming into the room. "John!" he said, smiling, "they told me you were here. How wonderful!" I stood and he shook my hand. His grasp felt weak, his hand chilly. "Madeleine, my darling," he said going over to his sister. "What are you doing up? You should be in bed. I *told* you to stay in bed. How do you think you will get over your flu if you persist in working at your desk? Now say goodbye to John and do as the doctor orders. At once!"

She smiled at him, and they embraced tenderly. Over her shoulder he caught sight of the daisies, gleaming in the shadows of the deep window embrasure. He started. "Madeleine! Look! The flowers of death. Get them out of here!" He clutched her tightly, trembling, trying to interpose his body between her and the window, as if to protect her from some evil emanations.

"Rod, calm down. Those are just some late autumn daisies I picked for you. . . ."

"They are the blooms of death! They are the harbingers of doom! I don't want flowers nourished by the accursed soil of this place in your room. Can't you smell them? Can't you smell their evil, poisonous fumes?" His voice frantic, he turned to me. "I don't dare touch them, John. Take them, take them out. They are killing Madeleine. Look at her, look at how ill she is . . . she is dying, dying. . . ."

Over his shoulder, I saw Madeleine's look of concern and compassion. "Don't worry, Rod," she said gently. "John will take away the flowers if they upset you, won't you John?"

I nodded.

"And I will go to bed and rest, if that will make you feel better."

This seemed to calm Usher. He released his sister and turned to look at me. "Forgive me, John," he said, his voice pleading. "I must sound mad to you. I warned you, we must be on our guard here always. The House has so many ways of reaching us."

Madeleine pressed her hands on her brother's arm in a soothing gesture. "I'm going now. Talk to John. Tell him what is on your mind. I know he will do you good." She turned to me, smiling weakly. "Just a couple of sick old Ushers, John. But don't worry about me. I will be up and about in a few days and then we will finish our chat."

I agreed.

"Promise you'll come back and talk to me?" she said, tilting her head in a coquettish gesture that might have been charming had she not looked so weak and ill.

"Of course," I said.

"Promise?" she said again, and suddenly her dark eyes bored into mine with that same intensity I remembered from her better days. "We have things we must discuss, John. Rod and I trust you and we are counting on you."

Then she was gone. Rod stared after her, on his face that same confused look I had seen in my previous visit. "Madeleine is going to die," he said, his voice full of dread. "It is written in the walls of this house, in its very stones . . . and there is nothing you or I or anyone can do to prevent it."

Ma Boynton was not amused. "We have a deadline, Mr. Poe," she said, shaking a set of galleys at me. "The *Crowley Sentinel* has come off the presses at two o'clock on Thursdays for a hundred years, and no lazy, hungover reporter is going to mess that up while I am still in my boots, you hear me?"

"Yes, ma'am."

"Don't hang your head in that boyish way, young man. I know that trick. Now get onto that computer and get that accident story written up. And be sure that you don't slang Mayor Winsome. He's up for reelection and we don't want the town to think he was driving while under the influence."

"Ma'am, the whole town knows Mayor Winsome was driving under the influence, and they like him the better for it."

"You may be right, John Charles," Mrs. Boynton said, a slight smile crossing her face before being replaced with her usual termagant expression.

Mrs. Fanny Boynton was a stout woman in her middle sixties, the epitome of a certain kind of Southern womanhood. Tough as nails, she ruled her domain with an iron hand and brooked no resistance from anyone. But underneath, she couldn't resist a little flattery and she had a vast and cynical understanding of human nature, which could always be appealed to in a pinch.

"Yes, you may be right," she said, fingering her pearl choker with the diamond clasp, which was her signature, and which, I am sure, she wore to bed. "But that doesn't mean Jackson Lee wants it written up in the *Sentinel* in black and white. We don't want to give that tart, Larue, reason to think she can sue and take the mayor to the cleaners, either. Jackson would not appreciate that one little bit. Do you get my drift?"

I got her drift. She was sticking closely to her policy to avoid telling the truth, the whole truth, nothing but the truth. I just needed to stick to *my* policy of outwitting her. "I hope Jackson Lee will remember he owes the *Sentinel* a big one for our . . . discretion," I said.

Mrs. Boynton smiled. "I'll see to that, don't you worry."

I turned on the computer. Now I only had to figure out how to write up this story so as to satisfy Ma Boynton, to not foul up my chances with Marilyn, and to hide the truth between the lines, where it could be available to the alert reader.

But instead of typing, I began to daydream about my evening with Marilyn. It had been promising. We had had some good laughs over drinks and dinner at The Old Forge, and Marilyn had told me that she thought I was "just the cutest little thing that has come my way in a month of Sundays." She had invited me in for "one for the road" when I took her home and allowed me a few passionate embraces before sending me home with a look that promised more, later. The woman had a truly bewitching smile and a most attractive figure, and a man could waste a lot of time thinking about her when he should be rushing to meet a deadline.

Ma Boynton coughed, and I began to tap away at the keyboard. "On Friday, November third, an unavoidable accident occurred at the intersection between Central Ave. and the Turnpike ..." I wrote mendaciously, as Mrs. Boynton watched over my shoulder. . . .

I was late coming home that night. The damn accident story turned out to be more challenging than butting heads with a bull. Right after Ma Boynton gave up hanging over my shoulder, Buzz Marco, the other writer at the *Sentinel* decided to give me a hard time.

Actually, calling Buzz a writer is a bit of an exaggeration. He is, in fact, an intern from the Columbia School of Journalism who has graced us for a term while on his way to a Pulitzer. There has been a major culture clash between Buzz and the staff at the *Sentinel*. For his part, Buzz has found it difficult to comprehend that, despite the fact that he is a bona fide journalism graduate student, and from New York City to boot, he is still junior at the *Sentinel*. Mrs. Boynton writes any important articles that need to be written, I write the rest, and Buzz's job is to organize the articles we get from various syndicates and to write "Goings-On Around Town," the most widely read article in the *Sentinel*. "Goings-On" tells whose relatives are in town, from where, and for how long, and also who went away, where, and why.

Of course Buzz thinks we are a bunch of rubes, and if we would only listen to his ideas we could be winning as many prizes as the *Hartford Courant*. It's no use telling him Ma Boynton is as interested in prizes as she is in the news of the latest red dwarf. Contrary to Buzz's fixed opinion of his potential greatness, Ma Boynton took him on because he was cheap labor.

"I hear you are investigating a big potential scandal at the Usher Sanatorium," Buzz hissed over my shoulder. Or I thought that was what he said. Buzz talked so fast one had to make a proximate guess at his meaning. Most Yankees do that; it makes us contrary and we tend to talk even slower. So what I heard was: "Iheryr vestiging shulchol at the Usherum."

"Kindly back away from my chair, Mr. Marco," I said as slowly as possible. "I am attempting to write an article and a certain solitude is required for concentration."

". . . skating a scandal?" he repeated.

"How's that?"

"I - hear - you - are - investigating - a - scandal - at - the - Usher. . . ."

I swiveled in my chair, planning to put the kid in his place when I realized that Ma Boynton was standing in the door to her office taking in every word.

"Mr. Poe! May I see you a moment?"

"Be right there, ma'am," I said, giving Buzz a now-look-what-you've-done glare as I followed Mrs. Boynton into her office.

She wasted no time in coming to the point. "What was the New York idiot going on about? What's this about a scandal at Usher's?"

"There's no scandal, ma'am. Rod Usher is an old friend and he is not well." I lowered my voice. "It seems like he might be on the verge of some kind of a nervous breakdown."

Ma Boynton sat down in her big leather swivel chair. With what appeared to be an effort, she put a look of concern on her face. "I'm sorry to hear that. And of course, what you do on your own time is your business. But let's get one thing straight. You're *not* investigating Usher House. We don't investigate Crowley Creek people. We show the town the face the town wants to see, you know that. The Ushers have contributed a great deal to this town. The family has been respected in this country since before the revolution."

"I do know that."

She swelled up importantly. "I know you know, John Charles. But sometimes you need reminding. I wouldn't want you to catch the Columbia journalism disease. That kid is a real pest. You keep him in his place, you hear?"

I nodded. I knew minding Buzz was part of my job.

"And you stay away from all the business doin's at Usher House. They're going through a rough patch right now and they don't need us adding to their troubles."

"How is that? What rough patch?"

"No you don't, no you don't. Don't you try to pump me. And I hear you've hired Edith Dunn to help you with some of your family business. That's your affair. But I don't want to hear you have her messing around the Ushers. You understand me, John Charles?"

This had to be bad news. It was Ma Boynton's way of telling me that already, she knew what Edith was doing. Edith had only begun to investigate the Usher's business dealings that very morning. Amazing how connected the Boynton was. How could she have found out so fast?

"I promised Roderick Usher I would help him and his sister," I said, starting to get angry. "That is all I am doing."

"Is it?" Mrs. Boynton said, fixing her cold blue eyes on me. I looked back at her. Her rough square face was not softened by the coat of powder that covered it, and the flattened coils of orangeish hair that crowned her face looked more like some sort of a battle helmet than a head of hair. "I'm not sure I believe that, John. I don't know what you are up to. But let me make one thing clear. You are not, I repeat *not*, going to investigate Usher House if you want to keep your job at the *Sentinel*. Is that understood?"

I stood up. "I sure hope nothing I do makes you want to fire me, Mrs. Boynton," I said, giving her my most charming smile. It didn't work.

"Do I have your word you'll call off this investigation of yours?"

"No, you don't," I said. What made her think she could stop me from helping my friend? What gave her the right? The tormented faces of Rod and Madeleine Usher were vivid in my mind's eye, as I turned my back on her and stalked out.

Behind me, I could hear her voice, "John? John Charles, you come back here, you're making a big mistake. . . ."

So after that kind of a day at the office, coming home late and finding that Edith Dunn was still there was like a charm. I tossed my jacket onto the hall table and glanced at my reflection in the dusty mirror. Behind me I saw the gloomy expanse of the front hall: two stories with a gallery running around the second story, the place was dim and cold and musty. I ran up the broad curving stairway two steps at a time and sped down the hall to her office. She looked up as I entered and smiled. She certainly made a pretty picture. Lit by lamplight, the room felt like an oasis in my old house.

I saw that she had the casket papers that I had given her

that morning spread out on her desk, along with photocopies of legal, bank, and real estate documents.

"Looks like you've got a lot done today," I said.

"I did, and I just can't wait to tell you about it. Listen to this, John Charles." She picked up a legal document and began to read, "Whereas I, Roderick Percival Usher, in this year of our Lord 1835. . . ."

A sudden wave of weariness passed over me. I had a strong intuition that what was coming meant trouble. "Edith, I've had a day that could kill a horse. How about you just cut to the chase?"

"Oh, John," she said sympathetically. "You do look tired. Would you like to get a cup of tea or a drink before we go over all this?"

"No, but just give me the gist. I confess, I have a lot on my mind."

"Well, the gist is, Roderick Usher willed the deed to Usher House to a trust so that his descendants who inherit it, and the money that goes with it, have to support poor and indigent people there. The way it affects the Sanatorium is, the Ushers have to have at least twenty percent of their patients be charity cases. The poor folks pay what they can. That's putting a real burden on the Sanatorium. State regulations only allow for a certain number of patients, and they're not averaging enough revenue per patient because of the poor ones. The result is, they are having trouble just breaking even."

"The heavy hand of the past," I muttered to myself.

"What's that?"

"Nothing. Sorry. But don't you think that kind of fits with the casket papers?"

She frowned and picked up the papers. "Do you mean where Edgar Allan writes," she skimmed the page and then read aloud: "in his Will he had bound his descendants to certain acts of Mercy and Goodness forever' "?

"Yes. That's what I was thinking of."

"Could be. John, is that why you asked me to look into the Usher will?"

I allowed as how the thought of a possible connection had crossed my mind.

"That's impressive," Edith said. "I would never have picked up on that. What else do you get when you read this thing Edgar Allan Poe wrote? To me it just reads like a lot of nineteenth-century romantic . . . I don't know . . . foolishness?"

I was starting to know Edith. A logical, clear-headed woman, she didn't seem to pick up the feelings behind things. But also, she didn't let her emotions interfere with her work. And she had an open mind. Still, I didn't feel I could tell her what I read in the papers, how I interpreted them. At least, not yet. And I still couldn't bring myself to give her the papers I had hidden in the library.

"I do have some ideas," I said. "But I'm not sure. . . ."

I was interrupted by the telephone. "Hello? John Poe speaking."

"John? John?"

I could not recognize the voice on the other end of the line. The sound of it was more moan than words. "This is John Poe speaking. Who is that?"

"John? It's me, Rod Usher. John?"

"What's the matter, Rod? I can barely hear you. What? Please speak up. What?"

Again that terrible moan, a sound of grief that sent a chill right to my heart.

"Please, John, please come. It's Madeleine. She's dead. They say she's dead. But . . . please come."

"Hold on there, Rod. I'm on my way."

# FOUR

Usher held himself under tight control. He sat stiffly on the sofa, twisting a water glass round and round in his hands, his face frozen and expressionless.

He had turned on all the lights in the big salon. Three enormous crystal chandeliers, candlesticks now electrified, blazed in the high ceiling, their droplets sparkling like tears. For the first time I could see the room clearly. Faded oriental rugs, overlapping upon one another, covered the blackened oak floorboards. Burnished antique chests gleamed, tall screens cast inky shadows, reflections glittered on glass-fronted bookcases, their doors hanging open. Books lay in disorderly heaps on the floor near high-backed, stiff armchairs, beside lamp stands with fringed shades. Valuable bric-a-brac, statues and porcelain, snuff jars and colored glass littered every table. A stack of old guitars and lutes leaned against one another in a corner, their strings broken.

"She died peacefully, John," Usher said. He lifted his glass of water to his lips and sat forward on the sofa. "When the nurse went to give Madeleine her evening medicines, she realized what had happened and called for me. But as soon as I saw my sister I knew I had come too late." He looked at me questioningly, as if waiting for me to explain, make it right. But I could think of nothing to say. He passed a hand over his face. "There she was, John, sleeping like an angel. At peace, finally."

"I'm so sorry, Rod."

He did not appear to hear me, completely absorbed in his own thoughts. For a moment he stared past me, as if he saw something beyond, in the shadowy corners of the room. Then he sat forward so suddenly that the water in his glass ran down over his fingers. A large, dark stain formed and slowly spread over the velvet of the sofa cushions. Oblivious, he began murmuring, as if talking to himself. I thought I heard him say, "But *is* she at peace . . . *is* she?"

"I understand how hard this is for you, how close you two were. It must be difficult to take it in," I said. I wanted to comfort him, but he seemed so far away, almost as if he were in some kind of trance. "I knew she was ill," I said, leaning toward him, trying to get his attention, talking in my most normal conversational tone. "but I never thought it was that serious. She said she just had the flu."

Now I had his attention. "She didn't have the flu, John." His voice sounded ominous.

"Well then, what did it, man? How did this happen?"

He just looked at me and shook his head.

"Come on, Rod. You must know something. You feared she was dying. No one believed you."

He got up and paced around the room. His nervous fingers raked up and then smoothed his hair, wild with static electricity. He moved from light to shadow. On every table, on every surface, candles burned. He had turned on all the lamps; the room coruscated with light. Yet here and there its gloom adhered, as if the shades of the past could not be dispelled. He passed into one of these dark areas now, a shadow cast by an ornate Chinese screen. I could barely see him, my eyes dazzled by the candlelight and the lamplight and the brilliant illumination cast by the gigantic chandeliers. Shadows shifted and folded over upon one another as the candles flickered in the draft. Rod murmured something.

"What's that? What are you saying, Rod?"

"Murdered, murdered by the curse of this damned old house, of this damned old family."

I stood up. "Come over here and sit down, Roderick. Pull yourself together." My voice sounded harsh in my own ears.

He came out of the shadows, and I saw that his face, no longer frozen and in control, seemed suffused with sadness. "Why should you believe me? I know it is absurd. It must be my grief speaking." He sat down, lifted his glass and swallowed the last of his water. Ice chinked in the glass. "Her doctors examined her yesterday, last week, the week before; each time they found her heart weaker. Did you not see it yourself? Yes, of course you did. It happened right before our eyes!"

The door opened. An elderly man with a stethoscope around his neck and carrying a ratty doctor's bag came in. Roderick sat up, stared at him, clasped his hands together. "Dr. Giron, may I introduce my dear friend, John Poe? John, Dr. Giron is our staff general practitioner. He has been looking after Madeleine, along with the specialists."

"Good God, man," Dr. Giron said. "What are you doing in here? This room is like a television studio. You'll blind yourself." Fussily, the doctor moved around the room, turning off lamps, turning off sconces, turning off the chandeliers. But when he went to blow out the candles, Roderick let out a cry that chilled my marrow.

"No! Do not extinguish her lights! We must keep her lights burning, burning, do you hear me?"

The doctor gave him a sharp look. He came over to the sofa. "Lean back, sir. Let me look at you." He examined Roderick quickly, taking his blood pressure, his pulse, listening to his heart. Satisfied, he took a seat across from Roderick.

"Now you listen to me, Roderick Usher. It is time for some plain common sense around here. You must get hold of yourself and not indulge these fancies of yours. Your sister fell prey to a particularly virulent virus. In her weak condition, she could not fight it; her heart just stopped beating. You must accept it. She is gone."

"No!"

Both the doctor and I stared at Roderick. I heard something in his tone that I, for one, did not understand.

"What do you mean, Roderick?" Dr. Giron said, pursing his lips. "No, she did not die of a virus, or no, she is not . . . gone from us?"  .

Roderick got up and began to pace again. "Listen to me, you must listen to me. I know she seems dead . . . God knows, I am a doctor, I too, examined her. All the vital signs had ceased. But this house . . . the things that have happened here . . . that happen here . . . we can take no chances. She must not be buried, must not be embalmed. Hear me, Dr. Giron. I want her placed in the copper crypt in our cellars for one week. It is refrigerated. But, well wrapped, she will not be too cold, should she. . . . I want television cameras on her day and night, I want sensors on her limbs . . . should she move . . . should she change her mind . . . she must not be buried, surely you see that? *Surely you see that!*"

Dr. Giron and I looked at one another. "Could I talk to you outside for a moment, John?" Dr. Giron said.

I nodded. "We'll be just a minute, Rod. I'll be right back." He smiled, but seemed not to be really listening.

Outside the salon we stood in the hall. Dr. Giron's face had gone pale, his flesh sagged and I noticed how much deeper the pouches under his eyes had become. "The man is clearly not in control of his faculties," Dr. Giron said, looking at me. "I understand you are an old friend. Can you do anything? After all, my God, he is a physician himself. At some level he must know perfectly well that his sister is dead. It is a terrible tragedy of course. Such a young, beautiful woman, so full of promise, to go like this. No wonder he is . . ."

"But go like how, Dr. Giron?"

The doctor shook his head. "I could give you all kinds of medical mumbo jumbo, but the truth is, we medical men only know so much about life and death. Why does one person pass away from a disease and another recover from a worse one? We have no idea. These things are mysteries. In Miss Usher's case, stress and a particularly bad strain of virus weakened her heart to such a point that she could no longer resist. Then her overburdened heart stopped and we lost her."

"You mean you don't know what killed her?"

"I didn't say that. I know what killed her. I just don't know why it killed her."

I didn't believe him. I thought the good doctor had got in over his head. I felt myself getting angry. "It's not convincing. What do her specialists say?"

"We are all of the same mind. Believe me, it's not just my opinion. I consulted with the best specialists available before I signed the death certificate. We agreed to state the cause of death as heart failure.

"It's not good enough."

"I don't understand you," Dr. Giron said, exasperated. "What more do you want? I could send the body to Richmond for further analysis, but you saw Roderick, he would never stand for it."

I could see no point in pursuing it. He would never back off his opinion now. In my experience, a doctor would rather be wrong than lose face. "What's this business about the copper crypt?" I asked him.

The doctor sighed. "Now there's another example of Usher's irrational state. The Usher family built this house before the Civil War. There is a room in the cellar designed for storing ordinance, lined, for some godforsaken reason, with copper. When they renovated, Rod and Madeleine had it refrigerated and use it for storing the Sanatorium's drugs and medicines. That's where he wants her put. But make no mistake, what Roderick requests is illegal, and in my opinion sacrilegious. I won't allow it. Let the poor lady rest in peace."

We talked for a few more minutes. The doctor would not consider any possibility but that Roderick had gone out of his mind with grief.

We went back into the room, and before Rod or I realized what he had done, Dr. Giron shot Roderick up with sedatives. As I watched, Rod sank into a passive state and I could hardly get a word from him.

There seemed to be nothing more I could do at Usher House until Rod recovered. I told Dr. Giron, in no uncertain terms, not to give Roderick any more sedatives unless Roderick requested them.

"I don't understand you," the doctor said. "The man is incoherent with grief. Why don't you want him to have a little peace?"

"He has things to say that I want to hear," I told Dr. Giron. I looked him right in the eye. "I hope you understand me on this, doctor. When I come again, Rod better not be sedated. He and I have things we must talk about." He tried, but failed, to meet my gaze.

The drug had tightened its hold. Rod's head sank deeper into the sofa cushions, his body limp. His eyes appeared closed, but when I approached him to say my farewells I saw them open a slit, his pupils racing back and forth under the lids.

"Rod," I said, urgently, "I'll be back soon, we'll talk again. I know something is wrong about Madeleine's death and I am going to help you. Don't let that doctor give you anything, you hear?"

He paid no attention to my words, just clutched my hands, and speaking with enormous effort to counter the tranquilizer, tried once more to convince me not to let them bury Madeleine. His hands trembled as they gripped mine.

Driving away, I thought that never had I needed a drink more. I headed directly for The Old Forge. Tommy did his usual magic, but this time, whiskey's power to soothe did not seem sufficient. I thought of Edith. Maybe she could help me put my thoughts in order. "Can I use the phone?" I said to Tommy.

He slid the phone across the bar to me. As I dialed, I stared at my reflection in the mirror beyond the bar. I saw dusty bottles lined up on shelves and behind them I saw myself, phone in hand, looking tired and tense. "Edith? It's John."

"John! Thank you for calling. Is Madeleine really dead? How is Roderick?"

"I'm afraid she is. And Roderick is taking it badly. There are some things we need to talk about. Any chance you can get away?"

"Oh, John, of course. You sound upset. Where are you? The Old Forge? I'll be there, ten minutes."

Hanging up, I noticed the fellow in the mirror looked cheered. Not for the first time, I felt thankful there were women in the world, for when men are troubled. It's hard to think how we would get through without them.

"You mean he doesn't want her buried?" Edith said, frowning. "But John, that's . . . that's *wrong*, plain wrong. The woman deserves to go to her rest."

I didn't say anything. I just looked into my Blanton's. We had moved to one of the booths in the back. Willie Nelson told the world about his sorrows softly, and the place had begun to fill up. Willie thought *he* had problems.

"Well, don't you think so, John? John? What's troubling you?"

"Did you ever read my ancestor's, E. A. Poe's story, 'The Fall of the House of Usher' "?

"Well, we all read it in school. But I can't see . . ."

"In that story, the sister of the hero dies and is put to rest in a copper-lined crypt in the House of Usher. But, in fact, she is not dead. She's been buried alive. I bet that's what's worrying Rod."

"But surely, John Charles, that's just an old story. That's fiction."

"Right. Of course." I took a big swallow of the bourbon. Edith made perfect sense. Why worry about an old story? Why did I feel the weight of the cryptic sentences in the casket papers? Why did I feel so sure Rod's obsessions pointed to something real? Maybe the Usher disease had got to my reason, too. "Tommy! Another round!"

"Not for me, John," Edith said. She had been sipping a glass of white wine and did not appear to have made much progress. "I can see that Poe's story worries you. Maybe there is more to your worries than you think. Sometimes our instincts are a way for our subconscious to alert us to something important."

Tommy brought over the whiskey. "So Miz Usher has passed on," he said. "What did it? I heard she had the cancer."

"They don't think so," I said. "Apparently a virulent virus took her."

"Say what?" Tommy looked doubtful.

"I know it sounds weird. But her doctor swears it happens like that sometimes. He claims she'd been overworking, had a lot of worries, got run down, resistance low, couldn't fight the bug off."

Tommy shook his head. "Hell of a thing, this stress. Seems more and more people complaining of it, saying they can't handle it." He went back to the bar.

"What do you think my subconscious is trying to alert me to?" I asked Edith. I felt grateful to her for not dismissing my fears.

"I don't know," Edith said. "But I'll tell you one thing. If you have something on your mind, I bet you there is something there. If you'll allow me, I am going to dig into it."

I looked at Edith and saw she felt just as determined as I did. For the first time since I had heard Roderick's voice that evening, the tight, fearful feeling that had gathered around my heart seemed to loosen. It seemed I wouldn't have to fight this one alone.

Mrs. Boynton glared at me. "John, are you behind this so-called 'research' Edith Dunn is up to?"

After the day I had yesterday, and after having downed a good part of a bottle of Blanton's bourbon the night before, I felt in no mood to put up with Ma Boynton's bullying.

"Yes, I am. Why?" My voice sounded angry.

It was eleven o'clock on the morning after Madeleine Usher's death. I had slept in, only to be awakened by a call from Buzz telling me that Boynton was on the rampage and I should "haul my ass over here pronto." Passing through the house, I saw that Edith had come in early, produced a pile of printouts and left. She left me a note saying that she had completed her on-line researches and had gone to City Hall to follow up. Her note said, "Things are going well and I have a lot to tell you."

My tongue felt like it had grown a coat of fur and my head ached. A sound behind me alerted me to the fact that another person was present, and I turned to see Mayor Winsome, sitting in one of Mrs. Boynton's guest chairs, smiling his genial smile. "Boy, you look like you was run over by the whole tractor pull. Sure hope you had a good time 'cause it's clear you're payin' for it today. Take a seat and let's talk this thing over. I'm sure we can see eye to eye."

Winsome looked his most oily this morning. A stout fellow of about fifty, today he wore a brownish suit, the jacket open to reveal a brown-and-yellow checked vest stretched tight over his large paunch. A matching yellow pocket handkerchief and yellow tie made me squint when I looked at him straight on.

Normally, we all tolerated Winsome. The town likes to go along with his pretense that he is a Southern gentleman of the old school and not—as is the truth—descended from unsuccessful carpetbaggers. His father had seen a change in the family fortunes when he won the Irish lottery, and the Winsome family has not looked back since. A lot of people in town have prospered from their connection with Winsome, and I had no doubt that Mrs. Boynton was one of them.

"See eye to eye on what?" I said, sitting down carefully in order not to jar anything—my brains for example.

"We can't have Edith Dunn prowling around the municipal real estate records," Mrs. Boynton said, "messing into people's private business." She gave me a look that suggested I was a silverfish she had just found in her linen closet. "It's the Usher thing, John. You've got to get off that. Didn't I tell you?"

I had no idea what the hell was she talking about, and for

sure I had no intention of letting her tell me what to do about my friend. What did real estate records and people's private business have to do with the Ushers? The woman had no heart. "Madeleine Usher is dead," I said. "Maybe you forgot that."

"A terrible tragedy, so young, absolutely terrible," Winsome said shaking his head so that his jowls trembled. His sharp little blue eyes looked at me, watching my reaction.

"Yes, truly it is," I said. "And Roderick Usher is not very well either. He doesn't believe she died a natural death and he wants my help to find out what happened."

"Face it, John," Mrs. Boynton said. "Roderick Usher has more screws loose than a broken baler."

"I don't see it that way, and I don't believe you know anything about it."

"John," Winsome said, "everyone in town loves the Ushers and our hearts are with Roderick in his time of trouble. You are to be commended for standing by him. But," here he leaned forward, "use a little common sense here. Usher needs psychological help. Have your Edith Dunn find him a good headshrinker. No good can come of her messing around in business dealings."

"Why?" I said. "Sounds to me like the only reason you and Mrs. Boynton would go on this way is if you have something to hide. Is that it?"

Mrs. Boynton stood up. "Let me handle this, Jackson," she said to our mayor. "Now you listen here, John Charles, because I am not going to say this again." She looked at me fiercely and I looked back at her just as fiercely. "The mayor and I and others are involved in some delicate land dealings. These things get around, prices go up. You're no fool, you understand that. You with me so far? Now, having Edith Dunn rooting around in real estate records may let our New York competition know our plans prematurely. That will cost us money."

The mayor interrupted. "John, this is confidential, completely confidential. Do we have your word on that?"

"I see no reason to give you my word on anything."

Mrs. Boynton frowned. "The property we are putting together must be assembled without everybody and their dog knowing about it. Dunn is fouling things up. I want her off this. And as for you, John Charles, I think you should go take a couple of weeks off, rest and dry up."

"I have no intention of taking a rest or drying up," I said.

Mrs. Boynton scowled. "Perhaps I haven't made this clear to you, John. Butt out of the Usher business or your position here will be terminated."

"Now Fanny, no need to be hasty," Winsome said. He turned to me, smiling his famous crocodile smile. "John understands, don't you, John."

I was about to tell them both what I thought of them and of their transparent attempt to get me off the Usher case. But I knew it would be a foolish move. Since I could see the two snakes hissing their way deep into Usher's affairs, I'd do better helping Rod from the inside, learning what I could. "Yes, I understand," I said, without making clear exactly what I understood.

I'm not sure I put anything over on them. A look passed between Winsome and Mrs. Boynton that I could not interpret.

"Well," Mrs. Boynton said, "just you watch your step. Keep out of matters that don't concern you or you're going to have serious problems. And you can take my word for it, they'll be problems a lot bigger than getting fired from the *Sentinel*.

I got in my car and headed back to Crowley House. I thought some gentle music might be helpful, and turned on the radio.

THE WEATHER OFFICE HAS POSTED HURRICANE WARNINGS TODAY FOR SAVANNAH AND CHARLESTON AS HURRICANE JEAN GATHERED SPEED AND HEADED NORTH. OVER THREE MILLION DOLLARS OF DAMAGE HAS BEEN REPORTED, CAUSED BY THE WINDS AS THEY CUT A SWATH OF DESTRUCTION ALONG THE COAST. COMMENTATORS NOW CALL JEAN THE "KILLER HURRICANE" AS THREE DEATHS HAVE BEEN REPORTED IN ITS WAKE. SERIOUS FLOODING . . .

I snapped off the radio and for the first time that day noticed the weather. Great masses of soot-colored cumulus clouds raced across the sky, driven by a strong wind. The bare trees bent in the gusts. A newspaper blew up suddenly on the road and passed over my windshield, temporarily blinding me. Flurries of rain struck the car's windows with force, as if handfuls of gravel had been flung at them. It looked like the storm system had hit Crowley Creek.

As I passed through town, I saw Beamis Jewelers boarding up their windows. Beamis is the town's worrywart, but he has a good nose for weather. The storm was definitely heading in our direction. I rolled down the car window and a blast of cold damp air and rain blew in, drenching my coat.

The soaking cleared my head and, as it did, the implications of the Boynton and Winsome duo trying to gang up on me also soaked in.

Edith sat at the kitchen table, eating her lunch out of a brown paper bag. She had unwrapped a sandwich and some potato salad and put them out on a plate with a leaf of lettuce. The food looked good and I realized that I was hungry. I opened the refrigerator and took out some cold chicken legs.

"Mrs. Boynton is threatening to fire me," I said to Edith. "Mayor Winsome put his two cents in. He tried charm and she tried threats. Wonder what they're so afraid of."

"John, they're up to something—the mayor, Mrs. Boynton—and it looks like your lawyer, Prynne, is mixed up in it too. They're buying land around Usher House. And they've gone to a lot of trouble to cover their tracks. The trail was real hard to follow."

Standing there, with the chicken leg in my hand, we stared at each other for a moment. I sat down. "What else did you find out, Edith?"

She took a bite of her sandwich.

The lights flickered, then went out. "Great. A power failure," I said. "It must be that wind." We could hear the wind now, much louder than before, making a strange deep roar outside the house, like cars going round and round the track in a stock car race.

I took the kerosene lantern from under the counter, lit it, and put it on the kitchen table between us. Outside the clouds drew in heavy and thick, so that it felt like evening. The kitchen grew dim. The lamp cast a glow around Edith and me, enclosing us. In this luminous circle, Edith looked very beautiful, the lines of sadness on her face softened. I could not take my eyes off her.

"You look tired, John Charles," Edith said softly, returning my gaze. "I know Madeleine's death and Roderick's strange behavior are wearing on you. I know how worried you are about him."

"I drank too much last night," I confessed, surprising myself. "I know better, but still I do it." I felt disgusted when I thought of how I had behaved with Edith the night before, though she hadn't seemed to notice. The more I drank, the sadder I got about Madeleine and the more worried about Rod. I wished Edith hadn't seen me so broken up.

"It weighs heavy on you, being his only friend and seeing him in such a bad way," Edith said. "I'm not saying you didn't drink too much, but you didn't show it much."

"Thank you, Edith," I said. "I appreciate what you say." We continued to look at one another.

The lights flickered back on and the moment passed. I got up, found a plate for my chicken leg, and began to gnaw on it.

"I've been doing some more investigation about Roderick and Madeleine," Edith said, picking up her sandwich. "I hope you don't mind."

"No, of course I don't mind. We need you to do that."

"There's not much to go on. Nobody has a bad word to say about either of them, but all their lives they've been kind of a world unto themselves. When they were kids, they even had their birthday parties together; seems like they were born on the same day. They've always been best friends. Both of them went to the same university, both of them went into medicine, both qualified at the same time, both went on to become specialists. They helped each other. Just before Rod started to have financial troubles at Usher House, Madeleine got offered a prestigious position at the Mayo Clinic. But she put everything on hold to support her brother. They're like this . . ." she held up two crossed fingers. "So it's not surprising that when she got sick he went around the bend."

"It's all very touching," I said. I hadn't been really listening. I couldn't stop thinking about Edith. How pretty she looked and how much I liked sitting in the kitchen listening to her talk. I thought about how she sounded when she said, "You look tired." Her tone, so gentle and warm, had made me feel very good inside. She didn't seem to hold it against me that I had drunk too much last night either; she understood.

"Do you think Mrs. Boynton is going to fire you if I keep on my researches?" Edith said. "I wouldn't want you to lose your job on account of me."

"Mrs. Boynton has been threatening to fire me once a month since I took the job at the *Sentinel*. She may mean it this time but there's nothing I can do about it. Right now, I'm going to play the polite young man around her best as I can. That way I can stay close. The *Sentinel* is a good place to investigate whatever's going on. And if she's mixed up in it, better to be in there than out."

"Is that going to work?"

"I don't know. But there's no doubt she has something to hide. Something we need to find out."

"That's what I think."

"What do you want to do? It's you she's complaining about most. She made some threats, probably she meant you too. Threatened us with 'serious problems.' I would understand if you didn't want to get mixed up in that. It would be okay."

Edith looked right at me. "I want to find out what's going on. I don't like the idea of the mayor and Mrs. Boynton and lawyer Prynne closing in on Roderick's property while he's down and grieving for his sister."

"Well, I'm with you there. I intend to get to the bottom of this. Too bad if Ma Boynton and old Winsome get their fingers caught in the wringer."

"So we keep at it?"

"We surely do."

# FIVE ·

I spent the afternoon and evening diligently completing various tasks at the *Sentinel*. I wanted to give Ma Boynton the impression that I had taken her warnings to heart, but more important, I intended to catch up on my weekly chores so I would be able to spend the next day at the Usher Sanatorium, investigating.

For the moment, I tried to focus my attention on my duties. As long as Edith and I thought it likely that Mrs. Boynton was involved in the Usher business, I figured it would be best to stay close to her action.

Running my eye over the letters we had received for our "Letters to the Editor" column, one caught my attention. Reading it, I sighed to myself. It looked as if our intrepid intern had caused trouble again. What was the fellow up to now? And why had Ma Boynton made me his baby-sitter?

"Buzz? Buzz! Come over here, will you?"

Buzz put down his copy of the *Rolling Stone Magazine* and sauntered over to my workstation.

"Do you know anything about this?" I handed him a letter, handwritten in a neat script of the kind one learns in fourth grade. The writer apparently hadn't had much practice since, and the handwriting had not evolved.

Buzz took the sheet of lined paper, skimmed it, and his ears grew pink around the rims. "This is garbage," he said, handing it back to me. "Just some redneck garbage."

I leaned back in my chair and read aloud:

Dear *Crowley Sentinel* Editor:
You should be ashamed of that New York boy you have working for you. We have enough troubles in Crowley Creek without you all bringing in Godless gamblers and New York Mafia to sow corruption. Tell him to take himself and his sinful friends back to New York City. We may be a small town here but we aren't stupid much as he might like to think so. Mrs. Boynton, your grandpa would turn over in his grave if he knew you was doing business with the sons of satan.

Sincerely,
A concerned friend

"What's it about, Buzz?"

"Oh, nothing."

Buzz was wearing his New York journalist outfit, investigative style. He had on a black turtleneck sweater with a hole in one elbow, faded jeans, and hiking boots. Now he put his finger in the hole of his sweater and wiggled it nervously.

"What 'nothing' do you think it was, triggered this letter, then?"

He smiled weakly. "It might have been my nothing cousin who came up last weekend, talking to Mayor Winsome? He wears fancy Italian suits and sunglasses. Maybe people in town thought that made him Mafia."

"And what might he have been talking to our mayor about?"

"He didn't tell me," Buzz said. "John, I have to go over to the church bake sale. Mrs. Boynton wants an article about it, so if you don't mind . . ."

"But I do mind, Buzz. You must have gotten some hint of what your cousin wants from the mayor, what he's doing in Crowley Creek. What kind of business is he in?"

He's kind of in the . . . the . . . this and that business, you know? Buying and selling."

"Come on, Buzz, you're a journalist. It's your profession to be observant. You must have some idea of the kind of business your cousin does. How does he connect to gambling?"

"Look, he's a lawyer. You know what they say about lawyers?"

I saw it coming. A lawyer joke. But I wasn't quick enough to avoid it.

"When the lawyer fell into the shark pond, how come the sharks didn't eat him?"

"Professional courtesy," I snapped. "Buzz . . ."

"John, I don't know who he's working for, or why he's in town. And to tell you the truth, I don't want to know either. My parents told me he's a wheeler-dealer businessman and that makes him of zero interest to me. I'm just not interested in him, so drop it, okay?"

His voice was both defensive and evasive. Although I doubted that he was telling me everything he knew, I could see that he was embarrassed by the topic and pressing him further wasn't going to accomplish anything.

I tucked the letter in my pocket, intending to follow up on it, and returned to my work. I had a lot of writing to do if I wanted to spend tomorrow at the Ushers.

Driving out to the Sanatorium the next day I was relieved to see that the weather had improved. The wind blew in gusts, the heavy cloud cover had broken up, and torn shreds of clouds raced across the pale blue sky. People had started talking about the hurricane and there were those who were sure it was headed direct for Crowley Creek. Last reports in the *Richmond Times-Dispatch* said that it had cut quite a swath along the coast, then veered out to sea, but that its course was so unpredictable, it could easily veer back our way.

As I drove up to the Usher's, the sun went behind the clouds. Then, as I got out of the Bronco, the sun suddenly broke through and the trees sparkled with moisture in the brilliant light. But as I walked toward the house, I saw the house's dark shadow fall over the tarn, causing the water to look even more black and fetid than I remembered. I hurried inside.

The reception area was deserted. Sunlight filtered through the dusty windows and shafts of dust motes swirled in the dead air. I rang the bell on the reception desk and waited impatiently, tapping my fingers, but no one appeared. Perhaps it would be a good time to check the garden, to see if any little old men were skulking around the bushes.

Outside, the air felt chilly and the grass damp beneath my feet. I avoided the reeking tarn and walked around to the back of the house. Off in the distance I saw a formal rose garden. The rose plants were shrouded in burlap and banked with dead leaves. Gravel walks surrounded the geometric beds of damp black earth. As I approached, I suddenly felt chilled through, despite my warm jacket. Looking up, I saw a figure in a dark cloak, carrying a basket, walking slowly through the garden. I rubbed my eyes, because for a moment, though of course it had to be impossible, I thought the figure was Madeleine. The cloak looked the same, the walk, though slower, almost dirgelike, reminded me of Madeleine, and surely that was the same basket she had used to gather daisies the day before her death!

I broke into a sprint, running as fast and as quietly as I could toward the rose garden, which looked to be only a few hundred yards distant. The lawn, spongy underfoot, seemed to hold me back and the rose garden to recede as I ran toward it. The cloaked figure glided away from me, moving from sunlight to the shadows cast by a grove of gnarled crape myrtle trees at the far side of the garden.

I reached the edge of the lawn and flung myself onto the gravel path, which crunched under my racing feet. I could hear my breath, loud in my ears. Perhaps the sounds alerted my quarry, because the person turned toward me for an instant. I could not see her face—the hood, pulled far forward, shadowed it—but only the shine of the whites of her eyes, and a gleam of blond hair. For a second the figure paused, looking in my direction, then turned, and increasing her pace, passed out of the formal garden and into the grove of trees.

With a burst of speed I ran through the garden, but the paths twisted like a maze, doubling back on themselves, and I lost sight of the cloaked figure as it disappeared into the myrtles.

Finally I reached the far edge of the rose garden and dashed forward, into the trees. In the distance I heard a strange echoing sound, a hollow thud, as if a door had banged shut, then silence.

I could see no one and I did not know which way my quarry could have gone.

I stopped, catching my breath. No longer gasping, I could now hear the sound of drops of water dripping from the branches above and the faint buzz of insects. A damp smell of rotting leaves filled my nostrils and I realized I felt chilled through with sweat. I walked further into the trees. Sunlight could not penetrate the interwoven branches, hanging with moss. There were no footprints to follow. The ground was covered with a carpet of decaying leaves, ferns, and small branches that snagged at my trousers. It seemed pointless to continue, but still I walked on, deeper into what now appeared almost to be a wood.

Through the trees I caught sight of what looked like a shack. Approaching, I realized it was some kind of a storage shed, completely dilapidated, the windows broken and the roof in poor repair. Could this have been where the cloaked figure had gone? I turned the doorknob, which hung loosely, and the door swung open. I peered in. When my eyes accustomed themselves to the dimness I saw that the shed could not have been my quarry's destination. It was completely empty; worn pine floorboards and rough pine plank walls, rotting window frames, a broken chair and some broom handles in one corner—nothing else. Then I looked closer and saw narrow, damp footprints on the pine boards. They crossed halfway into the room, growing fainter as they approached the midpoint, where they disappeared entirely.

I stared, baffled by what had happened. If the person I had been pursuing had come into this empty shed, it looked as if she had vanished in the middle of it. I walked around tapping the walls. They sounded the way uninsulated shed walls sound when you tap them. I tapped the floor. It sounded like a floor. There didn't appear to be any hollow points.

Nonplussed, I turned and left the shed. The door swung shut with a noise that sounded just like the thud I had heard when my quarry disappeared.

The thing was a complete mystery.

Matters did not improve when I returned to Usher House. This time the old man whom I had seen on my last visits sat at reception, his head down on the desk, snoring noisily. I cleared my throat. He sat up with a start and gave me an angry look, as if I were at fault for waking him. About to say something sharp to him, I looked more closely and saw that he was very old, his dark skin gray with fatigue, and the whites of his eyes yellow and rheumy. "I'm sorry about Miss Usher," I said, "I am sure it must be very hard on all of you here."

He recognized me then, and I realized that he had not done so when I woke him, despite my two previous visits. Perhaps he could not see well. "Thank you, sir," he said, with a melancholy smile. "Yes, it is a sad time at Usher House. O' course, we see much of death here, sir. In a manner of speaking, death is our business, this being an old folks home. Yessir, death comes calling more often than we would like. But it surely did surprise us when he came for Miss Usher, her being so young and all. It's been real hard on the old folks, too."

"And with Dr. Usher not well . . ." I said, pausing expectantly.

He shook his head, but said nothing.

"I saw something strange in the rose garden," I said.

His face closed up and he looked at me with an expression I could not read.

"I saw a person who, if Miss Usher had not passed on, I would have sworn was her. Wearing that cape she used to wear, with that big hood pulled down over her face, and carrying that basket she used to gather flowers."

"I don't know nothing about that." he said.

"I followed her, and she went into the little woods beyond the rose garden."

"Nasty in there. We tell our patients to shun the place. The damp will get into your bones and you don't know what you might come down with. Best to stay clear of it." He didn't meet my eyes and began to turn over some papers on the desk.

"The person went into an old shed and then just seemed to disappear."

"Don't know about no old shed. My job is to man this reception desk and that is what I do. You want to know about old sheds, you talk to the gardeners."

"Well, then, could I talk to the gardeners?"

"No gardeners this time of year. We let them all off until spring."

I gave it up. "I'd like to see Dr. Usher."

He brightened up at this. "That's good, Mr. Poe. He could use visitors, he's taking it hard, real hard. You know the way?"

"No, I don't think so. Last time you took me through the serving passageways. I think I'd get lost if I tried to find it on my own."

He led me up the stairway, past the office where I had met with Madeleine, along a broad, long corridor. We crossed over a kind of mezzanine, a gallery that looked down on a deserted ballroom, the floor covered with gleaming black-and-white marble. At one end I saw a stage, with chairs and music stands set out as if waiting for an orchestra. We walked around this mezzanine, through big double doors set with panes of beveled glass, down a long corridor, up a short flight of stairs, along another corridor and down another flight of stairs. Not the sort of journey you would want to take if you had had a few too many.

Eventually we arrived at the doors to the salon. The old fellow knocked and I heard Rod's voice. "Who is it?" He sounded frightened.

"It's me, John Poe," I called back.

"Come in, come in."

I entered and saw him lying on the sofa, huddled under a faded old quilt, his head propped up on a stack of tattered brocade cushions. On a small table by his side he had a silver pitcher beaded with moisture, an array of small pill bottles, and a tray of glasses.

"How are you Rod?" I said, pulling up a chair and sitting down beside him. "That tranquilizer Dr. Giron gave you worn off yet?" I knew sometimes sedatives could have a residual effect, leaving people confused or disoriented for days.

"I miss her, John," he said.

I patted his hand awkwardly. "She was a wonderful woman," I said, the words sounding clichéd in my ears.

"The patients miss her too." He struggled into an upright position, arranging the cushions behind his back. "We need her here. But I failed her, John. I failed her and that is why she left us. Now I must make amends."

"Dr. Giron said they did everything they could for her. And I saw how you looked after her. Don't say you failed her. You have to move on."

"Dr. Giron!" he said. I started. His voice sounded so malevolent that the name came out like a hiss. "The man treats me like I am a mental case. He never for once considers what I say to him."

"I saw that. I told him not to trank you anymore and he gave me a hard time."

"You believe me, John, don't you." He leaned forward, looking at me. "John . . ."

"Yes? What is it, Rod? Tell me, tell me what's on your mind."

"John, I've heard her, late at night, I've heard her step in the corridors." He stared at me, testing me, gauging my reactions.

I nodded, encouraging him to continue.

"I've heard her groaning, John, heard her crying out my name.

"Yes?"

He lowered his voice. "I think I saw her last night, John. She was wearing her cloak and carrying her flower basket.

She moved through the corridors, always ahead of me, like a shadow. I called to her, but she didn't answer. And then . . . I funked it. I ran away. I had a feeling of terror . . . of dread . . . John, I must be going mad. Tell me, tell me I'm hallucinating."

I hesitated. I knew I should tell him what I had seen in the garden, yet something warned me not to. "There must be a rational explanation," I said. My voice sounded unconvincing to me. "The old Poe story, it's in your subconscious, and in mine too. It's influencing us. We both remember what happened after *that* Madeleine died, how she walked the corridors of Usher House, how her brother heard her groans and ignored her."

"You saw her too! You know what I fear!"

"I saw someone in a cloak like hers in the rose garden," I admitted. "What does that prove? Look Rod, we have to get to the bottom of this. This 'sighting,' or whatever it was, it's not the first time. I saw an old man wandering around in the rain, and he too ran away when I approached."

"You did? What did he look like?"

I described the figure I had seen on my first visit.

"That's impossible," Rod said. His tone suddenly cold. "That's a description of old Alastair Mason, one of our charity patients who died last year. Why are you saying that, John? What are you trying to do to me? We were talking about Madeleine . . . Madeleine. . . ."

He got up suddenly and walked over to the corner and picked up a lute. He began to strum on it. The instrument sounded badly out of tune.

"Oh the river is wide, I cannot cross over," he sang, in a thin, doleful voice.

> And neither have I wings to fly.
> Give me a boat, that can carry two
> And both shall row, my love and I.

"Rod!" I said.
But he ignored me and continued singing,

> I leaned my back against some young tree,
> Thinking he was a sturdy oak,
> But first he bended and then he broke . . .

Rod sang, looking at me meaningfully.

I tried, but I could not get his attention. Full of rage at his incomprehensible behavior and of pity for his grief, I finally left. As I walked down the corridor, I heard his plaintive singing continue:

> I put my finger into some soft bush,
> Thinking the fairest flower to find.
> I pricked my finger to the bone
> And left the fairest flower behind. . . .

I was in a foul mood when I got back to Crowley House that evening. After my bizarre and inconclusive visit with Rod, I had talked to some of the staff and patients at Usher House. Several patients admitted that they too had seen strange sights, people walking around the grounds late at night, people who were supposedly dead. But the patients who told these stories had obviously heard them from others, and I realized that the stories of "those who walk" were one of the favorite forms of entertainment around Usher House. Was the place turning into a loony bin? If I hadn't seen "Alastair Mason" and "Madeleine" myself, I certainly would have thought so. The idea even occurred to me that old Ma Boynton might have had a point when she told me I needed to dry up. All my intuition told me that something truly strange and very wrong was going on over there. My mind told me that what I had seen and suspected were impossible and I should smarten up.

Edith was waiting for me at home, full of news. While she talked, I fixed myself a stiff Blanton's. The first one vanished with no apparent effect and it took another before I began to feel some of the day's tension and—let's face it—fear, melt away. I sat back in the leather chair in her office and let her talk. I listened with half an ear as she told me about her further researches into the property shenanigans of Mayor Winsome, Mrs. Boynton, and lawyer Prynne, a group that she called the "Crowley establishment." She told me that so far, she had just found a bunch of front companies. It looked as if lawyer Prynne had things so tangled up that more work would be needed to find out exactly what they were up to. They were applying for various zoning permits, too, but she needed to do more digging to understand the implications.

"Any sign of Dr. Giron being involved?" I asked. "He's Rod's personal physician and I've taken a strong dislike to the man. He seems real evasive to me."

"Not so far. Do you want me to look into it?"

I nodded, staring into my bourbon. Was I going to suspect everyone connected with Usher? Was the whole town involved? If I kept on thinking like this I'd soon be as loony as Rod Usher. I needed to get hold of myself.

But her next words reawakened my irritation and ill temper.

"John, have you heard about this Mr. Marco who came to town last week?"

Marco was Buzz's surname. "What did *you* hear?" I said.

"That he's a lawyer from New York, and that he's been talking to the mayor about his syndicate building a casino in Crowley Creek."

"Gambling's not legal in this state," I said.

"He swears he's got that all worked out in the capital. Now he just needs Mayor Winsome's support on zoning. John, the whole town is talking about it. They're in an uproar. I got the idea that it could have something to do with the shenanigans around the Usher property."

I took a gulp of whiskey. "Ma Boynton is going to go ballistic if Buzz's involvement gets the finger pointed at her and the *Sentinel*. This New York Marco is probably Buzz Marco's cousin. We got an anonymous letter about him yesterday at the paper. Where does Jackson Lee stand on the casino idea?"

"It's hard to know," Edith said. She ran a hand through her hair and took off her reading glasses. Maybe it was the two double whiskeys, but I thought she looked damned attractive, and it annoyed me. We had work to do. "There's some that say that the mayor's keen on the idea," Edith said, hesitantly. "But there are others that say he knows it would really upset the church-going folks in town and so he wants to keep it at arms length."

"Knowing old Jackson Lee, probably both are true. He'll find some way to approve a casino and wreck the town and blame it on someone else. But what's that got to do with what you're supposed to be doing today? I don't see what it's got to do with the Ushers."

Edith looked at me. I think she was shocked by my tone and I have to admit my voice did sound kind of belligerent. "Are you okay, John Charles?"

"No. No, I am not okay. I saw that twit of a friend of mine, Rod Usher, today and I think Madeleine's death has really driven him around the bend." What had happened to the second glass of whiskey? I could not have drunk it already. I must have made it short. I poured another.

"Surely that's a cause for pity, John, not anger," Edith said, her voice cold.

"Well how about this? Usher says he saw Madeleine walking the halls at night, groaning. And when I was out there today I saw her sauntering through the rose garden."

Edith stared at me. "What exactly did you see, John. Tell me."

I took a sip of the whiskey. How could I tell her? What could I say that would not make me sound like a complete idiot? I shrugged.

She leaned forward and touched my hand. "Please, tell me John." At her touch, I jerked my hand away. We both looked at one another for a moment. She leaned back. "I want to know what you saw."

So I told her. I described my pursuit of "Madeleine," how she'd disappeared on me, the rumors of the walking dead, my sighting of "Alastair."

"You say you think it's possible that the people repeating these stories are influencing one another? But if that's true, it doesn't explain what you saw."

"Maybe Ma Boynton's right. Maybe I'm drinking too much and having delusions."

"Madeleine Usher really is dead, John? There can be no doubt of that?"

"She's dead. Three specialists checked her body over. The funeral's tomorrow. She's been over at Porter's funeral home and I talked to Porter. It was embarrassing, but believe me, the lady is dead. She's dead, dead, dead!"

"Okay, okay John, calm down. I believe you, but there has to be some rational explanation. It follows that if Madeleine is dead, that was someone else you saw."

She had to be right, of course. But why that strange supernatural chill when I saw the cloaked figure? If it wasn't Madeleine, why did she have that unmistakable walk that I recognized at once? For some reason, I thought of the casket papers. I had a faint recollection of reading something there that might help. Of course, I had given Edith the casket with all the papers that related to Usher House, or all the important ones. True, there were papers I hadn't given her, but they surely would not be relevant. That's why I hadn't given them to her.

But could I be sure? I hadn't read them that carefully. Just sort of breezed through them. Every time I read the casket papers, I got depressed. Probably because they were boring and completely irrelevant in the 1990s. At least, that's what I told myself. Which is why I had not wanted to burden Edith with them. And too, the ink had faded, making them awfully hard to read. And . . . I was full of excuses as to why I didn't want to look at the papers I had hidden or show them to Edith.

I know what my father would have said. "There you go

again, John Charles, taking the easy way out. You're just lazy, bone lazy."

And he would have been right. I better get down to it, read them tomorrow. Of course, there was no way any hundred-and-fifty-year-old papers could help my friend in his grief or me to figure out what was going on. The way I saw it that night, I was so down, nothing could help.

But at least I would have tried.

# SIX

The funeral was not pleasant. Of course, they never are, but this one seemed worse than most. It rained heavily and the cemetery looked like a sea of dripping umbrellas. The sky was low, a gritty steel-gray color, and as I walked toward the open grave, my shoes squished in the damp sod, soaking through.

The old church cemetery had been full since the nineteenth century, but the Usher plot was off by itself in a corner and they had found space in it for Madeleine. I saw a large obelisk, dedicated to the Usher family, the stone worn, the figures pitted with age and now virtually indistinguishable. As the minister droned on, I studied it. Eventually I made out two broken columns flanking a weeping angel. Around the arched top, I could recognize a pattern of upturned torches. On both sides of the monument stood old cast-iron urns. Around it I saw the graves of the Ushers who had been laid to rest here in the eighteenth century, marked by stones at both the head and foot, as had been the custom then. I couldn't read the stones; the inscriptions on them had been worn away by time. Nothing left, I thought, but cryptic symbols that we no longer understand and grave markers now undecipherable.

Looking around me, I realized that almost everyone in town who could get the day off had come to the funeral. In addition to the owners of most of the retail businesses, whom the Sanatorium had tried to support, all the town's most prominent citizens stood listening to the minister, looking appropriately mournful. I guessed that rumors had gotten around about Rod's strange behavior because people seemed tense and unusually quiet, even for a funeral.

Rod stood next to me, not speaking. Rain—or were they tears?—ran down his face and from time to time he shook his head, as if arguing with someone. When I spoke a few words of condolence to him, he nodded his thanks without replying, but I had the impression he did not really hear me.

Afterward, Rod invited everyone back to the Sanatorium for refreshments. Long tables covered with white linen and lit by tall, branched silver candelabra had been set out at one end of the ballroom. Despite the large crowd, perhaps fifty or sixty people, the room was so huge people huddled in isolated knots, drinking ice tea or coffee and talking in subdued voices. The folks from town did seem to be making an effort to mingle with the old patients who were ambulatory enough to come to pay their last respects to Madeleine Usher.

On the stage, someone had arranged the wreaths and flowers sent by friends of the family and business associates. The masses of blooms looked stiff and out of place, as if part of a play that had been cut in the middle, unexpectedly.

I behaved badly by spending too much time talking to Marilyn, whom I had not seen or talked to since Madeleine's death. I even went so far as to use this occasion of grief to invite her out for dinner and dancing in Richmond. I figured I needed a break; I didn't want to end up looking like Rod. She seemed real enthusiastic about the idea.

I kept a sharp eye on Rod. Although he was acting normally, I thought it might well be pretense. Watching him, I saw him chatting to one person after another, accepting condolences, and then, when no one was looking, his face would slip into the wild, absent expression that I had come to dread. He would stare off at nothing, his mouth working as if he were talking silently to himself.

Old Roger Boynton was there. He had had his wheelchair rolled up to the food table and when I approached him, he started guiltily. "Hello, sir," I said to him. "A sad occasion here at Usher Sanatorium."

He nodded without much interest and continued to eye the food table intently. "See any of those little shrimp things?" he said. "Those ones in the puffy crust? They won't give me any fried food here, you know. Got me on a diet. What's the point? I'm not going to get any younger." His speech was difficult for me to follow, and it took a few seconds for me to understand him. While I puzzled over his remarks, he went on, "All gone, are they? You got the last one?"

I handed him the shrimp canapé I had been about to bite into. He greedily stuffed it into his mouth. "How about that one with the bacon on it?" he said. "Won't give me bacon either. Sometimes, I wonder, what's the point of it.

Howsomeever, there's folks who have it worse, much worse. *They're* lucky to get ham hocks and greens."

"Who might that be, sir?" I said. For the first time, I think, he realized who I was. "John Charles! So, what do you think? I outlived another half my age, not bad, eh?"

"That's true, sir. Especially considering all the good times you've had."

"You can say that again!" he said forcefully. Then, his head slipping slightly, he repeated, as if to himself, "say that again . . ."

"Who's lucky to get ham hocks and greens?" I repeated.

"Them as walks. But then if you've passed over, what does it matter, right?" He chortled to himself.

"I don't understand, sir. Who are you talking about?"

He leaned forward, as if to confide in me. Just then a nurse walked by and gave him a sharp look. "Now you behave yourself, Mr. Boynton," she said. "You keep to the diet we agreed to. We don't want to have another stroke, do we?"

"Don't you threaten me, you old bitch," Boynton muttered under his breath, "I'll eat whatever I damned well please."

The nurse, who had not heard, walked away, and Boynton leaned forward and began scarfing canapés off the table and putting them in his pockets. It was strange to see, because one side of him was vigorous and quick, while the other was completely inert. His eye darted, checking to see if anyone beyond me was watching, and at the same time he stuffed food into his jacket pockets and into the folds of his lap robe.

His spunk appealed to me, and I found a big linen napkin and made a nice collection for him of the best of the food he couldn't reach, and then tucked it under his lap robe.

When I did that, he looked up at me, and I saw there was a tear in his bad eye. "They'll be grateful," he said. "You're a good sort, John Charles. Poor souls. It's a miserable existence, living in the dark and cold of the other side. Not what they expected when they came to the famous Usher Sanatorium. When you pass over, you expect angels and golden harps, right boy?" He let out such a loud cackle that several people looked over at us. His good eye winked.

Rod Usher came by and put his hand on Boynton's shoulder. "You are looking much improved, Mr. Boynton," he said to the old man. "I see you have recovered complete use of your right hand." His tone was professional and there was virtually no intimation of the madness I had seen in him the day before. Either he was much better, or he could control himself more than I had realized.

Boynton grinned. "Y'all should have more parties like this one. Eating what a man wants to eat is the second best medicine. Now if you brought up some of the wine from that famous cellar of yours. . . ."

At the word "cellar" Usher paled. "You forget yourself, sir," he said stiffly. "We are here to mourn the passing of my beloved sister."

Boynton seemed to shrink up. "Lord forgive me," he mumbled. "I forgot. . . ." A tear trickled down from his bad eye. "This stroke. . . ."

"Of course, of course," Rod said. He turned to me. "Mr. Boynton is making a good recovery. We see improvements every week. If he keeps to his diet and his physiotherapy, the prognosis is excellent."

Boynton gave me a cynical look, and gestured like a

naughty child toward his pockets, bulging with stolen tidbits. "We all follow doctor's orders here, if we know what's good for us," he said.

Rod motioned me aside, and I followed him. The crowd had thinned out and the nurses were beginning to wheel and escort the patients out of the ballroom. "My apologies for yesterday, John," he said. "As you see, I am much better."

Actually, he did not look better to me. He looked like a man holding himself together with string and baling wire. "Perhaps it helps to see, with your own eyes, Madeleine laid to rest," I said.

He frowned. "But I saw no such thing, John."

"What do you mean, Rod?" I said exasperated. "We saw her in an open coffin in the funeral home. We saw her coffin laid to rest in the cemetery."

"So it seems," he said darkly.

"For God's sake, man, what do you mean?"

"What did you see, yesterday, John? Did you see Madeleine wearing her cloak and walking in her favorite rose garden or did you not?"

I did not reply.

"Well, I saw her again at dawn this morning."

"It must be someone else, pretending to be Madeleine."

"You know better, John. I saw her, I followed her. She turned to me, she beckoned to me. I saw her face. Madeleine is here; in this house.

"It's some kind of a sick practical joke, that's the only possible explanation."

"Don't say that, John! I saw her."

"Rod, listen to me. We need to get to the bottom of this. Let me search the house, look in the inside passageways. I might find some clues to who is doing this to you and why."

"I know and you know, John. Why are you pretending it's not Madeleine? Are you trying to tell me you think I am mad? When you yourself saw her? Is that what you're trying to do? I thought you were my friend!"

He was very close to the edge and I didn't want to push him over.

I spoke carefully. "Remember you said that you thought maybe there was some chemical in the tarn or in the moss that was causing you to hallucinate? Let me search, I might find something that will explain what is happening. Please, Rod."

He just shook his head. "The old story is working its way out. We are in the clutches of a fate stronger than ourselves, John. There is nothing we can do but wait for the moment when we hear her call to us. Then, and this I promise you, I will not make the mistake my ancestor made. I will go to her, John. I will rescue her. I will not let her be entombed far from the light. I have sworn it."

Driving home, I reflected on what I had learned from Boynton and what Rod had said. In particular, Rod's comments about my ancestor Edgar Allan's story reminded me of my vow the night before to finish reading those accursed casket papers. The unread bundle had appeared to be some preliminary notes of the kind writers make when developing their stories. Poe had written articles about his literary theories and these notes seemed to be drafts of such articles. I had not thought them worth more than a quick skim. But now, I wondered why E.A. had included them in the casket.

There must be something in there of importance. Or, more likely, something *he* thought was important. While there was no doubt that Edgar Allan Poe had been a genius, he had also been self-obsessed, unstable, neurotic, and possibly slightly mad. He certainly knew how to see the dark side, something I desperately wanted to avoid. I felt as if I were getting sucked into an irrational world where nothing was what it seemed and the normal rules did not apply.

At home, I went to the false drawer in my father's desk in the library and drew out the packet of papers I had taken from the casket and hidden before giving it to Edith. The papers were yellowed and crumbly to the touch. The ink had faded and was almost illegible in places. I sighed.

The room was cold and I made a fire, stacking the oak branches carefully. When it was drawing well, I turned on the lamp over my favorite armchair, untied the bundle and sorted through the sheets, looking for the papers I recalled, the ones that related to Poe's famous story, "The Fall of the House of Usher." Mixed among fragments of literary criticism and brief, preliminary notes to stories yet unwritten, I found the following pages.

> *Notes for the story: Fall of the House of Usher 1839*
> *I have often thought how interesting a magazine paper might be written by any author who would—that is to say—who could—detail step by step, the processes by which any one of his compositions attained its ultimate point of completion. For that purpose, I now propose to set down the steps by which I devised my extraordinary tale, "Fall of the House of Usher."*
>
> *Never losing sight of the object supremeness, or perfection,*

at all points, I asked myself: "of all melancholy topics, which, according to the universal understanding of mankind, is the most melancholy?" Death—was the obvious reply. "And when," I asked, "is the most melancholy of topics most poetical?" The answer here is obvious: "When it most closely allies itself to Beauty. The death, then, of a beautiful woman is, unquestionably, the most poetical topic in the world. And equally is it beyond doubt that the tragedy is greatest when seen through the eyes of one who loves her most deeply and most enduringly.

This chain of logic has provided us with the subject for our tale, so we turn our attention to the moral or intellectual underpinnings. For a tale without moral content and intellectual coherence cannot endure in the mind of the reader. Ephemeral, once read it will vanish from his mind, and thus be a cheat upon the public and a waste of its author's creative energy.

Dividing the world of mind into its three most immediately obvious distinctions, we have the Pure Intellect, Taste and Moral Sense. Just as the Intellect concerns itself with Truth, so Taste informs us of the Beautiful while the Moral Sense is regardful of Duty. Of this latter, Conscience teaches the obligation and Reason the expediency. All three must play a part in the tale to be constructed.

Having determined the theme, reminded myself of the moral, aesthetic and intellectual requirements, I now turned my attention to the requirements of the plot.

Nothing is more clear than that every plot, worthy of the name, must be elaborated to its dénouement before anything be attempted with the pen. So I needed a story whose conclusion contained the dramatic energy to provide the vital *thrust which would carry my reader forward. But where was such a tale to be found? In my view, either history affords a thesis, or one is suggested by an incident of the day.*

These then were my principles: *I wanted a story where the Death of a beautiful woman is the most important theme, I want a bereaved loved one, I needed a moral and intellectual underpinning to sustain my story and I required, to stimulate my mind, an "incident of the day" to launch my tale.*

*I cast my mind back through my recollections searching for that seed, that trigger that I needed, but alas, was unable to find one. My life, so full of events, of pressures, seemed to allow me no time to think. My friend and patron, Burton, pressed me for the story I had promised for his magazine, now long overdue. In desperation, I thought to spend a week with my friend, Roderick Usher, who lived in a desolate ruin of a house far outside of the city.*

*Perhaps solitude, away from the stresses and alarums of my daily toil would answer my cause. I confess too, that I could not but hope that Roderick, who had previously been immune to my pleas for funds, might consider helping me, Cissy and Muddy. But then, my life has been whim—impulse—passion. Chance so quickly seized, too often long regretted.*

*Roderick and his sister Madeline acceded to my request, albeit reluctantly. Their reticence did not surprise me as they had always been somewhat hermetical and had become more so in recent years. Their ultimate kindness did not surprise me either, for Rod and I had been as soul-mates since our days together at the University.*

*Now, to explain what happened, the events that provided the germ for my story. In truth I cannot. Could it have been the laudanum and the drink that Roderick and I fell* prey to? For it is true, that we drank. And for me, even the smallest amount of alcohol and I am sick, drugged, lost to myself.

Some of what I saw, what I feared, must surely have been drunken delusions. And then, too, I am profoundly excited by music. . . . Music is the perfection of the soul. And Roderick was a consummate musician. I can remember the two of us, day after day—in that salon—I only half conscious, hearing him playing upon his guitar, mournful, dirge-like love songs. Always he sang of an impossible, a cursèd love.

And once, late at night, when I rose, and walked—sleeping?—half asleep?—and opened a door—what did I see in that house? What unmentionable sin? But how could I have seen anything? Surely, I slept and I dreamed.

Yet I have always believed that at death, the worm is the butterfly—still material, but of a matter unrecognized by our organs—recognized occasionally, perhaps, by the sleep-walker directly, without use of his organs, through the mesmeric medium. Thus a sleepwalker may see ghosts. Divested of the rudimental covering, his being inhabits space—what we suppose to be the immaterial universe—passing everywhere, and acting all things, by mere volition, cognizant of all secrets but that of the nature of God's volition.

I drank again, and in my stupor, I seemed to hear an infant crying. I became insane, with long intervals of horrible sanity. During these fits of absolute unconsciousness, I drank— God only knows how often or how much. I dreamed of my darling wife, Cissy. I dreamed of a love so profound and so passionate that nothing could stand in its way, not even death. I saw and I recognized my darling's doom.

And then, Roderick was putting me on the train, his tor-

*mented face flying away from me as the train gathered speed
and carried me from what had become vague and terrible
memories.*

    *And as the train bore me toward home, toward my beloved
wife Cissy and our mother Muddy, there formed in my mind,
like figures limning out of a Crystal Ball, the cryptic story I
would tell. I would encipher in my story the terrible events I
had seen with my sleeping eyes and my tormented spirit: a story
of Death, Undying Love that endures beyond the grave, Evil
and Beauty. My moral sense would be regardful of Duty, my
Conscience of my Obligation and my story would yield to the
expedience of Reason.*

    *What did I see at the House of Usher? I do not know. Read
my story and it is all there, hidden in the cryptogram whose
power lies in its mystery and its terrible Secret.*

Sighing, I flung the papers aside. Poe's ramblings meant
nothing to me. As far as I could tell, these were notes for a
nineteenth-century literary essay combined with a disjointed
account of a drunken week with a friend. Sleepwalking,
ghosts, unmentionable scenes, terrible secrets, these were
standard elements of gothic fiction. What difference could
any of it make to the events I was trying to unravel? At best,
I could believe that my friend Rod was being subconsciously
influenced by Poe's famous published story. But these scrib-
blings, with their dark hints, meant absolutely nothing to me.
I put the sheets beside me on the desk. I should show them
to Edith. But as soon as this thought crossed my mind I felt
a profound reluctance to do so. It was if there was something
in the papers that was going to hurt both me and my friend,

Rod, as if I knew something I didn't want to know, something it was important that Edith not find out.

I retied all the sheets except the notes on Usher and replaced them in the false drawer in the desk. The papers I had just read I placed carefully between the leaves of the family bible, which sat on the desk exactly in the place where my father had kept it.

I stood there for a moment, holding the old bible in my hands. It was a large, heavy volume, its pages edged with gold, its cover darkened and discolored with age. Idly, I opened the front cover and read the inscription, handwritten in faded grayish ink in a nineteenth-century copperplate:

> O, Never on this Holy Book,
> With careless, cold indifference look
> Tis God's own word, and they who read
> Shall learn from each unfolded page
> A blessing for their heritage.

For a moment I thought of my beloved mother who had read this bible to me when I was little, every Sunday, until she died when I was eleven. How would she have felt if she knew I had put the Poe papers in the holy bible? What a strange thought. I put it out of my head and left the library, closing the door firmly behind me.

# SEVEN

Excited and happy, Marilyn walked proudly beside me through the spectacular turn-of-the-century lobby of the Jefferson Hotel, the grandest in Richmond. We strolled past the gleaming marble pillars and potted palms and then stopped while she admired the spectacular two-story staircase that Scarlett O'Hara had descended in the movie, *Gone with the Wind*. Marilyn confided to me that Scarlett was one of her heroes. I wasn't sure if she meant Scarlett or the actress Vivien Leigh. I told her I thought she would look sensational coming down the stairway. And if I were the fellow waiting for her at the bottom, no way I would tell *her* I didn't "give a damn."

We pushed open the glass doors at the back of the mezzanine and entered the Lemaire restaurant. Marilyn smiled with pleasure as the waiter pulled out her chair, then whisked the huge pleated linen napkin off the plate and placed it on her lap with a flourish. Marilyn's pleasure made me happy.

"Just listen to this, John Charles," she said, studying the menu. "'Grilled venison wrapped in smoked bacon with Thomas Jefferson's black root salsify and dried-currant foie gras sauce.' Can you believe it? Or how's about 'buffalo strip loin with sun-dried cherry sauce.' Wild. What are you havin'?"

"I need to reflect," I said. "It's a serious decision."

"You got that right."

"An *amuse-bouche*," the waiter said, giving us both little plates of salmon and grapefruit.

"Free?" Marilyn said. "That's a real good idea." She thought for a moment, perhaps assessing the business advantages inherent in freebies. I watched her as her sharp eyes took in all the details of the restaurant. She studied the ornate plaster cornices touched with gilt, the silver breadbasket, the single pink rosebud in the silver vase, the heavy yellow satin curtains, the other diners.

Only one thing disappointed her: the hairstyles of the other women. "I don't know who they think they're kidding, John Charles," she told me as the waiter poured our wine, "but there's not a woman in the world who doesn't look better with big hair. Now look at the gal over there," she pointed to a plain-looking blonde in a black dress, dining with an older gentleman at a far table. "She's got a big rock on her wedding ring finger, so they can't be hurting for bucks, but she's done herself up dull as a dishwasher. With her money, she could have some decent highlights, get a little sex appeal, know what I mean? That guy she's with's been givin' me the eye for the last half hour. She's prob'ly boring him to *death*."

Marilyn's hair had plenty of highlights. She had it piled up on her head, with long curly bits hanging down over her face. She wore glittery blue stuff on her eyelids, which gave her brown eyes a sparkle, and a dark-red dress cut so low in front that I found it hard to concentrate on what she was saying whenever she leaned over to reach for the breadbasket. No question of my getting bored. "Hey, John, I thought the way you wrote the article about me and Mayor Winsome was real clever. You know, he came round and thanked me in person for being such a 'real lady' about him smashing up my new Firebird. He even said he was going to give me a look-in on a new shopping-center development some of the boys are workin' on."

"More to the point, did he offer to pay for the Firebird?"

"You gotta be kidding. The mayor is tighter than Ma Boynton's corsets. But he told me he has a brother-in-law runs a body shop outside of Charlottesville who will give me a good deal."

"That's something, anyway."

Marilyn laughed and took a long drink of her red wine. We had already had drinks at the bar and now her cheeks flushed, and another long, curly bit came loose from the tangle of curls on the top of her head. I watched mesmerized as she lifted her arm to tuck it back in, causing the front of her dress to gape. "I wouldn't trust a Winsome farther than I could throw him. He'd prob'ly chop up the Firebird for parts and then stick it full of bits from all those old wreckers they got. Last thing I'd do is let anyone with that blood touch my Firebird. Say, how's it going over at Usher's? What I hear, is, they have real troubles over there and Dr. Usher is too broken up over his sister's passing to cope."

"Is that so? What else do you hear?"

"Maybe it's not right to talk about people's business problems. Gossip can really hurt and who knows if it's true or not?"

The waiter came by and our conversation about the Ushers took a backseat while Marilyn and the waiter discussed how you marinate duck in "rare Tennessee whiskey." Once he had our orders, I tried again. "So, tell, what are people saying about the Ushers and the goings-on out there at the Sanatorium? You know Rod is my friend. I'd never repeat anything that could give him problems."

Marilyn looked uncomfortable. "I know he's your friend, John."

"Come on, Marilyn." I smiled my most winning smile at her.

She ran her fingers through her hair, distracting me, then said, "Well, people think Usher is hiding something. Some say Rod Usher has a girlfriend in Roanoke who hardly anyone ever sees. Folks say she's staying up there now but she only comes out at night when all the dead walk, you know? There's people think she's really a ghost."

I looked at Marilyn to see if she was serious. They had brought a silver bowl of spoon bread with our salad. Marilyn concentrated on spooning it out, so I couldn't see her eyes. "Seriously, Marilyn, don't tell me you believe in those stories about ghosts walking at Usher House."

Marilyn looked up at me and gave me that bewitching little smile of hers. "But o' course I do. I just love a good ghost story. Everyone knows the old Usher House's been haunted forever. The first house fell down, you know. Then the Ushers built another one, and it has a bad curse on it. But Rod and Madeleine turned it into a sanatorium and did good. So folks figure that the ghosts are happy now. You can't expect them just to take off, can you? Where else would they go?"

I felt pretty sure Marilyn was pulling my leg. But I played along and we swapped ghost stories for a while. I figured Marilyn was either exaggerating to amuse me, or knew something she didn't want to say. I needed to find out which. "Well, ghosts are fine," I said, "but still, I'd have to say they have pretty strange ghosts at Usher House, looking to eat ham hocks and greens and nibbles from parties."

"How's that?"

I told her about what old Roger Boynton had said.

"Well, you know best, John Charles," she said, studying her dessert menu. "What do you think about this here dessert quartet? You get four different desserts on it. If I ordered that, I'd get to try four different pastries. You could help me out. But look, they have a peach and strawberry soufflé. That's not something you see every day. I could do with some coffee too, that French wine went right to my head."

"Have whichever you like best," I said, "and I'll have the other one. That way you get to try both."

"You are so sweet, John Charles," Marilyn said. "Let's just do that. Look, John, lots of folks in town have seen the ghosts. Most everybody who goes over there early in the morning to deliver or late in the evening will see old people who have passed on walking around. And there've been ghost stories about Usher House told for over two hundred years."

"I just don't believe you fall for that, Marilyn."

She looked up at me and I saw the sharp look in her eye that she usually kept hidden. "Well, it could be said there's something funny about the food they buy in town. Expensive stuff and cheap stuff. Seems like they're feeding two classes of people."

"That's interesting. But couldn't it be the fancy food for the patients and the other for the staff?"

"It could be, o' course," Marilyn said, her tone letting me know she didn't think so. "Another thing, whatever Rod is up to, it might have been getting to Madeleine. Maybe she didn't like the girlfriend. Because the two of them had been having some set-tos lately."

"Could it be they were quarreling about money? Tommy White told me he thought they were having money troubles and now you say you've heard that too."

The waiter brought the desserts and Marilyn oohed and aahed about the soufflé and the pastries. It was hard to concentrate on Usher problems when Marilyn was going all out to cheer me up and give me a good time. I didn't want her to think I didn't appreciate it, but the woman worked at the beauty shop that was the female gossip central in Crowley Creek. If I could get her to open up, I knew I'd find out things. "So do you think that's what Madeleine and Rod argued about, money troubles?"

"Could be," Marilyn said. "Madeleine wore her hair long and pulled back, you know? So she hardly ever needed to come into the shop. But when she did come in for a trim, we used to have a good natter. She always seemed like a real lonely lady to me. But then, who wouldn't be, stuck out in that place day after day, never seeing anybody but your brother and a lot of sick old people? Still I'd guess the problem had to be money because I know for a fact she wouldn't give much mind to Rod's girlfriend. She'd be happy for her brother. She told me she worried about him, wanted him to get out, have more fun, live a little."

"Did he take her advice?"

She winked at me. "Hey, that's enough about the Ushers. It's too damn gloomy a subject. Ghosts, money trouble, sisters dying on you, who needs it? Did you say we were going dancing?"

I didn't get back to Crowley House till after breakfast the next morning. Although tired, I was in a fine mood. Marilyn had invited me back to her place and demonstrated convincingly that her idea of a good time fit in real well with mine. Underneath that manner of hers, I thought, Marilyn is a truly nice person. Generous-hearted. I wasn't sure what to make of what she had told me about the Ushers, however, and I wanted to talk to Edith about it.

When I came in, still wearing my good suit from yesterday, my shirt looking rumpled around the collar and my tie stuffed into my pocket, I found Edith taking a coffee break in the kitchen. She looked up at me and frowned. "You were out early this morning, John Charles. Can I get you a coffee?"

"In late," I said, smiling to myself. "I've had breakfast."

"With Marilyn?"

Her sharp tone surprised me. And surely she knew a gentleman doesn't talk about the lady he spends the night with. "I did speak to Marilyn about the Ushers," I said. "I want to try out some of the things I learned on you. See what you think of them."

She didn't say anything. Just got up from the table, walked over to the stove, and refilled her cup.

"Well, do you want to hear?"

"Of course I do," she said, not looking at me.

"Marilyn said lots of people in town have seen the 'ghosts' at Usher House. She says everyone knows it's haunted, always has been."

"I've heard that too," Edith said. "*I* didn't pay it any mind."

She was real snippy this morning. Things hadn't been right between us since I snapped at her the day I got back from the funeral. Then too, I felt bad about not trusting her with the Usher casket papers I'd hidden in my papa's bible.

"I don't think Marilyn believes it either, though she plays along. I think she believes there are people there who are like second-class citizens, get poorer food, walk around at night."

"It doesn't make sense, John. Why would the Ushers do that? And then, if people know they've died, how can they walk around?"

"Then she told me some gossip about Rod having a girl-friend hidden away over there. She also hinted that Madeleine had encouraged Rod to go out with other women."

"Now *that* makes sense. Everyone knows Madeleine wor-ried about her brother. She probably wanted him to have some kind of personal life. I bet she thought it might help him, because he's been acting odd lately. Lots of people no-ticed. I've been wondering if the mayor, Mrs. Boynton, and the rest of that bunch were after the property because they knew the Ushers had problems. But something still doesn't hang together. And none of it explains your seeing Madeleine in the rose garden. . . . John?"

"Yes?"

"I really want to help. But it's hard. I think there are things you're not telling me."

I went to the cupboard and took down a mug. I'd changed my mind about the coffee. Actually, I had begun to feel the effect of the partying last night and I kind of wished Edith would lay off. I poured the coffee and took a sip. What it needed was a shot of Blanton's. However, that probably wasn't such a good idea.

"Nothing important," I said. "I found some old Poe papers, literary notes about the story 'The Fall of the House of Usher.' I've got a bad feeling about them."

"Why not show them to me?"

Why not? Because they make my ancestor seem like a deranged druggie alcoholic, and that bothered me? Because there was too much I didn't understand? I walked over to the window, and looked out. Weather reports said the hurricane had taken a sudden turn out to sea, away from our part of the country. The storm center had moved with it. A cloudless day, the sky a brilliant metallic blue. In the bright sun, the bare tree branches cast long, complicated shadows, almost like spiderwebs, over the ground. The lawn—sodden, colorless, and dead-looking—stretched toward a copse of tall hemlocks in the distance. "I'm real sorry, Edith. I know it seems like I don't trust you. I don't mean to act that way. That's not it."

Her face softened. "It does feel like that, John Charles. I want to help. I've got lots of information about the property dealings around Usher's, but you've hardly looked at it. And you know things about the history of the Usher family you aren't telling me. Without more trust, we're missing out on what we could accomplish. We have very different temperaments. If we work together, we'll learn from each other."

She was right. What held me back? What was I afraid of?

\* \* \*

I told Edith I needed to get on over to the *Sentinel* and do some work. We agreed to meet early in the evening to go over the things she had found out, and then to drive together over to the Usher's for their Thanksgiving party. The party was to be a kind of stripped-down version of the open house they had held in previous years.

But when I got to the office I found Ma Boynton waiting for me, looking fed up. "John, we just got a call from Buzz. Seems that junker car of his went off the road over near Belleville. He's waiting for someone to come by and help him. He's at Mill's filling station."

"What?" I was annoyed. "Can't Mills tow him out?"

"Apparently there was a five-car pileup on Highway 360 on the Narrow Creek bridge this morning, and you can't get a tow truck for love or money. Anyway, he doesn't need a tow truck. He just needs someone who knows how to drive to rock him out of the mud."

"But . . ."

"Do I have to spell it out for you, John Charles? The big city boy can't drive worth a darn. You know it, you've pulled him out before. What's the problem today?"

The problem was, I felt fed up, hungover and I had work to do. But Ma Boynton was right; I probably was the best one to help. As long as he didn't expect me to tow that junker of his with my Bronco. Last time I had to tow him out, the guy put his car in "park" and I almost lost my transmission before I figured out what was going on.

Buzz waited for me about six miles out of town, on the road that passed by the Usher property. It was getting on for three thirty when I picked him up at Mill's. He showed me where he had turned off the highway onto a dirt track, driven in about a half mile, and then got stuck. As I drove carefully down the rutted laneway, I asked him what in the hell he had been doing on this cow path anyway.

He was silent for a moment, then said, "if I tell you, you have to promise that this is my story, okay?"

"What are you talking about, Buzz. What story? This is a road to nowhere, how could there be a story down here?"

In fact, I knew the track, as I did so many in the area. It led into a nice marshy area where my papa and I had gone duck hunting when I was a kid. Just driving down the road on this beautiful late-fall day brought back memories of those times. I wanted to think I had happy memories of this place, but truth to tell, my dad had been so bad-tempered, so irritable, so hard to get on with, that hunting with him had been a trial for me. I had stopped as soon as I could. No matter what I did, it was wrong. According to him, I shot too soon, I shot too late, I spooked the dogs, you name it—if anything went wrong, I caused it. If nothing went wrong, that was despite my incompetence and stupidity. When I got older I realized that the thing that got to him was my getting more birds than he did. Once I cut that out, he could give me advice, and things went better.

Remembering, I decided to go easy on Buzz. After all, he was younger than I, from the city, and I shouldn't have been surprised that he didn't know how to get a car out of the mud. But what could he have been doing out here, on this road that didn't lead to anything but a marsh?

He lowered his voice and practically whispered, "I was following my cousin, Aldo. He came out here with two surveyors. I wanted to see what they were doing but they were driving a rented Jeep, and they went on down the road and I lost them."

We came over a rise and I saw Buzz's junker about two hundred yards ahead, skewed off the track, the rear wheel sunk to the axle in mud. I stopped the car and we both jumped out. The ground was low and swampy. Mosquitos and flies buzzed around us and you could see standing water in the wheel ruts. But it was still kind of nice. I could hear the birds singing in the underbrush; the sun's rays slanted down through the trees, lighting the ground cover of sumac, ferns, buckwheat, and burdock.

"Damn!" Buzz said, swatting his face with his hand. A spot of blood appeared on his forehead. "Mosquitos any bigger they could tow my car. What do you think, John, think you can rock it out? Mrs. Boynton said you're real good at things like that; said if anybody could, you could."

Mrs. Boynton saying nice things about me? Why? And why had she sent me out here to help Buzz, anyway? Why not just let him cool his heels at Mill's until a tow truck came free? She couldn't care one way or the other about saving him money. Had she been trying to get rid of me, for some reason? I'd have to find out if she'd had any visitors to the office while I was off rescuing our intrepid intern.

I walked around his car, checking it out. A 1968, dark-green Ford Falcon. What little chrome it had had rusted through, and I saw rust pockets around the license and the odd pellet bullet hole here and there—kind of poor-man's air-conditioning. The car blended into the surroundings, the rust patches like camouflage on the green body. I imagined if Buzz had been following someone, he wouldn't have been that easy to see against the forest backdrop.

Buzz hadn't had a car when he arrived; said you didn't need one in New York. He'd got this one off Tommy White's brother, Earl, who always had a few around the place in the process of being worked on. Earl thought it was pretty funny that he got rid of the Falcon to a guy from the big city, but Buzz had the last laugh, because it turned out to be a tough little car and had done fine by him. He'd got his money's worth on the two hundred and fifty he'd paid for it.

Walking around the car, I noticed how the left rear wheel had sunk down to the axle in mud. Looked as if Buzz had tried to accelerate out and dug himself in deeper. I saw the Jeep tracks, too, coming and going, indicating that it had driven off, then come back and detoured around the stuck Falcon. The Jeep's tracks were the only recent ones; they still looked soft; all the other tire tracks had hardened up.

"Look here, Buzz. I want to see where the Jeep went. How about you just rest here awhile, I'll be right back."

"Hey, no way. I want to see where the Jeep went, too."

The kid stuck to me like a limpet. Still, the fact that he suspected his own cousin meant he knew something about him, something I might want to know. If Aldo Marco was mixed up with the property dealings around the Usher's, Buzz might be able to contribute some useful information.

I felt pretty sure the swamp where Dad and I used to hunt was on Usher property, legally speaking, although we didn't bother about things like that in this county. I started to wonder if maybe Ma Boynton didn't want anyone else getting Buzz out because she didn't want others sniffing around that particular parcel of land.

While I thought I made good time, striding along the laneway, my eyes following the Jeep tracks. Buzz trotted behind me, slapping at mosquitos and swearing to himself whenever he splashed into a flooded wheel rut. The ground felt firm in some places and still wet in others, having had just a day to dry after all the rain. You had to watch where you walked or you could find your foot sucked into a pothole.

The quality of the sound changed. The buzzing of insects grew more intense, the calling of the birds crisper, then the trees thinned out and we were on the edge of the marsh. I stopped, but Buzz, who probably didn't recognize the way the ground cover changed to reeds, cattails, and a thick coat of algae, continued walking until he splashed into it. He cursed under his breath and backed out, his expensive hiking boots soaked and covered in thick brown muck.

I looked around. Now in the late afternoon the shadows had grown long. The far side of the marsh was completely in shadow and dragonflies skimmed across its surface. Here and there on our side of the pond black pools of stagnant water reflected the afternoon sky. Mirrored on the surface you could see the thin wisps of cirrus clouds, and the reddening light of the sun, now sinking behind the ridge toward the Usher's. It seemed as peaceful and idyllic and untouched as when I was a kid. I could even imagine I saw the ruins of what had been our duck blind over on the far side of the marsh. But as I looked closer, I picked out orange surveyor flags and surveyor tape among the reeds and underbrush. Then I saw stakes in the marsh. The longer I looked, the more stakes I saw. It looked as if the place had been completely surveyed.

What had they been doing, surveying Usher property? Did Usher know? How had Aldo Marco found out about his land anyway? Buzz couldn't have told him about it. Had to be locals involved. It wasn't the sort of place you accidentally stumbled on, and it certainly wasn't for sale. The Usher will and trust made it clear that Usher had obligations to maintain it. Edith's research revealed that the trust had the property completely tied up in ancient covenants.

"What a lot of absolutely nothing," Buzz said. "What the hell could they have been doing out here?" I turned to look at him. His face had swollen up with mosquito bites and a thin line of blood had dried on his cheek. His boots and jeans looked soaked halfway to the knee. He had his hands stuck deep into his jacket pockets and seemed to be shivering. It *was* damp, and now with the sun going down the air had grown chilly. I turned around and thoughtfully headed back to the cars.

I stuck my head out the window of the Falcon, checked the position of the car one more time, gripped the steering wheel firmly, and shouted to Buzz, "Now when I say push, you push, you hear?"

I rocked her back gently, then oh so gently forward. "*Push!*"

The rear wheels spun and mud spurted out onto Buzz. I could hear him yelp, "Hey!"

Back, gently, gently, then . . . "*push!*" No luck. Damn automatic transmission, anyway. He had really dug the thing in.

"Watch it, Buzz, this time lucky!" I called out. Back, sweet as a caress on a lady's soft skin, then put her in gear so gently and just slide her out of that sucking pothole. . . . "*Push dammit. Buzz, push!*" I shouted, and she shot out like a greased pig. Damn, it felt good! I drove her gently back onto the track, then got out, grinning. It made me even happier to see Buzz, covered with mud from head to foot, sweat rolling down his bug-bitten face, grinning like a monkey.

"You did good there, Buzz," I said.

"I got a six pack in the trunk of the Falcon," he said.

The man wasn't as hopeless as I thought. He got out the beer and we each took one and sat down on a dry fallen log by the laneway. The beer was lukewarm but it tasted just right. As the sun slipped below the tree line, shafts of sunlight pierced through the trees, shining on the clearing where we sat, and a big flock of Canada geese circled overhead, calling to each other before settling down on the marsh for the night. Buzz was thirsty. He chugged down his beer and snapped the pull tab off a second. The boy was growing on me.

"Man, I thought I'd bust a gut, the last time, but it just took off, all of a sudden," he said, happily. "You must do that a lot around here, rock cars out of mud holes?"

That remark would have got my back up a day ago. I'd have seen it as an example of a big-city put-down. But this time I just let it roll off me. "So, tell me about your cousin, Aldo," I said. "What's he up to?"

Buzz leaned his back against a tree trunk and stretched his legs out in front of him. The expensive hiking boots were caked in mud and his jeans plastered with it. One good thing—the mud all over his face probably helped ward off the mosquitos. "I don't like to bad-mouth a relative," Buzz said, "but to be honest with you, I'm no big fan of Aldo's."

I always suspected people of lying when they said, "to be

honest with you." "Why not, Buzz? Why aren't you a fan?"

"He's a real wheeler-dealer. All he cares about is the big score. He told me his syndicate has some giant deal cooking with the mayor."

"What's his syndicate about?"

Buzz hesitated. "It's real estate. They build big developments outside of small towns. You know, apartment buildings, minimalls, stuff like that."

"Crowley Creek is too small for a shopping center I'd say."

He looked sad. "That's what I think. So I started investigating, following him. But all we saw was a big swamp, right? So that doesn't get us anywhere."

Obviously, he hadn't seen the surveyor stakes. "Can you find out anything by talking to him or to anyone else in your family?"

"Maybe, but it's my story." He finished his beer and pulled the tab on another. He chugged half of it down in one pull. "I hate it when Italian guys act like mobsters. I hate it. I think I'll change my name to 'MacSwain.' "

"Well, MacSwain," I said, identifying with his name problem—how'd he like to be named "Poe," for God's sake— "why do you think he's acting like a mobster?"

"Anyway," he said, slightly slurring the word, and I realized the beer was starting to get to him, "the mayor's a bigger crook than anyone. I get the impression from Aldo that your good old boy Winsome would shoot you in the back if you crossed him, then slice you up, toast you, and serve you around to his friends as pork crackles at the county fair."

I laughed. "That's good, Buzz. Keep on talking like that and we'll make you an honorary citizen of the county. And you're dead on about the mayor. You never want to show old

Winsome your back. Unless he's got money invested in you, of course."

"The thing about Aldo," Buzz said, "is when he has a big deal in the works, he doesn't like to screw it up. He works for some rough characters. If he said he could put together a parcel of property around here, he better do it. I feel bad. I bet he got the idea of Crowley Creek from me. When I got here, saw what it was like, I told my family the place was full of dumb rednecks. How the town hides everything under the rug. I couldn't believe the *Sentinel*. Tommy White gets busted for selling moonshine and the *Sentinel* just reports it as a 'city ordinance violation.' The thing isn't a newspaper, it's an advertising sheet with filler."

"Don't get your shirt in a knot, son," I said. "That's just how it is."

"But, John, how can you go along with it? How can you stand it? There's lots of real news in this town and you just bury it! Don't the people have a right to know how Winsome and Prynne and their buddies are ripping everyone off? They're stealing the town right out from under everyone's noses!" His tone, which had been plaintive, turned nasty. "Maybe you don't care because you are so rich it doesn't matter to you."

It had grown dark. The moon had not yet risen and the woods seemed suddenly full of black shadows. I could hear faint rustlings in the underbrush, the buzz of insects, and suddenly the sound of an owl that had found its prey.

"You want to help Crowley Creek?" I said. "You're here for six months and you have it all figured out, who's ripping off who, and why, and what needs to be done—is that it?"

"Well, but . . ."

"Well, but you don't know damn all about it. So why don't you grow up and try to find out. Find out what your cousin is up to with the mayor. Find out what he was doing on Rod Usher's property this afternoon."

"I will!"

"Sure you will," I said, in a sarcastic tone, goading him. "Then, when you really know what's going on, you'll be in a position to do something about it, right?"

"Right!" he said loudly, finishing his beer and standing up.

"In a pig's eye," I said to myself, standing up in my turn.

We both walked back to our cars, our good feeling completely evaporated. He got into his, slammed the door, and drove slowly and carefully back out to the road. I sat in mine for a moment, letting the sounds of the evening wash over me. I could hear the wind rising and the trees bending in the gusts, the branches rustling and creaking. I listened for a moment. It was as if someone was whispering to me, telling me what I needed to know about the things that troubled me, about what Buzz knew and was hiding, about Madeleine's death and Rod's madness and the strange goings-on at Usher House. I strained my ears, but the whispers remained cryptic, their secrets undecipherable.

I put the Bronco in gear and drove back to town.

# EIGHT

It was almost six when I opened the front door of Crowley House, removed my muddy shoes, and tossed my jacket over the banister. The lamp on the hall table had been lit, and I took a quick look in the mirror before going to find Edith. I was late, but not that late. Peering into the mirror, I saw that I needed a haircut; my hair, which is brown and unruly, had gotten all ruffled, and I ran a comb through it. I could use a shave and I would need to change. Better tell Edith I would be another ten minutes.

I took the stairs two at a time and sped down the hall to her office. It was dark, but a Post-it note stuck on the door said: "In the library, waiting, hope you don't mind."

I had told Edith she should make herself at home at Crowley House, so of course she was welcome to go into the library. But it felt strange. My mother had never entered it that I could recall, although I did not know why. In fact, except for Mrs. Slack, the housekeeper, I don't recall ever seeing a woman in the library.

Still in my stocking feet, I padded along the hall and down the back stairs and along to the library. One of the two tall, oak-paneled doors stood open and a rectangle of light shone out from the doorway. I looked in. Edith sat on the old horsehair sofa, twisted around, with her face buried in her arms, pressed into the sofa back. For a moment I thought I heard her crying. Edith crying? I could not imagine it.

"Edith?" I said gently.

She sat up with a start. "John! I didn't hear you . . . I must have dozed off." Her face looked drawn and in the shadowy light of the library I saw deep circles under her eyes, making them look hollow and sad.

"What's the matter, Edith?" I said. I turned on a few lamps, went over to the drinks tray and without asking her permission, poured each of us a Blanton's. I handed her the drink; she smiled at me and took a delicate sip.

"Oh nothing, don't worry yourself about it."

She wore a soft, draped, cream-colored wool dress with a string of lustrous pearls and a brown suede belt with a pearl buckle. She looked lovely, even tired and drawn as she was.

"Please, tell me Edith."

She smiled, a small, sad smile. "It's just, I'm tired . . . I haven't been sleeping well these last weeks. . . ."

I remembered how harsh and unfeeling I had been to her, how little attention I had paid to her hard work. What was the matter with me, anyway? Here this gracious woman was working to help me and I hadn't taken the time to give her a kind word. "I'm so sorry, Edith, I know I've . . ."

"Oh, John, it's not you," she said in a rush. "You're saving my life. It's my husband. He's messing up my kids and I'm at my wit's end."

I didn't know what to say.

"He promises to come on weekends to see them and he doesn't show up. Then he buys them presents to make up for it. We have hardly enough to get by, and he buys the kids an expensive Nintendo. He's so irresponsible.

"Last weekend . . ." she closed her eyes for a moment, then wrapped her arms tightly around herself, as if pressing her feelings in. "He promised to come for Bobby's football play-offs, then take them both out for dinner after. They were so excited, looking forward to it, talking about it all week. He never showed up. It'd break your heart how all weekend they kept looking out the window, expecting him any minute, inventing excuses why he hadn't come. But he never showed up at all. Didn't call either. Just . . . seems like . . . he forgot them. Bobby was crushed. Of course, he decided somehow it was my fault.

"Then last night, a school night, without calling, no warning, he drove all the way out from Richmond, picked them up and kept them out till 3:00 A.M. I didn't sleep a wink, watching for them, worried sick that something terrible had happened. I even called the hospitals and the state police to see if they'd been in an accident. This morning the boys told me he took them to a strip club—said I was stifling them and they needed to see life. What kind of a club would let in boys that age, John Charles? I don't like to think. They're only fourteen and sixteen.

"They used to be such good boys, responsible, worked hard, polite, kind, but now . . . now they've started skipping school, they're rude to me, and when I try to discipline them they say 'cut it out' or they'll go live with their father. He tells them the separation is all my fault. And what can I do? I can't tell them the truth, run him down to the boys. It would just hurt them more than they've already been hurt. He's their father and they miss him and want him back and don't really understand . . ." her voice tailed off in despair.

"Maybe he feels guilty. He wants them to love him and he doesn't know how to go about it," I said.

"You think that's it?" She reflected for a moment. Then she said, "I wish, just once, he'd think about the boys, what he's doing to them. But no. It's how *he* feels that matters to him. Not how anybody else feels. Thinking about himself all the time, feeling hard-done by, it makes him so unhappy. Sometimes my heart aches for him. He's going down and down, looking for the good time he remembers from when he was young."

I wondered if she still loved him. He sounded like a total jerk. Why had she married him in the first place? I never get why smart, pretty women seem to go for the wild, irresponsible guys—the losers. The nicest guys I know seem to have no luck at all with women. "I don't blame you one bit for being mad at him," I said. "But I bet he knows he's acted badly and let down you and his sons and he's hurting."

"I sure hope so," Edith said. She laughed, but it was not a happy laugh, and I noticed that she had finished her whiskey.

"Want another?"

"No, thank you. Hadn't we better be going along to the Ushers?"

"In a minute, but first I need to change. Listen, Edith . . . uh . . ."

"What?"

"You know those papers I mentioned to you? The old Poe papers? I'm sorry, I thought they weren't important, but now that I've reread them I think maybe you better read them too."

She looked at me.

I went over to the desk, removed the papers from the bible and handed them to her. "They seem to be some kind of notes for E.A.'s story, 'The Fall of the House of Usher.' Remember when you told me my instincts were a sign my subconscious was picking up on something?"

"Yes. I believe that."

"Well, my instincts tell me there's something important in these papers, but I just can't see what it could be."

"I'd be glad to have a look," she said. Her face had brightened with interest, her troubles seemingly set aside for the time being. She took the papers to the desk, settled them under the desk lamp, and began to read. I watched her for a moment, then went on upstairs to change.

Every year the Ushers had a Thanksgiving open house. I'm ashamed to say I had never been to one. I thought of them as business promotions for the Sanatorium, and as I had no aged relatives I was looking to stash away, and no need to sell the Sanatorium anything, I had always given the open house a miss.

But the townsfolk saw it as a chance to get free eats and free booze and party a little, and I guess Rod didn't want to disappoint people, so he had decided not to cancel, despite Madeleine's death. Actually, I was kind of surprised the party was on, considering his grief, but I had a plan and the party could be the perfect opportunity to put it into practice.

As we walked out to the car I realized the wind had picked up. I could hear it gusting. The branches of the oak trees in front of the house whipped back and forth, the wind ripping off the weakest branches and flinging them over the lawn and driveway. I held the car door open for Edith with some difficulty, and as she climbed into the Bronco her skirt billowed up and her hair streamed out from her face.

As we drove off Edith said, "You know, they say the killer hurricane has veered back inland and is coming this way. Some people are leaving town for higher ground. They're afraid Crowley Creek will overflow its banks and flood the town like it did in '67."

"Some people just love disaster," I said, feeling uneasy. "Probably Beamis has left town with a load of canned goods and a ton of ammo for his hunting guns. But hurricanes never come this far inland."

"They're saying this one is really unpredictable. Maybe cause it's so late in the season."

It had begun to rain. The rain came in gusts on the wind, flooding the windshield as if a giant hand was flinging buckets of water at us.

"Edith, I have a plan for tonight, and if you're willing, I'd like for you to help me."

"Of course."

I paused for a moment, waiting for the wipers to clear the windshield so I could see the road. Headlights coming toward me looked blurry and indistinct, reflecting off the wet road, as if ghost cars were riding along under the surface. A huge oak branch, twigs spread like grasping hands, blew past, and

I slowed to avoid it. "I want to search Usher House, especially the cellars. The only thing that makes sense is that there is some kind of passageway from the house out to the grounds and that people are moving around through the serving passageways and then through the underground tunnels to get outside. That's how come they can appear and disappear like they do."

"But why would they do that?"

"I don't know. But I'd feel a whole lot better if we could be sure there were real people behind all these sightings. Then maybe I could get Rod to tell me what's going on."

"Do you think he knows?"

"I hate to say this, but I just can't tell. He used to be my best friend. I'd have said I understood him as well as I understand myself—whatever that means. I'd have sworn that Rod is too proud of his honor ever to do anything deceitful. But now, he just acts so crazy sometimes. I think we have to find out what is doing that to him, and we can't count on him at all. The things he says just don't make any sense."

The Usher House parking lot was full. A lot of pickups, but also the fancy cars of the town's leading citizens: Cadillacs, Lincolns, Grand Ams, and big vans. The gravel surface of the parking area was awash with deep puddles, and we had to step carefully as we picked our way toward the house. Passing the tarn I saw that it was frothing and turbulent, like a boiling pot, and I could hear the rain hiss as it struck the surface. I held my umbrella over Edith's head but it turned inside out and our raincoats were soaked through in the few minutes it took us to run to the grand doorway under the *porte cochère*.

The open house had been scheduled from four to eight, and it was close to eight as we came into the ballroom.

Candles burned in the candelabra and the big gilt chandelier glittered with tiny lights. The crowd was still going at it with no sign of letting up any time soon. At the far end of the long table I saw piles of decorative pumpkins and squash and big sheaves of Indian corn. A huge canvas hung on the wall above the center of the table and someone had twisted a wreath of dried flowers and berries around its frame. Edith drifted off to greet some friends, and I went to take a closer look at the painting.

A brass plaque mounted on the ornate frame said: "Portrait of Roderick Usher and his sister, Madeline, by James Lawrence Usher, 1837–1864."

I did not recall seeing the painting before and studied it with interest. It showed a man and a woman dressed in the Puritan garb of the seventeenth century. The painting had a Thanksgiving theme. In it, a long table was set out in a clearing in an improbable wood. Indians, dressed as nineteenth-century painters liked to think of them (in feathers, war paint, and beads) filed out of the woods bringing a feast to the table—cornucopias of fruit, vegetables, and a large turkey on a wooden platter. Among the trees in the wood, peering out, lurked wild beasts: wolves, foxes, even a bear. Hidden in the high, dark branches of the trees, vultures watched. In front of the table, accepting this largess with grace, stood the first Madeline Usher. She wore a black dress with a crimson hieroglyphic on the breast. On her shoulder was an evil-looking monkey eating a large, juicy red plum whose drops had stained the white lace collar of her dress. Next to her, looking not at her, but at the 'noble savages,' stood Roderick Usher. He held a hunting rifle in the crook of one arm, the stock on the ground, the barrel leaning outward so that it drew the eye into the dense forest on the margin of the painting. In the same hand he clutched a leather-bound bible, the cover darkened with what looked like a bloodstain. In the other hand he held an apple, with one bite missing. The skin of the apple was the same dark, glistening red as the monkey's plum, while the eaten-away meat was a pearly white. This white flesh irresistibly drew the eye, as if the light that streamed through the trees and lit up the trestle table all focused on the apple.

I stared at this painting, mesmerized by it. "Our namesakes," said a voice behind me. It was Roderick. He looked exhausted, his face pale, his hair lank. But he seemed under control.

"I don't recall ever seeing this picture before," I said, continuing to stare at it.

"It's really an amateur work," Rod said dismissively. "We only take it out and hang it up at Thanksgiving because of the theme. It's my great, great, whatever grandfather, James Lawrence Usher's idea of his father and aunt, who were the progeny of the Jamestown Ushers. You've probably heard the story. Supposedly our ancestor, Sir Aubrey Usher, came over from England with Lord de la Ware in 1610 and settled in Jamestown. His son was said to have built the Usher House that fell down. According to family legend, they were Puritans who thought it was a sin to eat a plum. But the family legend is all wrong. The Usher House that fell down came down much later, in the eighteen-thirties. The fellow who painted that thing was the son of that nineteenth-century Roderick Usher whose house fell down. And *those* nineteenth-century Ushers in the picture, our namesakes, weren't Puritans, no matter what their son wanted the world to believe. No," he smiled a strange little smile, "far from it."

"I thought the Usher whose house fell down was the 'last of his line,'" I said. "That's what old E. A. Poe's story says. So how could they have a son who painted that picture?"

"Look," Roderick said. "It's all myths. Probably there weren't any Ushers who came over with de la Ware. I've re-searched and researched and all I can find proof of was that our ancestors were established in Virginia in the early eigh- teenth century, got rich off tobacco and merchant trading, and built a big house, which successive generations added onto. That house was destroyed, probably by an earthquake, in the mid-nineteenth century. Your ancestor, Edgar Allan Poe, might have known the Ushers, might even have stayed in the house. But he was wrong about their being the last Ushers. Roderick married, had a child. His wife died in child- birth, but her name is in the family Bible. Their son, John Lawrence, was a dissolute fellow who drank himself to death. But before he passed on, he painted that and had two sons and one survived to become my great-great-grandfather."

I had not really followed all this. "You're saying that the fellow who painted this Thanksgiving picture was the son of the Roderick Usher in Edgar Allan Poe's story?"

"Probably."

"So the picture is really of his father and aunt, but he dressed them in Puritan clothes for the hell of it?"

"Right. He would never have seen his aunt. She died right after he was born. Who knows, maybe her death gave Poe the idea for the story."

I turned and saw that Edith had joined us, had been lis- tening to the explanation. She was studying the painting intently. "There's something really strange about that picture," she said. "I think it's the effect of the way he painted that apple. It just jumps out of the painting."

"I think it's the weird monkey," I said. "And all the stains. Look. The stain on her dress, the stain on the bible, there's wine spilled on the tablecloth, and even the shadows of those vultures looks like stains in the grass."

"What vultures?" Roderick said, "I don't see any vulture."

"I don't either," Edith said.

"See?" I said, "High in the tree branches, painted in a green just darker than the shadows, here . . ."

"Oh!" they both said, speaking at the same time. Then they both laughed, but Roderick's laughter was that high, strange laugh I had grown to dread.

"Rod," I said quickly, "you've met Edith Dunn, haven't you?"

"Yes, of course," he said, "Welcome to Usher House, ma'am." He shook her hand formally, then turned back to the painting. "I never saw those birds before, John Charles," he said in that doom-filled voice that signaled to me that he was about to go off the rails. "How did they come to be there? That painting is kept locked in the climate-controlled copper room eleven months a year. How did they . . ."

"Oh get with it, Rod," I said. "You didn't see them until I pointed them out because they are really faint and you are not a hunter and don't look for birds in trees. Edith didn't see them either, right Edith?"

She nodded, but kept looking at the painting with a puzzled expression.

"You see what you are meant to see," Rod said in a mysterious tone. "John Charles," he lowered his voice to a hiss,

"I saw Madeleine again tonight. I should never have had this party. It's an insult to her, she cannot rest in peace, she . . ."

"Rod, I really think . . ."

"You don't believe me? She's been walking this evening, she hears us celebrating heartlessly on her grave. Stay awhile, you will see her." He turned away from me, his face working, and disappeared into the crowd of guests.

"Edith, did you hear that?"

"I surely did."

"What do you think?"

We walked away from the table toward the window, where we could speak in privacy. We stood for a moment in silence by the tall, small-paned French doors flanked with heavy, deep green moiré satin curtains fringed with gold and held back with gold swags. The windowpanes ran with water as rain beat against them and coursed down the glass. The wind gusted and the French doors quivered in their frames. I noticed that they were not completely airtight and that the heavy curtains billowed slightly with each attack of the wind. Edith shivered slightly. "John, I see what you mean about him. One minute he seems fine, but then he goes off and you realize he is just holding himself together by force of will."

"Yes! Just what I think."

"I'd have to say I don't think you can trust anything he tells you. I think he's not completely lucid. But then, you never know, there may be a grain of truth in what sounds . . . crazy. Why don't we both ask around, find out if anyone else has seen this 'Madeleine.'"

"Good idea."

\* \* \*

The party was heating up. The guests showed no signs of leaving, despite the fact that the official closing time had come and gone. The noise had risen, the punch bowl had been refilled, and those who preferred their own, harder stuff were now drinking from pocket flasks. Mayor Winsome was too cheap for that; he was sticking to the Usher punch. He fished an orange section out of his punch glass and sucked on it happily. "Just love to see folks havin' a good time," he said to me. "Town deserves it. 'Work hard, play hard,' is what I say. Hear you've been doin' some playin', son." He winked at me. "Wild women are the most fun, that's what I allus say."

I was annoyed. "I'm not sure what you are referring to, sir," I said.

"Right, right, the perfect gentleman," he said, his smile even broader as if he were onto some joke that he had no intention of telling me. "Women are mysterious creatures; we men will never understand them."

"You got that right," I said. The punch was too sweet for me but I had brought along a flask of Blanton's for emergencies. I figured talking to Winsome could be classed as one, and took a discrete swig.

"Even when they've passed over," he said, lowering his voice and looking around in an exaggerated conspiratorial way. I realized that the punch had gotten to Winsome. "You see that Madeleine traipsing around in her cape? The woman don't want to miss a good time, even when she's dead."

"No," I said, as if he had just repeated a normal piece of gossip. "Do tell. You say you saw her tonight? Where was that?"

"I went down the hall to the facilities, and there she was,

just slipping around the bend, gliding along in her big cape like she does, carrying a basket of dead daisies. What a sight. Hell, it could turn a man to drink!" He laughed. "I told Usher I expected all those who 'walk' round here to give me their votes in the next election. Man didn't get the joke. Usher may be a fine fellow but something's missing there, in the sense of humor department. Know what I mean?"

"Man's sister just died, Jackson Lee," I said. "It's no laughing matter."

"Lighten up, John Charles. I know his sister died. Tragedy." He slurped down the last of his punch and gestured with the empty glass. "But as they say, life goes on, and fortune and the big buck wait for no man." He lurched off toward the punch bowl.

"John Charles!"

It was lawyer Prynne, and he too was looking somewhat sozzled. He had removed his jacket and his vest was unbuttoned. He had a silver flask in his hand. "Could I interest you in some excellent brandy? Usher's punch leaves much to be desired."

"Thank you, sir, but I came prepared."

"Hell of a storm out there, hurricane's approaching, bringing trouble and disaster, it's on it's way, John Charles. Have you been out? Trees coming down, land flooding, wind rising . . . rising . . ."

I noticed that Prynne's trousers were damp around the ankles and that his shoes were soaked. "You've been out in this weather, sir?"

"Someone playing a stupid joke, pretending to be Madeleine. Thing's indecent. I followed her to give her a piece of my mind. She went right out into the storm and disappeared into the wind! Blew away. Serves her right, I say. Act like a ghost, blow away like a ghost." He took a huge gulp from his flask, shook it, turned it upside down and shook it again. A few lone drops emerged. "Time to go home. Party's over for Mr. Ambrose Prynne."

"Have some of mine," I said, tendering my flask. "Blanton's single barrel bourbon."

He looked over my shoulder, started, paled. "No thank you. I think, yes, I think it's time I was moving on, departing this vale. Yes sir. I shall depart."

I turned and looked in the direction where he had been staring. He seemed to be looking at the French doors where Edith and I had chatted. Now, I saw, Edith was standing there, staring out the window, which was open a crack. Rain was coming in, pouring onto the polished marble floor, while Edith pressed on the door, trying to shut it against the wind. I ran to her side and gave the door a shove, then latched it firmly shut. Rivulets seeped in under the door and spread on the black marble.

The front of Edith's dress looked soaked. "I saw her, John, I saw her in the garden. I opened the door and called to her, but she vanished!"

"There's someone out there in that storm?"

Edith shivered. I took off my jacket and put it around her shoulders. "We should get you home and dried off, Edith."

"No! Now we really have to follow your plan. She was standing at the window, staring in. I saw the white shape of her face. For a moment I couldn't believe it, then I opened the door and she took off into the rain and . . . I couldn't see her anymore. I should have followed her, dammit."

We hurried out of the ballroom to the main, formal reception area and began looking for the way to the cellars. We opened one door after another, finally finding one that revealed a staircase going down. "Here it is, Edith," I called. I had brought a flashlight and I needed it because the lighting was dim and flickering, perhaps due to the storm. The stair was broad, the risers of oak worn with generations of footsteps. At the bottom we found ourselves in a short corridor with doors leading off in all directions.

"We should have brought bread crumbs," Edith grumbled. "This place is a maze."

We opened all the doors. Several led to storage areas, but one opened onto another, narrower descending staircase. A strong smell of stone mold and damp rose up from the stairwell. "What do you think?" I asked Edith.

She shook her head. "I don't have a clue."

"My instincts tell me this is it," I said.

She gave me that look women give you when you are driving and lost and won't ask for directions.

"Let's go for it," I said. We descended the staircase. The light was dim, barely revealing a stone staircase, worn and pitted. I could just make out the stone walls, sweating with moisture. The air smelled of damp stone, of rot, of age. Edith's heels clicked behind me, and underneath that sound I could hear a faint rustling that might have been rodents and a susurration, as if the stones themselves were inhaling, exhaling. That must have been the wind.

The staircase twisted gently downward. When I reached the bottom I paused to wait for Edith. She came down carefully, and when she stepped off the last step she sighed with relief and looked up at me, her face very pale. "John," she said softly, "do you hear it?"

"Hear what?"

"Nothing."

We stood in a large room with a stone floor and stone walls. Along one wall we saw dusty bins and along the other walls ran old, rotting shelving. Perhaps the room had been a food storage area at one time. It was very cold. In one corner, on the floor, we saw a granite basin with a drain hole. And at the far end of the room, a giant door.

It stood perhaps seven feet tall and five feet wide. Made of rusting cast iron, it was bolted with a long rod placed across wrought-iron brackets. A brass-trimmed keyhole gleamed in the middle of the door, an ornate, old-fashioned key sticking out of it. Edith and I looked at one another. I walked over to the door, removed the rod and set it aside, turned the key, and gently rotated the knob. Then, with an effort, I pulled open the heavy door, dragging it across the uneven stone floor. As it passed over the floor it made a sudden, loud, grating noise that echoed eerily, bouncing back and forth from the stone walls—sounding for a moment like someone screaming. Edith involuntarily clapped her hands over her ears.

I shone my flashlight inside. For a moment we both stood there, transfixed with astonishment.

We had found the copper vault. The room stretched before us, its walls gleaming the dull green of tarnished copper. The flashlight beam reflected off the copper, over television cameras mounted in the four corners of the room pointing toward the center. Their lenses glimmered as if eyes looked back at us.

When I passed the flashlight over the center of the room

and we saw the coffin, it stood upon a trestle that had been placed on a magnificent oriental carpet. The coffin, identical to the one in which Madeleine had been buried, gleamed in the flashlight's beam—polished ebony wood lined with lustrous white silk and ornamented with shining brass handles, each formed in the shape of a winged seraph.

The coffin lay open. Empty. Draped across it, we could see Madeleine's cloak. Water dripped from the cloak, soaking into the coffin lining. Next to the cloak, a basket filled with dead daisies. On the floor, under the coffin, dried brownish daisy petals had fallen on the dark red figured carpet.

Beside the coffin stood a small table covered with a white linen cloth. Upon the table someone had placed a Thermos, a silver goblet, a loaf of bread wrapped in plastic, untouched, and a bowl of fruit. The fruit had withered, spoiled; the apples wrinkled, the pears covered with brown spots. On a pewter plate, a piece of cheese, covered in mold, a silver sawtoothed fruit knife. Near the knife lay a blood-pressure gauge. The air had a bitter, acrid smell, as if the copper exuded metallic fumes.

Edith found a light switch and turned it on. The room's details sprang into view. Bright halogen lights lit the coffin and fluorescent lights illumined the rest of the room with a cold, aseptic light. On one wall we saw glass-fronted medicine cabinets, labeled, numbered, and locked. Fine steel security mesh glittered in the glass cupboard doors and clipboards hung from each cabinet. Locked medical refrigerators stood against another wall. Air-conditioners and dehumidifiers hummed, keeping the room cold and dry. In the middle of all this medical paraphernalia, bizarre, inexplicable, the coffin, like a relic from another century.

Edith and I looked at one another. We began walking around the room, looking into the cabinets, not ready yet to examine the coffin. We saw every conceivable medicine. I noted one cupboard in particular, which contained medicines I had seen often in my father's last years, for use in coronary conditions—digitalis, digitalin, nitroglycerin. In the log on the clipboard attached to this cabinet I noted Dr. Giron's name as prescribing digoxin for Madeleine. I pointed it out to Edith, and without a word she withdrew a pad and pen from her handbag and began copying out the prescription record.

While she wrote, I approached the coffin and stared in. But there was nothing to see. I touched the lining. Under the cloak it felt damp, but not soaked through. But what did that mean? The room was bone-dry. Powerful humidifiers throbbed, sucking every drop of moisture away.

When Edith finished writing we approached the double oak doors at the far end of the room and opened them, revealing another stone corridor. Narrow rail tracks led away into the darkness. Obviously, once upon a time, ammunition had been brought here in trolleys, stored, and taken away again. The tracks would lead upward to an exit. We turned off the light in the copper room, shut the door, and followed the tracks.

My flashlight did not succeed in lighting the corridor completely but we could see that several smaller passageways led off it in different directions. Eventually we reached the end and pushed open the hatch.

The storm assaulted us. Rain coursed down so heavily it was impossible to recognize our location. I told Edith to stand inside while I tried to get my bearings. A useless effort. I could see nothing but rain, trees bending in the wind, debris flying through the air. It didn't matter, I thought. I knew now, that as I had suspected, the denizens of Usher House could come and go as they wished. The house and grounds, a rallying point for confederate activities during the Civil War, had been honeycombed with interior and exterior escape routes.

Still not speaking, Edith and I retraced our route. We returned to the copper room, passed through it, locking both sets of doors behind us and leaving the keys in place as we had found them. We ascended the twisting stair and eventually found ourselves in the reception area to the ballroom. This was not the Sanatorium wing entrance, but rather the formal entrance to the main wing of the house itself. Lights blazed in the *porte cochère* as cars drove by to pick up the last stragglers leaving the party. I told Edith to wait, I would bring the car around.

Just then, Mrs. Boynton came up, bundled in furs. Roderick followed along behind her, saying his goodbyes. When he saw me, he turned away from her. "John! Are you leaving? Can you stay for a moment, there is something I want to show you."

"I'm sorry, Rod, can it wait until tomorrow? I have to get Edith home." She stood beside me now, looking very white and exhausted. She had begun to shiver again, and I remembered that her dress was wet.

"No, it can't wait," Rod said.

"You poor thing," Mrs. Boynton said, looking at Edith.

Why you're soaked through. John, whyn't you go get my car for me and I'll run Miz Dunn home. She doesn't live far from me. That way you can stay and talk to your friend."

"Thank you, ma'am but I . . ."

"That would be wonderful," Edith said, interrupting me, "I sure would appreciate it, Mrs. Boynton."

Edith was up to something. I played along, took Mrs. Boynton's car keys, ran out into the rain, started her car up, and drove back to the house. "Are you sure you can manage in this storm?" I said, looking out beyond the *porte cochère* into the night. Torrents of rain lashed the ground, the sound of the wind rose and fell, as if animals circled around the house, roaring.

"Don't you worry about a thing," Mrs. Boynton said, putting a heavy, furry arm around Edith's shoulders, "I'm a whole lot more sober than you, young man. She'll be home and dry in no time. I've driven through plenty worse than this in my day."

I watched the big white Cadillac Seville move off at a measured pace until it was swallowed up in the darkness.

"Come this way," Rod said impatiently. He had put on a raincoat but the rain beat down on his blond hair, plastering it to his scalp. I turned up the collar of my coat and followed him. We walked along, hugging the side of the house, past two sets of French doors leading into the ballroom. We reached the third set. Looking in, my face pressed to the glass, I saw the ballroom was now empty. This was the window where Edith and I had talked, where she had seen "Madeleine." I tried the door knob and it opened easily.

Rod turned back, saw me looking in. "John!"

I hurried toward him. He was standing, staring at the wall

of the house. As I approached him, I saw we were just opposite the tarn. It had overflowed its banks. Black water, whipped by the rain, rose and fell back, almost reaching the house. The noise of the wind was very loud, but even so I could hear the water making a hissing, sucking sound, the way tidal waters do when the waves pull in across the sand.

Rod took my arm, drawing me toward his side. "Look, John," he said, pointing to the house. I looked and saw nothing, just the dark, shadowy bulk of the house, rain pouring down.

I took out my flashlight and pointed it in the direction of his gaze. Then I saw it. A crack, a dark, sinister crack had appeared in the stone. From the foundation, it rose up, jagged, disappearing under the eaves—almost as if a black lightning bolt had burned its way deep into the House of Usher.

# NINE

When I got home after a harrowing drive through the storm, the telephone was ringing. I raced in, dripping all over the front hall, and grabbed at it.

"Hello, John?"

"Edith! You make it home okay?"

"Yes, John, thanks for picking up so quickly on what I wanted. I thought it would be a chance for me to talk to Mrs. Boynton, try to find out what she was up to."

Edith sounded energized, excited. I remembered her pale, exhausted face as she stood in the Usher House doorway. I know she had heard the same strange whispering sounds in the cellar that I had, and I regretted not admitting to her that I had heard them. I knew she had felt the overpowering atmosphere of dread in those cellars, as I had, and that she too had just driven through the same driving rainstorm. Now she bubbled with enthusiasm.

"I noticed she'd had a few, I hope she drove okay."

"She went very carefully. I invited her in for a cup of hot tea before she had to drive back over to her place, and we had a real girl-to-girl chat!"

Mrs. Boynton and Edith, girl-to-girl? What a thought. "What did she say?"

"Well, John, we agreed that men were just hopeless, hopeless. I told her that I found you to be not very serious and she agreed. She said she had the same problem with you and took pity on me that I have to work for such an irresponsible scapegrace." Edith laughed.

I knew Edith was teasing me, but somehow I didn't like it much.

"Then we talked about husbands who couldn't be counted on, and we agreed on that too."

"Good work, Edith," I said. Sometime I'd like to be a fly on the wall when two women are talking. I've always wondered how they can go on for hours and hours and never once touch on anything important, like, say, cars, hunting, or sports.

"We talked about how Mayor Winsome and lawyer Prynne made fools of themselves at the party tonight. And listen to this, John. Mrs. Boynton—or should I say Fanny; we are best girlfriends now—Fanny told me she worried that the mayor and Prynne had drunk too much and might spill the beans about the deal to get the Usher property. She claimed Marco is their big competitor, and is going to be making an offer to Usher tomorrow."

"I thought she and Prynne and the mayor and Marco are all in on it together."

"I asked her about that, and she got all fussed. She said,

'No way I'd have anything to do with the New York crook, and if that fat weasel Winsome is two-timing us with the New York slimesters, I'll see he never wins another election in this town.' What do you think about that, John?"

"I think Mrs. Boynton is as twisty as a backwoods trail and may have said that to put us off."

"John! Just what I think! So I said to her, 'but I heard *you* are working with Mr. Marco.'"

"And what did she say to that?"

"She said, 'Did John Charles tell you that?' And I said, 'No, I heard it around.' That really seemed to upset her. She was just fuming, you know how she does?"

"I sure do."

"She thinks you are behind a lot of her troubles, John. She told me that until you started meddling around in Usher's business she had a sure thing to make a lot of money, but now her deal is in, to use her words, 'one unholy mess.'"

"What did you say to that?"

"Oh I sympathized like all get-out. You know, I've had my problems with men. Meaning my husband. So I could be real sincere in agreeing how they can be so self-centered that they screw things up for other people without paying much mind to what they are doing. She let down her hair some more and told me that you never came in early after partying but that *she* always came in on the dot. Then she said she had to get going because she had an early meeting in the morning and off she got. I'd say she's not expecting you at the *Sentinel* office first thing tomorrow morning, so if you were there early, you might see something interesting, don't you think?"

"Edith, you did real good. I'll be there. That's just great.

In fact, I'll be there before she is, see if I can listen in somehow. And Edith, you were terrific tonight—at Usher's. Tomorrow we'll talk about the Poe papers you read, and what we saw in the cellar and . . ."

"And what Rod Usher wanted to show you?"

"Yes . . . yes, we'll talk about that, too."

When the alarm went off the next morning it felt as if the same, strange night had not ended, as if morning had not come, would not come. At six thirty it was still dark and the storm howled around the house worse, if anything, than the night before. I staggered into the kitchen and turned on the coffee machine. Then I opened the back door and looked out. Dense, coal-black clouds, layer upon layer of them, raced across the sky. Rain blew in diagonal sheets, littering the lawn with branches and debris. The heavy, wrought-iron lawn furniture had blown over and lay in disarray, like a windbreak against which the storm had piled huge pieces of wood, branches as big as saplings, and young shrubs ripped up by their roots. Just beyond my field of vision I could faintly make out unfamiliar, indistinct shapes in the blackness, as if the storm had changed the landscape. The air smelled of damp, of water, and of earth newly uprooted.

I gulped down the scalding coffee and drove through the storm over to the office.

Central Avenue looked deserted. Many more of the storefronts had been boarded up. Municipal garbage cans had blown over; one lay wedged against the door of the *Sentinel*'s office. I slid it aside just enough to unlock the door, replaced it in its former position and slipped inside.

I realized I had never been first in the office before. It felt kind of eerie. I looked around at the deserted workstations, at Mrs. Boynton's office. The thought crossed my mind to go in there and prowl around. I was toying with the idea when I heard the garbage can out front being rolled away from the door and turned upright. I dodged into the supply closet and swung the door to, leaving it open just a crack.

Mrs. Boynton came in. She turned on the lights and began talking out loud to herself. "First in again. Always the first in and the last out. Do you ever see one of them lazy good-for-nothings putting in a full day's work? Not a one of them that earns their salary. Not a one." She sniffed. "I got home at midnight last night and I'm here at seven. Where are they? Sleeping it off, most likely. Well, it's the early bird that catches the worm, and no mistake." She stalked into her office, stalked out, plugged in the coffeemaker and banged down a box of doughnuts. I watched, peering out of the crack in the door. "We'll just see who has the last laugh."

The front door opened and with astonishment I saw Rod Usher walk in. He walked slowly, his head down, and barely spoke as Mrs. Boynton greeted him effusively and welcomed him into her private office. She then rushed out and opened the front door to a man I had never seen before. Broad shoul-dered, stocky, and dapper, dressed in a long, light-colored trench coat glistening with rain, his hair very black and slicked back from his pale face. He strode in with a cocky step. He had a large, beaky nose and heavy, dark brows and car-ried a big black umbrella, which he shook carelessly, spat-tering Mrs. Boynton. She ignored this and fingered her pearl choker obsequiously. "Aldo, come in, come in, Dr. Usher is already here. Can I get you some coffee, a doughnut?"

"You think the hurricane is going to hit the town? It's hell out there," the man said. He had a thin, high voice that gave me a chill of distaste down my spine. If a snake could talk, that's what it would sound like.

"No, no," Mrs. Boynton said. "Hurricanes never come this far inland. Never have, never will. It'll blow over."

"Blow over, that's a good one," Aldo Marco said. "Looks like the whole town is about to blow over. Rains any harder we'll need an ark." He snickered, making a high, ugly sound that turned into a cough. "Coffee would be great, thanks. Black. I'll take a pass on the doughnut."

"Go on into my office," Mrs. Boynton said, her voice so honeyed I didn't recognize it. "Dr. Usher is there. I'll join you in a moment."

She poured three coffees, put some doughnuts on a plate and marched into her office, shutting her door behind her. Her private office backed up to the supply closet. I put my ear up to the thin particleboard partition and prepared to eavesdrop.

"Dr. Usher, I have all the necessary documents here," Marco said. I heard briefcase locks snap open and the rustle of papers. The wall had been made so thin it sounded as if they were in the closet with me. An unpleasant thought.

"I haven't agreed to anything," Rod said. "Just to meet and listen, that is all, and only because Mrs. Boynton asked me to do so."

"I can't believe you are in a position to turn down a million two," Marco said.

"One million two hundred thousand dollars," Mrs. Boynton said. "That's an exciting offer, don't you think, Roderick?"

"It's an insulting offer," Rod said, his voice angry. "A million dollars for Usher House and 250 acres of some of the most beautiful and historic land in the county? In the state? Land that has been in my family for over four hundred years? Land that I could never sell, will never sell? Land that . . ."

"Roderick," Mrs. Boynton said soothingly, "no one denies your family their fine history. No one can ever forget what you have contributed to our community and our state. Hear Mr. Marco out. He has some splendid ideas on that score. He . . ."

"No Harvard Law School ideas can make right what is wrong," Rod said.

"Just a minute, Dr. Usher." Marco's voice now had a steely edge to it. "I don't believe you are in a position to take that tone. Your property is in a very decrepit condition. The west wall of the house has a large crack two storys high. There is severe structural rot, and you may well have very serious problems with polluted soil. I have checked and you have no insurance regarding possible pollutants. Normally, we would require an indemnity in such circumstances. You need to keep in mind that we are proposing to take on a large, unfunded, potentially significant legal liability in regard to those pollutants. Now . . ."

"Crack!" Rod said. "How did you see a crack? It only appeared late last night."

"And that's not all," Marco went on, as if Rod had not spoken. "I have had an opportunity to look at the books of Usher Sanatorium Corp. Do you take my meaning?"

"Oh . . . oh . . ." The words came out as a despairing cry. I could the hear fragility, the weakness, the fear. All Rod's belligerence seemed to suddenly melt away. "You can't do this," he said, his voice so soft it seemed as if he were talking to himself. "I won't listen to these insults. You can't come down here from up North and just . . ."

"Rod, you really need to consider this offer," Mrs. Boynton said. "Why don't you reflect? It's no use you flying off the handle. You have to face reality."

"The house and the land it sits on are held in a trust, with certain conditions attached . . ." Rod said, but his voice sounded defeated, almost begging. Why had Aldo's threats about the books of Usher Sanatorium Corp. wiped out all his resistance?

"I'm sure Ambrose Prynne, our lawyer here in town, and Mr. Marco, a lawyer with a degree from Harvard Law School, can deal with that, Roderick." Mrs. Boynton said in a patronizing tone. "Where there's a will there's a way."

Both Mrs. Boynton and Aldo Marco laughed heartily at this pun.

"I need to think about it," Rod mumbled. I heard footsteps and looking out the door, saw him walk across the front office, as if in a trance, open the front door, and vanish into the storm. I wondered if I should follow. Once Mrs. Boynton came out into the main office I would be trapped in the closet.

"He'll come around," Mrs. Boynton said. "He'll wimp out. He has the spine of an eel. All the Ushers are like that. Inbred."

"I hope so, for his sake," Marco said. His voice gave me the willies. I wonder if they teach that sinister tone at Harvard Law School.

"Why did he spook so bad when you mentioned the books of Usher Corp.? And how did you get to see them anyway?"

"Prynne got me a copy from the Crowley Creek Bank. I didn't ask how."

"He acted strange," Mrs. Boynton said thoughtfully. "What's he hiding?"

"No need for you to trouble yourself about that, Mrs. Boynton. This deal is moving along. Just keep the rest of the players in line and keep the deal quiet, like we agreed. That shouldn't be a problem for you, should it?"

They came out of the private office. Opening the closet door a crack, I saw Boynton bidding Marco farewell. "Best you're gone before the staff comes in and the town wakes up," she said. "The gossips will soon be gathering at Shelton's. I'd like for you to be on your way."

He went out into the storm and she had to shove the door closed after him. Then, to my surprise, she walked over to my computer, turned it on, and began reading my files.

I opened the closet door as quietly as possible and came up behind her. "Mrs. Boynton!" I said, looking over her shoulder. "What are you doing reading my personal Usher files?"

She started like a singed calf. "John Charles! I didn't hear you get in. How come you're here so early?" she glared at me.

"I don't believe you answered my question, Mrs. Boynton."

She hit a key, closing the file and stood up, glaring at me. "I believe this is *my* office, these are *my* computers and this is *my* business. The question is, when did you get in and where were you? I never heard the door open."

"You were too busy snooping."

I could see she was not fooled, but I had her on the defensive. She looked around, and her eyes lingered on the supply closet for a moment. She sucked in her breath. "There's been a lot of damage from the storm. I think you better get out, check around, write it up, you hear?"

She wanted to get rid of me. I saw her eyes fasten on the telephone. Worried about what I had overheard, she wanted to consult with her cronies. Well, I wanted to consult with Edith. We had a lot to talk about.

"Don't read my personal files—ever again," I said. My voice sounded angry. "That's way over the line. Way over." I grabbed a doughnut from the box and shrugged on my raincoat while I swallowed a mouthful.

"Don't push it, John. I think we both know what's going on here." She stormed into her office and I went out the door. I needed to see Edith.

Past nine o'clock in the morning and daylight had not yet come. The wind still raged but the rain had lightened. It came in gusts now, rather than the heavy sheets that had made visibility so poor when I had driven over to the *Sentinel* office earlier that morning. I wondered about the hurricane's course and turned on the news radio. Perfect timing.

AND NOW FOR AN UPDATE ON HURRICANE JEAN. THE HURRICANE WATCH CHALKED UP THREE MORE DEATHS TO THE KILLER HURRICANE YESTERDAY AS RIVERS FLOODED THEIR BANKS AND WINDS UP TO NINETY MILES PER HOUR BATTERED TOWNS IN THE HURRICANE'S WAKE. WEATHER EXPERTS ARE NOW SAYING THAT HURRICANE JEAN WILL BE WORSE THAN HURRICANE HAZEL,

THE 1952 STORM THAT TORE THROUGH THE MAINLAND. PLEASE KEEP TUNED TO THIS STATION. WE WILL BE AN-NOUNCING EVACUATION ORDERS FOR TOWNS AS INFOR-MATION BECOMES AVAILABLE TO US.

OVER TEN MILLION DOLLARS OF DAMAGE ESTIMATED IN VIRGINIA BEACH LAST NIGHT AS THE FLOODWATERS ROSE, DRIVING CITIZENS FROM THEIR HOMES, AND HURRICANE-FORCE WINDS RIPPED THE ROOFS OFF BUILDINGS AS THOUGH THEY WERE TINDER.

THE GOVERNOR HAS DECLARED A STATE OF EMERGENCY THROUGHOUT THE COMMONWEALTH. AS THE COURSE OF THE STORM IS ERRATIC, WE CANNOT YET BE CERTAIN WHICH COUNTIES ARE AT RISK. THE HURRICANE WATCH AT THE NATIONAL WEATHER SERVICE HAS ASKED CITI-ZENS IN THE RICHMOND AREA TO MONITOR THEIR LOCAL RADIO STATIONS FOR BULLETINS . . .

It did not sound good. I turned into the driveway and saw that a huge pine tree had fallen across it, blocking access to the house. I pulled up, turned off the motor and got out. Wind tore at my raincoat, whipping it around my legs. I walked around the tree and saw Mr. and Mrs. Slack and Edith. Mr. Slack chopped away at the tree while Edith and Mrs. Slack hauled away armloads of branches as he cut them loose. Edith wore a bright-yellow rain slicker, big black ga-loshes and a yellow rain hat tied tight to her head. Her eyes shone with enthusiasm as rain streamed over her face. "John Charles!" she called out to me as she saw me. "Look at this? Isn't it terrible? Tree must be at least two hundred years old . . . pulled up like a match stick!" She shouted over the sounds of the wind and rain. I nodded, took the axe from Mr. Slack, who was too old for this sort of thing, and began chopping away at the branches.

It turned out to be hard work. The tree must have been very old for the trunk was dense and resistant. The branches whipped across my face as I chopped, as if the old tree did not want to be dismembered, and rain flowed down my collar and into my boots. But it felt good, swinging that axe, with Edith by my side helping. Within ten minutes we had the tree cut up and pulled off the drive.

Back in the kitchen, Mrs. Slack made a big pot of coffee and took a tray of hot biscuits out of the warming oven. Edith and I carried our coffee and biscuits up to her office. Fortified with coffee and food, she brought out her notes, the Poe papers, and other documents I had not seen before.

"Now before I say anything, John Charles, you tell me what happened at the *Sentinel* this morning."

I repeated what I had overheard.

"That's Aldo Marco, Buzz's cousin?"

"Looks that way."

"So you think he's in on the deal, along with the mayor, lawyer Prynne, Mrs. Boynton, and maybe the Crowley Creek Bank?"

"I can't quite put it together. But I think there's more to it than that. Mrs. Boynton is pretty clever. And she gets her kicks from outsmarting people who underestimate her."

"How about this idea?" Edith said. "Aldo Marco thinks he is on a team with Boynton, Prynne, and Winsome. They lead him on, and at the same time, they're assembling property all around the Ushers, not telling Marco. They're letting Marco bully Usher, get a cheap price for his land and house, which is key to their plans, and then planning to squeeze Marco after he's got the Usher property, because they have all the rest. It wouldn't look good in the town for Winsome, Boynton, and company to pressure Usher. They could let Marco do it for them."

"You've got a real devious mind there, Edith," I said admiringly. "Let's see if I've got this. Marco wants to build a casino, right?"

"No, I think it's more. I think it's a whole resort complex. For a casino alone, Usher's property would be enough. I've found preliminary zoning applications, soil tests, traffic studies, tourist projections . . ."

"Edith, that's amazing," I said, impressed.

She smiled, pleased with my praise. "Marco is the 'representative' of a very big New York syndicate. There's a lot of money behind him, I think Mafia money, and they're planning something like Atlantic City—a whole gambling town. It's going to have a confederate theme, you know?"

"Oh boy, that would really upset Rod. He would see it as a travesty of his family, the noble history of his forbears commercialized for a gambling resort. If he knew they had that idea, I'm sure he wouldn't talk to them."

"He sounded to me as if he didn't have much choice," Edith said. "The way you tell it, they have something on him that he doesn't feel he can fight."

"Lord, poor Rod. His sister dies, he's struggling to hold it together, and now this."

"There's something else, John. It's those Poe papers you gave me to read?"

A feeling of dread came over me. Those damned papers. "What did you think?"

"I think they're important. The stories of the Usher family past are very real to Rod."

"Too real."

"Exactly. Too real. From what you say, I think Rod feels somehow caught in the past, doomed to repeat it. Funny the way he talked about that Thanksgiving picture. He's like a man who can't resist reading his horoscope, although he doesn't believe it, then follows its advice, know what I mean?"

"I do."

"Once he saw those vultures in the picture, he spooked."

"Yes, but why?"

"You know, in the papers, Poe talks about a sin and says he hears a baby crying?"

"Right . . ."

"And you told me you heard rumors Rod had a mistress hidden away at Usher House?"

"Marilyn implied that. I never heard it from anyone else. But Marilyn hears so much gossip, she knows the secrets of just about every woman in town sooner or later."

"Well, suppose old Usher—the ancestor, the one Poe wrote about—had a mistress. A big sin in those days. Maybe she had a baby. It could even be that the family descends from that illegitimate baby. And maybe Edgar Allan saw the old Roderick with his mistress. Maybe our Rod has a mistress too and feels guilty. Maybe . . . I know this is far-fetched . . . maybe Rod is worried that she had something to do with Madeleine's death. And here's something else I thought of. Maybe it's this mistress who's pretending to be Madeleine!"

It didn't feel right to me. Almost right, but far-fetched somehow. It didn't explain the "ghosts." And Edith hadn't seen "Madeleine" close-up, hadn't seen her walk, didn't know how much she looked like the real, the dead, the very dead Madeleine and . . . even . . . though it sounds ridiculous, *felt* like Madeleine. And why would Rod need to hide a girl-friend? This isn't 1839.

"I don't know, I don't see it. My instincts tell me that whatever is bothering Rod goes a lot deeper than a lover. But I like the idea that the original Usher had a mistress and that the Ushers are descended from their illegitimate baby. That would explain why Poe's story said they were the last of their line, but there're still Ushers today. Though why we put any stock in E.A.'s writings, I don't know. After all, they're fiction. Fiction," I said again, louder.

"You're trying to talk yourself into that, John. You don't believe it. You think there's something important buried in that story."

She'd read my mind again. We smiled at each other.

"What did Rod want to show you?" Edith asked, finishing off her biscuit and delicately wiping her fingers with a napkin.

"Now there's another weird thing!" I said. "Rod took me around the side of the house by the tarn and showed me this big crack in the wall. Said it had just appeared. But Aldo Marco know all about the crack."

"Was Marco at the party? He could have seen it then."

"It's possible. I didn't notice him. But Rod seemed awful surprised that Marco knew about it. You know why it's such a big deal to him, don't you?"

"Because it's in the original story?"

"That's it. But in the original story, the fissure runs from the roof to the ground. This one seems to be coming from the foundation. Rod claims not to have seen it before. But I wonder. It seems hard to believe a house so old would just

crack like that. In the story the fissure is a symbol. Probably
of heaven's wrath. And of a family cracking apart. A fault in
his house, coming up from the foundation would make Usher
think his life is coming apart at the foundations, see what I
mean?"

Edith shook her head. "It's more likely to wreck the property value, if you ask me."

We sat in silence for a moment.

The phone rang. Edith answered, then handed it to me.

"Hello, John, that you?" Mrs. Boynton's voice sounded
high and aggravated. "John Charles, this is the last straw.
You're supposed to be out working, finding out about the
damage to town. Didn't I tell you to do that? And then you
go on home. Listen up. I just heard that Crowley Creek has
overflowed its bank, the Narrows bridge is down and people
are evacuating all of East Narrows. And what are you doing
to get the story?"

"Don't worry. I'm on top of it," I lied.

"That's not good enough, John Charles. You and I have
things to talk about it. You get that story and then come on.
Be here by three o'clock. You hear?"

"I'll be there." I banged the phone down in her ear. What
was she up to now? Had I finally gone too far? Was I going
to get the boot?

"What did she want?" Edith asked.

"I think I'm about to be fired," I said. I was mad. I grabbed
my raincoat, my notebook, and headed out into the storm.


Well after three thirty that afternoon I came into the *Sentinel* office, stripped off my dripping raincoat, shoes, socks,

and hat and sat down at the terminal to write up the storm story. Downstream, Crowley Creek had overflowed its banks and several small towns had been evacuated. The storm had veered away again but no one knew if it would hit the town of Crowley Creek. Some people had fled the town, others had stockpiled large supplies of fresh water, canned goods, beer, candles, and batteries. One good thing, the Sanitorium was on high ground, had its own emergency power supply, and it had room for evacuees. The mayor had announced that anyone made homeless by the storm could seek refuge there, Rod having opened his doors to the homeless. The storm made good copy and I concentrated on writing it up until Ma Boynton came out of her office, where she had apparently been in conference for some time.

"Mr. Poe, could you join me in my office please?" she said.

I padded after her, barefoot, my trousers soaked to the knees, dripping slightly.

"I see you have been out in the storm, John." It was lawyer Prynne, sitting stiffly upright on Mrs. Boynton's visitor chair.

"I am surprised to see you here, sir," I said.

Prynne looked uncomfortable. "Mrs. Boynton asked me to join her, to see if I might talk some sense into you. It's this Usher story, John. You must stop investigating it, you must drop it."

"I should fire your ass for listening in this morning," Mrs. Boynton said. She was still fuming, but even so, her language surprised me. No matter how angry she gets, Mrs. Boynton has always been ladylike.

I looked at her. "I can't believe that you would threaten Rod Usher in his time of grief," I said. "Take advantage of him when he is vulnerable. Extort his family home away from him."

"Extort!" Mrs. Boynton screamed, losing her temper entirely. "I offer the man the best business deal he will ever see in his lifetime for a moldering, polluted ruin of a house and a bankrupt business and you have the unmitigated gall to accuse me of extortion? Why you . . . you . . ."

"Now let's not lose our tempers here," said Prynne. He looked meaningfully at Mrs. Boynton. "Let's not forget that John Charles is a close friend of Roderick Usher's and Usher will depend upon his advice. I'm sure John Charles only meant . . ."

"I meant that I will do everything in my power to prevent Rod Usher from being taken to the cleaners by whoever it is who is after his land," I said, looking right at Prynne. "And I intend to find out what Aldo Marco is doing in town and what plans are underfoot for the Usher property and the land around it. And nobody is going to stop me. Nobody."

Silence. For a moment, everyone looked at my bare feet and the pools of water dripping off my trouser cuffs, soaking into the faded carpet.

"Just what do you mean, sir?" Prynne said. His voice sounded defensive. "What do you know about the property around the Ushers?"

"I told you he was listening, snooping, reading my files," Mrs. Boynton hissed under her breath to Prynne. She mistakenly imagined I could not hear her. "We can't allow it!"

"What did you say, Mrs. Boynton?" I said. "Do you object to my helping my friend? Because if so . . ."

"Now you just listen here, John Charles," Mrs. Boynton said. She had got her temper under control, her voice icy.

"You work for me and you do what I say, or else. You stop your prying and your snooping and you butt out of Usher's business dealings with me. You can be assured I have his best interests—the town's best interests at heart. . . ."

I had had it with her and her threats. I stood up. "Now you listen to *me*, Mrs. Boynton. My friend is in trouble and no one is going to stop me from helping him. And you and *your* friends better stop threatening him. Rod Usher may be sick with grief and not thinking clearly. But I'm not. Do I make myself clear?"

Boynton stood up too, and leaned toward me. "I just told you to butt out, John Charles. Are you telling me you refuse?"

"Yes, I sure as hell refuse and I'm telling *you* to butt out!" We advanced toward one another and for a moment I thought one of us was going to throw a punch. I didn't intend for it to be me, and controlling myself with an enormous effort, I turned and headed for the door. Prynne cleared his voice, trying to speak.

"Shut up, Ambrose," Mrs. Boynton said. "John, don't you dare leave without . . ."

I opened the door and stomped out.

"You're fired!" Mrs. Boynton shouted out after me.

I grabbed my coat and umbrella, stuffed on my sopping socks and shoes, and headed for the front door. Mrs. Boynton flung open her office door. "Did you hear me, John Charles? You're fired!"

I tore out the front door. "No, I'm not," I yelled at her. "I quit! Hear that? I quit!"

I slammed the door and swept out into the roaring wind.

* * *

"Make it a double, Tommy," I said, stretching out in the back booth at The Old Forge and removing my soaking shoes and socks. "And throw in a dry pair of socks while you're at it, would you?"

The Old Forge was jammed, the air full of cigarette smoke, the jukebox playing full tilt, as Travis Tritt told the world how his papa never warned him about T-R-O-U-B-L-E. *He* had better luck than me. My papa never stopped warning me about the trouble I would find if I kept on acting like I did. But had I listened? It didn't seem so.

Tommy brought my drink and a bowl of peanuts. "Want for me to put those socks and shoes on the heat vent?" he said. "Got a whole mess of them back there already, so I can't guarantee you'll get the same ones back."

"Thanks, but no thanks, Tommy. I like these socks. . . . Looks like the storm's good for business," I said.

"In a manner of speaking, but lots of folks have left town. Lucky the town is on a bluff above the creek, but the trailer park is awful low, and most everybody's gone from there, or so I hear. Guess your place is on high ground? I heard the roof blew right off Jackie Winsome's body shop. Place is a wreck. You okay, John Charles? You look like you're not havin' a real good day."

"You could say that, Tommy," I said, gulping the Blanton's bourbon. "But there's a great deal of consolation in a good measure of whiskey, as my father always said."

"Well, hello John Charles!" It was Marilyn. Her hair had kind of wilted, but she still looked beautiful in a tight cowboy shirt with silver fringe, open three buttons at the front, faded jeans, and red tooled snakeskin cowboy boots. "Hey Tommy," she called, "get me Long Island Ice Tea, will ya?

Thanks kindly. John Charles, you're lookin' kind of down in the mouth." She slid into the booth, took a few peanuts and popped them into her mouth. The gesture pulled at the buttons on her shirt, and I watched, fascinated, wondering if they would hold up.

"I guess I'm not feeling all that great," I said, draining my drink and gesturing to Tommy for another. "Ma Boynton just gave me the sack . . . but that's okay 'cause I quit."

"You quit? Now why'd you go and do that? Everyone says you're gonna be editor when Ma Boynton retires. You just got to hang in and take it. Her bark is worse than her bite."

Tommy came up with our drinks. "Hi Miz Larue," Tommy said, smiling at her and looking with interest down into her shirt. "You're looking good this afternoon. Some storm we're having."

"Did you hear it blew Jackie Winsome's body shop right off its foundations?" Marilyn said. "Wind just came up and took that tin shack right to Kansas."

Tommy and I smiled at one another. "News sure travels fast around here," he said, putting our drinks down and taking away my empty glass.

"Do you think Boynton's bark is worse than her bite, Tommy?" I asked. "Do you think I should hang in and take it?" I was feeling bad because I remembered that Edith and I had agreed that I would stick by Boynton so I could pick up as much information as possible. Now I'd lost my temper and blown it. Just when I most needed to know what was going on.

"I'm not goin' to touch that," Tommy said, marking my tab and drifting off into the crowd.

"I sure had a good time the other night, John," Marilyn said, smiling at me.

Her smile reminded me of our night together, but instead of feeling happy and lustful, I just felt my misery deepen and wished she would go away. The noise in The Old Forge had grown to a dull roar, as if people were trying to drown out the sound of the storm.

"I had a real good time too," I said, smiling back at her dutifully. It wasn't her fault, after all.

She could see my heart wasn't in it. "You feel real bad about being fired, don't you, John Charles?"

But I didn't want her sympathy. I felt too much like a fool as it was. I drained my whiskey and looked around for Tommy. "Where is that guy?" I mumbled. "Can't anybody do anything right nowadays?"

"It's not as if you need the job to make ends meet, that's one comfort."

What did she know about it? Nobody understood what that job meant to me. You'd have to have had a father who told you every day of your life that you were a lazy-good-for-nothing who would never amount to a hill of beans and were only good enough to sit on your duff and spend money other people had earned, to understand.

"I need a drink," I said, and went off to find Tommy.

When I came back, Marilyn had buttoned up one button of her shirt and was scowling into her drink. Perhaps she resented the fact that I had stopped to say hello to one or three people.

"Took you any longer you could have distilled it yourself," she said.

I hadn't asked her to join me. I just wanted to get quietly

drunk all by myself. But I couldn't be rude to a lady who had been so generous to me, so I tried to pull myself together. "Please excuse me," I said, sitting down and taking a big gulp of the double I had brought with me. "I just lost my temper with Ma Boynton, the old bag. No wonder Roger Boynton took a stroke." I looked into the glass. The ice cubes reflected the light, shiny with the promise that lies in the bottom of every glass of whiskey. "You should have seen her. She swelled up like a puff adder and started spitting poison. That old fart Prynne was there. But she told him to shut up. That was good."

Marilyn looked at me. "I think maybe you should ease off a bit, John Charles. You have to drive home in the storm and I wouldn't want anything to happen to you."

It was none of her business. "I can handle it," I said.

"Of course you can."

She was humoring me. "Tommy! Another double. And another round for the lady."

"I'll have a burger," Marilyn said. "No way I'm going to cook tonight. Bet you anything we'll get another power outage. Why don't you have something to eat, too?"

"I'm doing fine," I said. What was Usher hiding anyway? How could Boynton, Prynne, Winsome, and Marco make him sell if he didn't want to? Tommy brought my drink and took Marilyn's order. I stirred the whiskey with the little plastic sword, then bent the sword until it broke. I took the little pieces and bent them until they snapped, too. I ate some more peanuts and studied my whiskey. Strange, not much left in the glass. Whiskey has a habit of disappearing unexpectedly like that. The ice cubes hadn't had time to melt, however, which was good, because when they do, they dilute the whiskey and that's nasty. You have to keep an eye on them, not let them get away with that melting business. Some cubes are sneakier than others and it's hard to tell which are which, because they all look so alike. I kept an eye on them. They seemed to be behaving.

"That looks good," Marilyn said, as Tommy set down her order. "I like the burgers here, don't you? And I like how they make these puppies so crisp." She buttered one of the hush puppies and took a bite.

I had forgotten she was there. I felt annoyed. Couldn't she see I was trying to think? I needed to concentrate. "I need to concentrate," I said to her.

"Well, thanks a lot!" she said.

I could see she was upset. One bad thing about women. They don't understand when a man needs to concentrate. "Nothing personal," I said carefully. "I just have to figure this thing through. Tommy! Another round."

"Don't you think you've had more than enough, John Charles?" Marilyn said. She was really mad now.

"No I don't." What business was it of hers?

"Well, let me tell you one thing, Mr. Poe. I've had it up to here with hard-drinking men and I don't intend to have any more of 'em. You can't handle the whiskey, you can't handle me, you get my drift?"

I got her drift, but I had other things to think about, so I didn't say anything. What was there to say, anyway?

"I'm going now. You think on what I said. You drink too much, John Charles. You're a great guy, but you drink way too much."

She got up and I watched her good-looking ass, in those tight jeans, sashay out of there. Quite a few other men watched it too. It's unfair, the way women do that. They always get the last word even when they don't say anything.

I studied my whiskey closely, certain the answers to this and my other problems were hiding there in my glass, just waiting for me to ask the right questions.

# TEN

Usher House loomed up out of the rain suddenly. Lights blazed in the tiny windows, but they barely penetrated the gloom of the night. Clouds raced across the heavens, from time to time revealing a starry expanse of sky and a sharp, cruel sliver of moon. In the moments of moonlight, Usher House glowed, as if exuding a moist, pearl-white phosphorescence, then the clouds covered the moon and it sank back into shadow.

In the past, when visiting the house I usually entered through the Sanitorium wing. But tonight I saw that, as at the Thanksgiving open house, lights shone in the *porte cochère*. Rain hissed down, soaking through my raincoat. I ran under the *porte cochère* and opened the large double doors into the ballroom foyer.

Piles of wet coats lay helter-skelter on the marble floor of the foyer. The door to the ballroom stood open. Inside, I saw townsfolk, camping out. A table at one end held a coffee urn, a basin full of ice and soft drinks, and plates of sandwiches. You could hear a babble of voices, babies crying, the sounds of portable radios and tape players. I recalled Tommy saying Usher had opened the ballroom for people evacuated from the low-lying areas.

I passed through the ballroom and out into the hallway. It seemed as if no one saw me. Nobody spoke to me.

In the corridors, drafts whistled around me and the tapestries fluttered on the stone walls. The lights flickered and went out. I turned on my flashlight.

How long I walked though those dark corridors, I cannot now remember. I saw old Alastair Mason, the supposedly dead Alastair Mason, the fellow with the wisp of white beard and eyeglasses smeared over. We spoke. About what? I cannot say.

The whiskey I had drunk at The Old Forge made everything both clear and comprehensible and at the same time opaque and confusing. I had to find Roderick Usher. I held onto this one idea as I traversed the passageways, heading always toward the salon he had made his headquarters. Tall shadows cast by my flashlight followed me as I passed though corridors, mounted steps, entered empty rooms. From time to time I thought I heard footsteps behind me, but whenever I turned, I saw only shadows and heard only the rustling of the drafts of cold air borne by the storm that now filled the old house.

Suddenly, the double doors of Rod's studio appeared before me. I flung them open. The long room stretched away, dimly lit by a few flickering candles. "Rod? Rod!" The cavernous chamber seemed to swallow up my voice. "Rod?" I called again. No answer. I snapped the light switch. It must have been on the emergency generator system because the overhead chandelier came on and the room sprang into view: garish, disordered—empty. On the floor near the door I saw a small drift of brownish dried daisy petals.

I retraced my steps, finding my way to the stairway leading to the copper vault. I wanted to see if Madeleine's cloak was still there. I wanted to see if that Thanksgiving painting, now no longer in the ballroom, had been returned. Would the vultures still be watching from the woods? I needed to know.

Some time is missing in my recollection. I recall that I came to the copper vault. I remember the heavy grating sound of the iron door as I pulled it open. Or did someone open it from inside? A chill wind blew out of the vault. The door on the opposite side leading to the earthen passageway lay open.

Madeleine stood in the doorway. She held a silver candelabrum in her hand; two candles flickered in the draft, casting her shadow upon the floor.

"Madeleine!" I said. My voice rasped from my throat, faint in my ears as if in a dream.

"Hello, John Charles Poe," she whispered. Her voice blended into the wind, yet I could understand her every word.

A cold chill passed into my bones. "Is that you, Madeleine?" I said, the hair standing up on the back of my neck, prickling along my arms.

"Yes, John Charles Poe, it is I." The whisper carried Madeleine's characteristic intonation, her curious old-fashioned pronunciation.

I started toward her. I wanted to see her face, so shadowy under the hood of her long cloak.

"Come no closer," she said, stretching out her arm and holding up a warning hand. "I wish you no harm."

"Why are you here?" I asked. It took all my will to force the words from my mouth.

"I cannot rest, John Charles Poe, I have come back to ensure that the terrible secrets of this House of Usher see the light of day. They must not remain buried . . . buried. . . ."

Her whisper, soft and sibilant, sounded barely louder than that strange susurration of the walls I had heard before, that vibration that I now felt in the stones under my feet and thought I saw in the wavering candlelight.

"Show me your face, Madeleine," I pleaded, "let me help you. . . ."

"I cannot rest because of the evil I did in this place," she said, her voice like a faint sigh. "It must be undone. . . ."

Her voice faded into nothingness, she turned and glided into the passageway.

I sprang after her. She would not get away this time.

Ahead of me, in the dark corridor, I could see the flickering light of her candles. Then the light disappeared. I turned on my flashlight, but its beam could barely penetrate the heavy darkness. Damp oozed from the walls and wind roared down toward me, as if the hatch at the end of the corridor had been suddenly opened. I ran after her and I smelled the putrescent smell of the tarn mixed with the scents of rain, water, damp earth. The whiskey I had drunk coursed in my blood and my steps were unsteady. The walls closed in on me, yet I staggered upward.

I reached the end of the passage and stepped out. I stood in the woods. Around me, trees bent and groaned in the wind. Rain gushed out of the heavens with a force so great I could barely stand upright. Behind me, the hatch blew shut with a crash.

I could see nothing. Sick at heart, exhausted, confused by whiskey and sorrow, I made my way back to my car and drove home.

The next morning we had no power. The electricity and telephone lines had been downed by the storm. Edith had not come in. I couldn't blame her. The radio announced that the hurricane had been sighted forty miles from Crowley Creek and heading our way.

I sat at the kitchen table, drinking the coffee I had made on the Coleman stove, trying to swallow some cold cereal and to remember what had happened the night before.

I remembered seeing Madeleine. I remembered every word she had said. Or had she? After all, I had had a lot to drink.

I tried to recall the conversation with Alastair Mason. As soon as I made the effort my brain shut down, and I could feel my head heavy and clanging and sparking like a hammer hitting an anvil.

I poured myself a big tomato juice and added a raw egg, a heavy dash of Tabasco and a half measure of bourbon. Whipping the concoction up until it frothed, I chugged it down. I felt a little better, but my memory had not improved.

I remembered I had called Edith from The Old Forge, told her about being fired. This recollection made me even more unhappy. Had I sounded as drunk as I now feared I had? And my blackout, not remembering what Alastair Mason had said, a bad sign. A very bad sign.

Then I recalled how I had treated Marilyn. I put my head down on the table. She would never talk to me again. Sweet Marilyn. What a beautiful woman; she looked so great in that cowboy shirt and tight jeans. I might never get another chance with her. How could I have been so foolish?

Oh, Lord, I had been fired. Old Boynton had really canned me. I had mouthed off and she had canned me. Fired and drunk. Just what Daddy had predicted. Worse, I had been close to "Madeleine" and too drunk to catch her and find out who she was, what she was. Or too scared? This "Madeleine" had driven my friend Rod Usher mad, I knew it. If only I had caught her, I might have unraveled the mystery.

I heard the front door slam and then Edith came into the kitchen. She carried her dripping raincoat, rain hat, and umbrella, which she hung on the coat pegs by the back door. "Have you been out yet, John Charles? It's unbelievable out there! Hot coffee? Great! I could use some." She poured herself a mug of coffee, tore a piece of paper towel off the roll and began to blot dry her wet face and neck. "It's as dark as night out there and as thick as grits. The wind is still rising. I'm pretty sure the hurricane is on its way. Most of the town is deserted."

I made an effort. "How is it at your house, Edith? Everything okay? Your kids okay?"

Edith looked sad. "Our house is on high ground. But Gerald took the kids to Roanoke for the rest of the week. They closed the school because of the hurricane, so I guess it was good of him."

She didn't look happy about it, but I didn't want to push her.

"You okay, John Charles? You seemed pretty depressed when you called last night."

I didn't want to tell her that I couldn't remember our conversation very well. Strange how some parts of the previous night were as clear and vivid as a dream when you are awakened suddenly, in the middle of it, and other events remained nothing but blurred memories.

"I didn't handle Mrs. Boynton well." I said.

Edith looked at me sympathetically. Seeing that look, I felt something inside me relax. "Then I stupidly got drunk. After that I had the bright idea to go over to Usher House and confront Rod. I couldn't find him, but I saw 'Alastair Mason,' who is supposed to be dead, and I saw 'Madeleine,' who is supposedly even deader. I talked to her."

"You did? What do you think?"

I shook my head. "I just don't know. Whoever it was sounded so much like Madeleine that it made my hair stand on end.

"Do you believe in ghosts, John Charles?"

"I never did before last night, that's for sure."

"Do you now?"

I thought about it. "I don't know. I don't know anything anymore. Do you believe in them?"

"No, I don't. There's got to be another explanation. Someone is playing games over there, and I believe it is connected with the property sale. That's the only thing that makes sense. Maybe someone's trying to scare both you and Rod, trying to make Usher House seem haunted, lower the property value that way."

"You didn't hear her, Edith. She walks like Madeleine, what I could see of her face looks just like Madeleine. She's her height, the voice intonations are the same. Although, truth to tell, she spoke so softly, I couldn't swear to the tone of voice."

Edith took a sip of her coffee and walked to the window. "Two big pine trees are down in your backyard," she said, peering out. "Did you see that?"

I went to stand by her. I felt her closeness, smelled her perfume. I had a sudden impulse to touch her, to hold her close. What was I thinking of? She was at least ten years older, and she worked for me. It must be the hangover. Outside, we could see nothing but inky blackness, rain, and the shadowy forms of the downed trees. Although it was almost noon there was no sign of daylight.

"I feel bad about you getting fired, John Charles," Edith said. "I hate it that Mrs. Boynton fired you for trying to help your friend. I don't trust her one bit."

I walked back from the window and sat down at the kitchen table. "I thought you two were buddies," I said.

Edith smiled. "Mrs. Boynton knew my mother. I guess she thinks of me as her kind of person. She can't really believe I'd cross her in any way. And now that my husband has left me, she feels superior and she enjoys that."

Edith could be cruel. She had a toughness about her that I admired; I don't like soft women. "Well," I said, "you and I agreed I'd stay close and watch what she's up to, and looks like I blew it."

"Mrs. Boynton's definitely mixed up in all the land dealings around the Usher place," Edith said. "We're not going to understand what's going on unless we know what she's up to."

"Why don't you talk to her, girl-to-girl, tell her to take me back," I said. "Tell her she's better off with me under her nose, where she can keep an eye on me, than she is having me running around investigating at Usher House."

"You told me you quit. Could you handle it, going back, if she agreed?"

"Well, that's the idea. You tell Mrs. Boynton you'll try to convince me, but you're not sure if I'll accept, I'm so mad at her."

Edith looked at me. Or I should say, she looked into me. Her voice was gentle. "Okay, John Charles, if that's what you want, I'll give it a try." I could see she knew how much I hated the idea of going groveling back to Boynton, and even more, having Edith help me do it. But I thought the idea would work better with Edith to intervene than if I tried it directly. And after what I had seen last night at Usher House, I wasn't going to let anything stop me from getting to the bottom of things there.

The phone shrilled and we both stared at it. It had been dead when I awoke. I picked it up.

"Hello, is that Mr. Poe?"

"Yes . . ." I didn't recognize the voice on the other end for a moment, then realized it was Dr. Giron.

"Please excuse my bothering you, but we have a problem here. I wonder if you could tell me, have you seen Roderick Usher recently?"

This was strange. "What do you mean?" I asked. "Is he missing?"

"Yes," Dr. Giron said. "We are getting quite worried. We last saw him around six thirty yesterday evening, when he made evening rounds. No one has seen him since. It's not like him to . . . just disappear like this . . . and with the storm . . . well you can understand our concern."

"Is his car there?"

"I'm afraid we can't tell about that. Unfortunately, a tree came down on the old carriage house where he keeps his cars and until we clear away the debris, there is no way to be certain."

"You don't think he might have been in the carriage house when the tree hit it?"

"No, that happened yesterday morning, early, well before he vanished. You haven't seen him or heard from him?"

"Sorry." I didn't mention that I had been in Rod's studio at around eight the night before and not seen him. I didn't ask the doctor about that little heap of dried daisy petals. What would be the point? Was I going to suggest that the ghost of Madeleine had gotten him? In any case, I had never trusted Dr. Giron. "But I'll certainly let you know if I hear anything," I said. "And will you do the same, doctor?"

He promised to call me at once if Rod turned up.

"What was that about?" Edith wanted to know.

"Dr. Giron says Rod Usher went missing sometime after six thirty last night. He probably couldn't have gone in a car, because a tree crashed on the garage, but I suppose he could have had a car out of the garage at the time. Old houses like the Usher's, the garages are away from the house and in this storm, he may have kept a car parked nearer the house. I recall Usher House has several cars; Rod has one, Madeleine had one."

"You haven't heard from him?"

"I looked for him last night. Didn't see him. This morning the phone had gone dead. This is the first I knew they got it working again."

"Probably not for long, the way trees are coming down," Edith said. "Do you think Mrs. Boynton will be at the office? I could try talking to her right now. I should go upstairs and see if any faxes came in, too. I'm waiting on some news about Aldo Marco from New York."

"Give Boynton a try," I said. "If she can get in to work, she will. Woman's a workaholic."

Edith went upstairs to make the call and check her fax machine. I went to the cupboard and took out the bottle of Blanton's I keep in the kitchen for emergencies. The pounding in my head had settled down to a dull ache, but I still felt miserable.

Hurricane lights shone out of the glass chimneys on the tables at Shelton's. Coleman stoves behind the counter held tubs of boiling hot dogs and water for coffee. The place was packed. I saw Mrs. Shelton grilling burgers and chicken on a propane barbecue brought in for the occasion. People in town prided themselves on their survival spirit; they didn't intend to let a little thing like a hurricane get them down. Those who were afraid had left, folks said; those of us still in town were the tough survivors. Our ancestors had stood their ground when the Yankees burned everything in sight. No way we'd let a little hurricane drive us away.

Water ran in under the door and around the windows, but Mrs. Shelton had put rolled-up towels along the door and windowsills to catch the worst of it. A portable radio blasted out hurricane updates from time to time, and people shushed one another, then passed the word. "Still headin' our way." "Should be here by tomorrow." "Crest of Crowley Creek only twenty miles upstream, flooding everything in its path." "Low-lying areas all evacuated."

I found Edith waiting for me in a back booth, her eyes bright with excitement. I decided that Edith liked a crisis. She liked to be tested. "I did it, John Charles!" she said, as I slid into the booth across from her. "I did it!"

"Did what, Edith?" I said, admiring her glowing cheeks, her eager expression. I was glad I had not drunk that whiskey after all. I started to feel almost perky, looking at her.

"You should have seen me flimflam Mrs. Boynton. I said to her, 'You know Fanny, I'm real worried about John Charles.' " Edith put on an exaggeratedly worried expression. "We were sitting in her office—did I tell you, she agreed to meet with me at three this afternoon? Anyway, when I said I was worried, she said, 'How's that, Edith?' So I said, 'He's real mad at you, Fanny. No telling what he'll do, now that he feels no responsibility to you or to the *Sentinel*.' So then, she looked worried. Then I said, 'Too bad, now that he's not working for you, you can't keep your eye on him. Why he was all night at the Usher place, digging around.' When I said that, she made that face, you know the one, where she squints up her eyes and looks like a bull about to charge, and she said, 'That young man needs to get married and settle down and take on some responsibility. He's a loose cannon. I hear Marilyn Larue couldn't take his drinking anymore so she just dumped him, not that she's the marrying kind. . . .' " Edith broke off her imitation of Mrs. Boynton to ask me, "Did you break up with Marilyn, John?"

I just shrugged, and she paused for a moment, waiting to

see if I would say anything, then went on, "Mrs. Boynton gave me a real hard look and then she said: 'You say John was at Usher's last night?' I allowed as how you were. 'He say anything about seeing Roderick Usher? We have a business deal we're trying to close with the man and he's taken off.' I said I had no idea, but that you and Rod Usher were like this." She crossed her fingers. "Mrs. Boynton didn't like that one bit. I said, 'Why don't you ask him, Fanny? He won't tell me what he doesn't want to, but if you're his boss, you have a right to know.' "

Edith was eating a tuna Caesar salad. She took a mouthful and crunched it enthusiastically. She saw me looking at it. "Help yourself, John. There's way too much for me."

I took a coffee spoon out of the glass full of them on the table, and spooned up some lettuce and tuna. My appetite had started to come back.

"So then," Edith continued, "Mrs. Boynton says to me, 'The problem is, John got mad and quit. I don't think he'd come back even if I asked him to. He's got a real independent attitude lately.' "

Edith smiled at me. What a lovely smile that woman had. It just lit up her face.

"And I said to her," Edith went on, "I said, '*You* could talk him in to it, Fanny. You're so good at persuading people. And after all, he loves the *Sentinel*. Just apologize.' Well you should have seen her face when I said to apologize, so I real quick backtracked. 'I mean,' I said, 'just say you're sorry about the misunderstanding.' Mrs. Boynton thinks about this for a while, then she says, 'But I can't have him spying on me, I can't have that, you hear?' So I say, 'But Fanny, surely you don't have anything to hide? After all, John Charles is a born reporter, naturally he's curious. You wouldn't want it any other way.' You should have seen the look she gave me when I said *that*!"

"Surely by now she'd figured out you were pulling her chain," I said.

Edith laughed. "She was too busy worrying about the fact that you were loose and prowling around to notice that maybe I *was* a little bit over the top."

"So how did it end up?"

"She's going to come crawling back and apologize. And I have some information from New York that came in by fax, about Aldo Marco. It might help you get to the bottom of what she's up to with Marco, lawyer Prynne, and Mayor Winsome."

"What's that, Edith?"

Edith looked around, then lowered her voice. Not that anyone could overhear us in the din. What with the wind howling outside, the rain smashing down on the roof like buckshot, the Coleman stoves hissing, the pots of water boiling, and everyone talking at the top of their lungs, the place was a madhouse. "Aldo Marco manages a money laundry for the mob!" she hissed at me.

Astounded, I said, "Edith! How would you find out something like that?"

Edith looked proud. "I researched in all the newspaper files on-line. Then I went back into some of the reports of the RICO Commission. Aldo Marco's father is a big gangster. He sent Aldo to Harvard so he could put a legitimate front on crooked syndicate business. Aldo is known for being slick and cutthroat in business. It's said that he tries to do his deals legally, but if he can't, he finds a way to do them with 'help' from his father's associates. He puts together deals on casinos that the mob uses to launder dirty money."

"I don't get this casino business. The town would never, never go for it. How could they get permission? And then the governor would never approve. . . ."

Edith leaned toward me. I smelled her perfume. Her eyes shone. "Prynne, Winsome, and Boynton have created a series of numbered holding companies. I've been tracking back through the companies. It turns out that one of them has a contract with Marco's company. I'd say they're getting paid off for something. I think all this business about competition for the Usher land is a smoke screen. They're all in it together. They're buying up the land around and they want Usher's cheap. All these 'ghosts' are stories they're telling, just a way to lower the value of the property!" She sat back with a smile. I could see Edith thought she'd cracked the case.

"And Madeleine's death? Rod Usher's strange behavior?"

"Rod is unstable, you know that John. His sister's death was a tragedy and it sent him over the edge. The sightings you and I saw, of this 'Madeleine,' I don't know. But it doesn't really matter. Maybe Boynton and Marco and company paid someone to walk around dressed like Madeleine."

I didn't buy it, but I couldn't think of a good reason not to. It made sense. "What about that theory you had about Rod's mistress? What about the Poe papers? The crying baby?"

Edith looked thoughtful. "You got that story about the mistress from Marilyn, right?"

"Right."

"Well, I'll talk to her about that. See what she knows. And I think we should both reread Poe's story, 'The Fall of the

House of Usher.' I get the feeling you have some kind of memory of a clue in that story. Probably we should reread the Poe papers too. Will you check in the stack you haven't given me? Be sure there's nothing more in that?"

I said I would. I appreciated her taking my doubts seriously. "It's just," I said, hesitantly, "it's just, I *saw* 'Madeleine.' I talked to her. I'll never believe she was an actress, or someone pretending as part of a business deal. There was something really . . . I don't know . . . uncanny about her. And then, where's Rod? What if something has happened to him? How will that fit into your solution?"

"I don't know," Edith said. "I wonder who inherits the house if something happens to Roderick? I am pretty sure Madeleine and Roderick really are the last of their line. I better look into that. I guess there's more work to do before we really get to the bottom of what's going on. . . . Uh-oh, look who's coming."

I turned and saw Mrs. Boynton, a huge shit-eating grin pasted across her face, heading right toward us. Edith slid over and Mrs. Boynton sat down next to her.

"Edith, hello. Why, John Charles. What a surprise!" Mrs. Boynton said, smiling at me. "May I buy you dinner? I'd like to try and straighten out our little misunderstanding."

# ELEVEN

I left Edith and Mrs. Boynton drinking coffee at Shelton's, my job reinstated, and went out into the storm. According to the latest bulletins, we were now in the leading edge of the hurricane, and unless it changed course, the eye would pass directly over Crowley Creek. The town itself stood on high ground, and a place like Shelton's was probably as safe as anywhere. People intended to go into the cellar when the full force of the hurricane struck. I had done my best to protect my house, having boarded up windows where I could. But I couldn't stop thinking about Rod Usher. Where could he be? Could he be wandering about in the storm? What if "Madeleine" had come to his studio and so unnerved him that he had fled? I remembered that little pile of dried daisy petals on the floor of his room. The "ghost" had carried the daisy basket, and the dried flowers shed their petals from time to time. It had taken every ounce of my willpower to confront

Madeleine, to challenge her, to pursue her. I had felt a terrible dreamlike lassitude, a desire to simply slide into the horror of seeing such an apparition, and to let fate take its course. Rod had been acting so unstable, I couldn't imagine what he might have done if the ghost of Madeleine confronted him in the room he used as his retreat.

I remembered the old Edgar Allan Poe story. *That* Roderick Usher had opened the door to *his* studio and seen his supposedly dead sister standing there, reproach in her eyes. He realized he had entombed her in the copper crypt, alive. Struck dumb with horror, he had confronted her accusing eyes, and then her blood-soaked body had destroyed him in its death throes. This scene, the fear of Madeleine's return from death, had surely haunted Rod, explaining the TV cameras in the copper vault. But nothing explained the apparition *I* had seen there.

I had hoped Rod might be starting to recover. True, he had acted weird about the Thanksgiving painting, and our last conversation had not been what you could call normal. But he had been showing signs that he could pull himself together if he wanted to. I would feel better if I knew that he had shown that capacity before he vanished. Then perhaps I could believe that he had left town for business reasons. Though if that were true, why tell no one at the Sanatorium?

I felt too worried about Rod to go home; instead I headed for Usher House. I drove directly up to the *porte cochère*, now surrounded by cars and pickups. Inside, the number of people had increased, as had the hubbub. A stack of six-packs suggested that people planned on dealing with the hurricane in the time-honored fashion. Several friends and acquaintances hailed me as I passed, offering me a beer, but I just shook my head and hurried down the corridor toward the Sanatorium reception area.

Once there I asked for Dr. Giron, and a minute later he appeared, looking flustered. "John! How good of you to come," he said. He seemed to have aged since I last saw him. He walked more slowly, and his arrogant posture had become a stoop. The pouches under his eyes had grown deeper. "Have you had any news of Dr. Usher?"

I shook my head. "I came to see if you'd heard anything."

"Let's go to my office," he said, leading the way up the same flight of stairs I had climbed with Madeleine, passing the room she had used, and entering into the next one. With only skeleton generator power augmented by a kerosene lamp and rain beating on the leaded window, the room felt more like a shadowy cave than a doctor's office.

"Usher House is holding up well to the storm," I said.

"Oh, you think so?" Something in his tone puzzled me, but for the moment I was more concerned about Rod than the solidity of the old building.

"Tell me, when did you last see him?" I asked.

"I saw him yesterday morning. All the doctors have a ten o'clock meeting to review patients' progress. He was present."

"How did he seem?"

Giron hesitated. "Better . . . not really well, but better. He was coping. Just that one incident . . ."

"What incident, doctor?"

"It happened as I gave a report on the care of one of our patients. I had recommended digoxin to control the heart arrhythmia, and for some reason Dr. Usher flew off the handle. He said that digoxin was an evil drug and he would no longer allow it at the Usher Sanatorium. Completely irrational. We all tried to calm him down, but there is no arguing with Usher when he takes these fits. The man has become a complete compulsive-obsessive. I'm sure you noticed it."

"Is digoxin a dangerous drug?" I said, remembering having seen it about. Had I glimpsed it in the copper vault, or on Rod's table on the day of Madeleine's death? When? I couldn't recall.

"A dangerous drug? All drugs are dangerous when misused . . . aspirin, you name it. But digoxin is one of the most-prescribed drugs for certain heart problems. Usher's reaction was totally unreasonable. You can only see it as a sign of his mental instability."

"What are the symptoms of digoxin poisoning?" I asked.

Dr. Giron stared at me. "Are you implying . . ."

"I'm not implying anything. I'd appreciate an answer."

"There's no answer to such a question. Digoxin must be properly prescribed. Some of our older patients suffer potassium problems as a result of taking it. Treatable, perfectly treatable."

"Suppose you got too much?"

"How much is too much, that depends . . ."

"Dr. Giron! We're not writing a book here, just give me a general idea."

"Well, I suppose . . . the side effects of an overdose could be nausea, vomiting, diarrhea, blurred vision, tachycardia, arterial fibrillation, atrioventricular block . . . who can say . . . all these are possible."

"Sounds like Madeleine Usher's last days to me."

Dr. Giron's face grew purple. "Are you implying . . ." he spluttered.

"I told you, I'm not implying anything. I'm just wondering if Rod Usher had begun to suspect that his sister had been poisoned by digoxin, that's all. It would explain his reaction to the mention of the drug."

"So would his unstable state! What you're saying, why its monstrous . . . are you suggesting that a medical error led to her death? The best doctors in the state monitored her treatment! An accusation of malpractice . . . well sir, all I can say is, you better not repeat that outside this room . . . you . . ."

"I'm not suggesting medical malpractice. You misunderstand."

"What are you suggesting?"

"Murder, Dr. Giron. Murder. It is the only thing that explains Rod's peculiar behavior. He feared his sister had been murdered, and that someone here at Usher House was responsible. He suspected she was being poisoned slowly and that his failure to deal with it led to her death."

He stared at me, color draining from his face. "But . . . but that's . . ."

I saw from his expression that he now realized Madeleine's symptoms matched his own description of digoxin poisoning. He faced the choice of attributing her death to malpractice or to murder. Of course, he could continue his pretense that a virus caused her death, something that had been extremely hard to believe from the start.

"Was she being treated with digoxin?" I asked.

"Yes, a low dosage . . . it could not possibly have harmed her, not possibly. She was a doctor herself, surely she would have . . ."

"If someone had given her more, in food say?"

"This is outrageous! Outrageous! You are taking a button and sewing a vest on it. This conversation is at an end, at an end! You are free to leave, sir."

I remained in my seat, not taking my eyes from his face. "Who has access to digoxin at Usher Sanatorium?"

"There are several doctors here," he said, his shoulders slumping, the outrage in his voice replaced by a tremor of fear, "a consulting pharmacist and perhaps twenty nurses come and go on shift. All of us have access to these medicines. But the medicine logs show if unprescribed drugs have been removed. If that had happened, both the Ushers would have been informed by our pharmacist."

"If Rod *had* been informed, do you think he would have told you?"

Giron gazed down at his desk, where his hands lay, helpless. They looked old, knobbed with arthritis. Blue veins bulged and crisscrossed them like spiderwebs. Neither of us spoke and we could hear the roar of the wind, despite the thick leaded windows and deep walls. The windows vibrated in the tempest. Suddenly, we heard an eerie sound, a deep, wrenching, boom. The house vibrated for a moment, then it seemed to shudder upon its foundations.

Above the wind, merging into its howl, I thought I heard men's voices shouting. We stared at one another for a moment; then, as the room returned to normal, we both rushed out into the hall, along the corridor, and down the stairs toward the sound of shouting. We entered the ballroom. A crowd had gathered at the far side of the room, staring at the wall. There I saw that the crack Roderick had shown me had now widened. A jagged, narrow fissure had opened up in the outer wall of the House of Usher.

\* \* \*

Outside the wind howled so loudly it sounded as if the air were full of banshees. I could barely stand upright, as, leaning into the wind, I skirted the side of the house and approached the fissure. Rain lashed the side of the building and coursed down the cleft in the stone wall. Standing before it, inspecting it intently, I saw Aldo Marco. I thought I saw him put something shiny in the pocket of his raincoat as I approached. "Marco!" I shouted through wind.

He turned and watched me approach. The tarn had overflowed its banks and the west side of the house now rose out of the dark waters, which sucked and lapped at the foundation. Sloshing through the water, I came up to him and for a moment we both looked at the aperture in the wall. It looked like a giant earth tremor had shaken and cracked the house. The dark stones, overgrown with sodden moss, had broken apart along a hidden flaw. The fractured edges revealed the inside of the stone, still dry, which glowed a pallid bone-white color. Rain dashed against the wall and the black, fetid waters of the tarn seeped inward.

"Hell of a thing," Marco shouted, his words carried away in the wind.

I remembered that Marco had worked with building contractors. He probably understood what the crack meant better than I did. "Think the house is in danger?" I shouted back at him.

"Can't hear a word you're saying!" he shouted back at me. He took my arm and walked me back to the *porte cochère*. I went along with it.

Inside, he dropped his sopping raincoat on the marble

floor. I did the same. We stood there for a moment, dripping, looking at one another. Both of us wore jeans, windbreakers, rubber boots. He thrust out his hand to me. "Aldo Marco, from New York," he said.

I realized we had never officially met. "John Poe," I said, shaking the hand, which grasped mine in a bone-crushing grip. "I work with your cousin, Buzz."

He eyed me with heightened interest. "Oh yeah? I know your boss too. I've heard quite a bit about you. Fact is, I hear you think you can screw up a deal I'm working on in Crowley Creek."

"I hope so," I said.

"Looks like you and me need to talk. Let's see if we can find somewhere private in this mausoleum."

We began mounting a huge spiral staircase that led up from the ground floor of the ballroom to the gallery that ran around it at mezzanine level. "You think the house will hold up?" I asked. "If that crack is serious, maybe we should be helping people to evacuate."

He turned to look down at me. His face looked very pale. Water ran in rivulets down from his wet black hair, soaking his collar. "This place is built like a fortress. It will take more than a little crack like that to put it at risk."

"Even in a hurricane?" I said, as we reached the mezzanine and began walking along it.

Marco stopped and leaned over the railing. We both looked down at the people below, sitting around on sleeping bags, drinking beer, laughing, listening to their portable radios. It looked more like a party than a forced evacuation from flooded homes.

"There is that," Marco said. "I'm no expert in hurricanes. But I'm not rushing outta here."

"I guess that's a good sign," I said, the sarcasm obvious in my voice.

"You seen your friend Usher around anywhere? He's only got twenty-four hours left on the offer we made him."

"I understood he refused your offer."

"Nah, where did you hear that? He just said he needed to think about it. He won't refuse."

"What makes you say that?"

He laughed, a horrible sound, like a hiss, reminding me again of a snake. No, serpent was the only word for him. He took a large, white, monogrammed handkerchief out of his pocket and began to wipe the moisture from his face and neck. "Usher can't refuse. He has too many problems here, and our offer is his only way out. The man may be crazy, but he's no fool."

"Rod will never never sell. He has obligations he can only meet by keeping the Sanatorium running."

Marco turned toward me and thrust his face very close to mine. "Oh yeah? Well, let me tell you something. It's those obligations that got him into this mess. He show you his books?"

I could say nothing to this. He smiled a slow, satisfied smile, the smile of a man playing poker who has raised your bet, knowing he has the better hand, and is now watching you realize you will have to fold.

"Think the ghosts will go over big with the gamblers?" I said.

He threw back his head and laughed. "The ghosts! Poor

Usher. The man is a loser, that's all. But don't worry." He put his arm around my shoulders. His coat sleeve was wet, and I could feel the moisture soaking into my own jacket. How long had he been out in the storm, so that the water would soak through his expensive raincoat and his water-repellant windbreaker? "We're paying enough so he can deal with his ghosts, all of them," he said, talking into my ear.

I jerked away from him. "Now *you* listen to *me*, Marco. I've lived in this town all my life. Long after you're gone, I'll be here. So will Winsome, Prynne, and Boynton. You can take it from me, they won't piss in their own well. And if they get any ideas to the contrary, I'll be sure they remember they have to get on here after you take off for New York."

"You better stay out of it," Marco said. "If you care about your friend."

"Is that a threat?"

We stared at one another. Now his body tensed; he leaned toward me menacingly. I am close to six feet and wiry. He could not have been more than five-ten but he easily had thirty pounds on me, and at such close quarters I could see that most of that extra poundage was muscle. His brilliant black eyes looked into mine, measured me, then dismissed me. "Yeah, if you want to take it that way, it's a threat."

I smiled.

For the first time, his composure wavered. "What are you grinning about? You think you got nothing to lose? You got friends, you got a pretty lady business associate, I hear. They could have real problems if you don't see reason."

Now I was really mad, but I didn't intend to let him know it. "Sorry," I said. "I guess I'm just heartless, but they'll have to take their lumps. Usher is my oldest friend, this house means more to him than anything else, and I won't stand by and let you take advantage of the man when he is down."

I was bluffing but I could see he believed me. If he thought I would let him hurt Edith. . . .

"You know what your fine aristocratic friend is up to?" he said, raising his voice, pushing his face up close to mine, his eyes glittering. "I just got to let the county officials know about the scam he's running here and he'll be tied up in court, bankrupt, maybe inside for five to ten. He knows I know. He wants to go on looking good, playing lord of the manor, let him buy another piece of property to do it on. I want this one. You tell him what I said, okay? And tell him soon. Our offer expires in twenty-four hours, and I'd hate to have to go back to New York and tell my backers Usher won't play. Know what I mean?" He rocked back on his heels, satisfied with his threats, waiting for me to say I would back off.

But I said nothing. Instead, I turned and began walking along the gallery, toward the staircase. "Poe!" he called after me, his voice hissing with rage, "Poe! You tell him. Tell him we'll turn his books over to the state board at the end of the twenty-four hours! Tell him. . . ."

I looked back at him. In the dim light, his dark clothes blended into the shadows and I could see his white face glimmering and that slash of a mouth fixed in a grimace of fury. "*You* tell *your* partners," I said, not shouting, but projecting my voice upward, "they will never get Usher House. Never."

He stared after me as I continued down the stairs, walked through the ballroom, and out into the night.

\* \* \*

The drive back to Crowley House seemed endless. Even with the back filled with sandbags, the Bronco turned out to be barely heavy enough to make it through the howling winds. In several places the road had become a sheet of black water and I drove through, up to the axles. Once a tree crashed across the road just behind me. Twice I had to drive around fallen trees and other debris, taking the risk of going off-road through the flooded fields. I only saw two other vehicles; an ambulance and a big four-wheel-drive truck loaded with road-clearing equipment. According to the car radio, the hurricane was on its way.

It took all my driving skill to make it home, so I was astonished as I drove up to the front door to see both Edith's little green Taurus and Marilyn's red Firebird parked before the door. What could Marilyn be doing at Crowley House? I knew I owed her an apology but I didn't feel in the mood for it right then.

I came in the front door, hung my soaking wet raincoat over the umbrella stand, where it dripped on the floorboards, and carrying my wet boots, headed upstairs to dry off and change. I threw my boots and clothes in the bathtub, put on dry jeans and a sweatshirt and then went to the kitchen to get something hot. The house shook in the wind, and I could hear water leaking through the roof and falling into the buckets we had put out. The boarded windows vibrated in the storm. It felt strange. All my life this house had seemed as solid and eternal as my family; now it trembled and leaked in the gale, fragile and vulnerable.

Kerosene lamps burned on the kitchen counter and in the middle of the table. A pot of Brunswick stew simmered on the Coleman stove. In one corner someone had placed a galvanized bucket into which rain leaked from the floor above.

When I came in, Marilyn and Edith looked up at me in surprise. They sat at the scarred old oak table in the center of the room, Marilyn drinking beer from a bottle and Edith, steaming coffee from a mug. They had a big bowl of popcorn.

"John! Where have you been? We were worried sick about you," Edith said, her face lighting up with welcome.

Marilyn, too, smiled, but she looked a little uncomfortable. "Hope you don't mind, John," she said. "When Edith heard I was flooded out, she invited me here."

"Marilyn was at Shelton's," Edith said. "And since your house is only half a mile up the road . . . John, where did you go?"

I checked out the stew. It looked almost done. I poured myself some coffee and sat down at the table with them. "I went over to Usher's," I said.

Marilyn looked kind of bedraggled. She had pulled her hair back into a ponytail and put on a sweatshirt of mine over her jeans. "I hope it's okay, me barging in like this, John," she said. "I thought my little house would hold up okay, but a big blast of wind blew out all the windows on one side. I should've boarded them up better. Rain just poured in . . . God, you should see it, carpet ruined, furniture a mess. . . ." She looked close to tears. Then she smiled. "I guess I'm like the little pig who built the house of sticks. Edith tells me she spent half a day boarding up her place and its holding up great, right Edith?"

"So far so good," Edith said. "But I hear we're going to get the full force of the hurricane tomorrow, so it can only get worse. It's scary, watching things that felt so permanent ripped up like they were made of paper."

"You should see Usher House," I said, drinking my coffee. "A big crack opened up in one side. I think Aldo Marco was measuring it, if you can believe that. I saw him out in the hurricane with a tape measure. He'll probably want to knock off some bucks from the price he's offering on the house. The man's a total sleazoid."

"Marco was over there?" Edith said. "Any sign of Rod Usher?"

"Nope," I said. "Not a hide nor hair."

"Hard on the ghosts," Marilyn said, "they'll have to come out of the woodwork with this storm blowing up, I figure."

"Come on, Marilyn," Edith said, "level with John and me about the ghosts. You don't believe in them, do you?"

Marilyn gulped down the last of her beer, got up and put the empty into the six pack and took another. "Sorry to disappoint," she said, "but matter of fact, I do believe in ghosts. Usher House has always been haunted. My mama told me about it when I was little. She saw ghosts around there, a woman in a cloak with a basket of daisies, and a tall blond man. She said the first Roderick and Madeline Usher from the nineteen hundreds couldn't rest their souls because of the evil in that house. That evil happened before the Civil War, Mama always said, then the old house fell down . . . and they've been walking ever since. Two of them, looking alike as two peas in a pod, wandering around. Stopped when this Rod and Madeleine came into the place, but then the old patients started up. Most folks in town have seen 'em. It's been worse the last little while."

Edith and I looked at each other.

"Well, all right, I admit I think there's something funny about the ghost patients ever'body sees." Marilyn said. "More and more of 'em, looking so poor and pathetic. Since Madeleine died they haven't really bothered to hide, neither. There's ghosts and then there's ghosts, if you know what I mean."

I didn't know what she meant, but Edith seemed to, because she nodded in agreement. "Marilyn," Edith said, "what's this story about Rod Usher having a secret girlfriend at Usher House?"

"There's something real strange about Rod Usher," Marilyn said. "He badly needs a girlfriend in my opinion. He's knotted up worse than a tangled fishing line. I did Madeleine Usher's hair, she said as how Rod needed someone. She'd introduced him to people, no luck. Seems he took her advice on most things, but not on that. She even asked me if I knew anyone, if you can believe that."

"Did you fix him up?" Edith said.

"That's what I'm tryin' to tell you, Edith. There wasn't any girlfriend . . ."

"But I thought you said . . ." I interrupted.

"Oh come on, John Charles, don't go all serious about a little gossip. It's fun to think of Rod Usher with a lover stashed away in that big mansion of his, but the truth is, who would want him? He's got real serious problems. Like, no kidding."

I realized Marilyn had been fantasizing—or telling tales—when she told me the rumors about a girlfriend. Who knew why? But with Edith there, she didn't want to maintain her fiction any longer. From the tone the women used to each other, I thought they liked one another. Marilyn, when she talked to me, acted like it didn't matter that much what she said, but when she talked to Edith, she seemed to be more particular. As if Edith could see through her in some way. I didn't really get it.

In fact, I felt fed up with just about everything. Sick at heart about Rod's disappearance, worried about Marco's threats and totally confused by Marilyn's contradictions. I needed time alone to think—and to let everything that had happened settle in. Sometimes some quiet, some Blanton's bourbon and some space will make things come clear.

I excused myself from the ladies and went along to the library, carrying one of the hurricane lanterns. I turned up the lamp and settled back in my chair.

The lantern cast shadows on the walls. Outside, the wind roared. Mixed into the deep growling sound, I could hear a high, keening, whistling note. The boarded-up windows rattled and rain leaked under the sills and dripped to the floor. I closed my eyes and let my mind wander.

I daydreamed about the original story of "The Fall of the House of Usher." I saw in my mind's eye the narrator of that story, old E.A. himself, riding his horse through the dismal, gray landscape, coming upon the ominous House of Usher, seeing the evil tarn, finding his friend half mad, reading and playing music with his friend, Roderick Usher, finding out that Roderick's twin, Madeline, had a cataleptic disease. Then Madeline dies, or seems to. Her mistaken entombment . . . the strange sounds, the increasing madness of Roderick Usher: I didn't doubt that this story haunted my friend. But it seemed as if the story had haunted my ancestor, Edgar Allan, too.

I got up from my chair and went to the desk where I had locked up the casket papers I had not given to Edith. I removed them from the drawer and put them on the table by my chair. I poured a glass of whiskey, and began to leaf through them. Their titles meant nothing to me until I came upon one which, for some reason, caught my attention. I laid the rest aside, turned up the lamp, took a hefty sip of whiskey, and began to read.

*Fordham, 1848*

*My Heart Laid Bare*
*If any ambitious man have a fancy to revolutionize, at one effort, the universal world of human thought, human opinion, and human sentiment, the opportunity is his own—the road to immortal renown lies straight, open, and unencumbered before him. All that he has to do is to write and publish a very little book. Its title should be simple—a few plain words—*My Heart Laid Bare. *But—this book must be* true to its title.

*But to write it—*there is the rub. *No man dare write it. No man ever will dare write it. No man* could *write it, even if he dared. The paper would shrivel and blaze at every touch of the fiery pen.*

*How heavy this truth lies upon me.*

*In my circumstances, where every fragment I produce, every drop from my pen, needs must be sold because we are in want . . . always . . . yet the soul of an artist thirsts for the beautiful, the sublime, the mystical—the true. I* must *write what is true, even if I steal bread from the mouth of my beloved mother, Muddy, by hiding these words. My bared heart's words cannot see the light of day in our era, but must wait for another time. To publish, in any but the most encrypted form, what I know, or have learned through the clear sight of my soul, would burn the hearts of men beyond bearing.*

*It is here, in these, my most secret Papers, that I lay bare my own longings, my most deepest intuitions into Good and Evil, into the nature of Man . . .*

*My love for Helen:*

*Let me describe my love for the woman I call Helen.*

*When she entered the room, I felt, for the first time in my life, and tremblingly acknowledged, the existence of spiritual influences altogether out of the reach of my reason. I saw that she was indeed Helen—my Helen—the Helen of a thousand dreams—she whose visionary lips had so often lingered upon my own in the divine trance of passion, and my whole soul shook with a tremulous ecstasy.*

*Her hand resting on the back of my chair, while the preternatural thrill of her touch vibrated even through the senseless wood into my heart—my brain reeled beneath the intoxicating spell of her presence (and it was with no human senses that I either saw or heard her. It was my soul only that distinguished her there). I grew faint with the luxury of her voice and blind with the voluptuous luster of her eyes.*

*I wrote to her and told her of my love. I told her the truth, that I felt in that inmost heart of hearts that the "soul-love" of which the world speaks so often and so idly, in this instance at least, was but the veriest, the most absolute of realities. I was so certain that it was my diviner nature—my spiritual being—which burned and panted to commingle with her own. In my letter I swore to the purity of my love.*

*"No oath seems so sacred as that sworn by the all-divine love I bear you." I wrote her.*

*"I swear to you my soul is incapable of dishonor—that, with the exception of occasional follies and excess which I bitterly lament, but to which I have been driven by intolerable sorrow, and which are hourly committed by others*

*without attracting any notice whatever—I can call to mind no act of my life which would bring a blush to my cheek— or to yours.*

*And so, with these words, these oaths, I gained her trust. And then, then I betrayed myself and her, I sullied her purity and our love. Yet how could this happen? What evil beasts men are, that our highest longings for these pure beings drive us to drag them into the mire? When I faced what I had done, I was plunged into despair. And she, betrayed, deceived, wrote that she could no longer love me. My heart, broken, grieving, I went to her, took her hand, and swore to her: ". . . if you die—then at least would I clasp your dear hand in death, and willingly—oh joyfully—joyfully—go down with you into the night of the grave."*

*We agreed that our promises to others must be kept. She had her beloved family. I, my obligations to her, the other, whose name was never uttered between us. I was poor, Helen was rich, our situation was intolerable. We longed for death but this we were not allowed.*

*How cruel love is, to draw us into its snares, clothing itself in the purest colors, and then, once we are entrapped, to pull us downward through the pitfalls of lust and passion. Helen and I swore never again to betray our love, but this has proven beyond our powers, and I now live, false to my oath and to myself, yet true—yes always true—to our love. Only the grave will free us from this terrible torment.*

*How clear it is, how easy to see, that death is the only respite from these horrors into which I have plunged us. She will be released from the intolerable pain in which she is now entombed, the pain of guilt and shame. She will rise up, pure and free, her soul one with the infinite. Forgive me, only laudanum offers me any release, for I cannot abandon those who depend upon me, much as I long for the restfulness of death.*

I set aside the papers. My glass, I saw, was empty. The wind roared. The shadows flickered. I leaned back in my chair, closed my eyes, and thought.

# TWELVE

The wind awoke me. Fiercer than the night before, it shook the house as if in a rage. It felt as if we had been living in a night that would never end, only grow darker and more violent. I looked at my clock radio but of course, with the power still out, I couldn't see the radio, let alone the time. I sat up in bed and lit the candle I had placed there before falling asleep. My watch showed nine thirty. Morning. Time to rise and get to it.

I sat up on the edge of the bed and put my head in my hands. Everywhere I could hear the sound of water. It leaked through the roof, ran under the sills, struck the windows, roared down the overworked drainpipes. I threw on a flannel bathrobe and went to the window at the end of the hall. This window was in a deep embrasure and I had not boarded it up. Outside, only darkness. Rain. Occasionally a glimmer of lightning in which I could see old trees, even those with trunks one or two feet across, bending and whipping in the storm. The hurricane had struck, I realized. Soon the eye would pass over us, then more of this and then it would be over.

I stumbled into the shower. The cold water chilled my skin, but I felt refreshed once I put on clean clothes. I skipped the shave, however. A man can go only so far with cold water.

Down in the kitchen I fixed myself some cold cereal and boiled some water for instant coffee on the Coleman stove. No sign of Edith or Marilyn. But on the table I found a note from Edith.

> Good Morning John!
> Marilyn and I stayed up late gabbing. I'm working in my office, she's still asleep (at 8:30). See you later,
> Edith

Where is Rod Usher? Where is Rod Usher? What has happened to him? The words beat in my brain, almost as if I could hear them in the sound of the wind. I couldn't stay at home, hurricane or no hurricane, with Rod Usher missing. And I had a premonition something was going to happen at Usher House. So many signs of the old story repeating itself, it seemed as if we had been caught up in events as inevitable as the hurricane winds. I would take my four-wheel-drive Bronco, which I had loaded with sandbags, and drive out there. I retrieved my raincoat, windbreaker, rubber boots and flashlight. I checked to be sure I had a good pocketknife and extra batteries.

Outside, the storm took hold of me. The winds had a will of their own. Strangely, the howling of the wind didn't sound as loud outside; the house itself, by interfering with the winds, must amplify the sound. But the force of the wind—it felt like standing in the prow of a fast-moving speedboat. I fought my way to the garage, started up the Bronco and drove toward town.

Town had been almost completed boarded up. Lights seeped out of the cracks in the boards on Shelton's windows. Folks had parked their four wheelers and pickups outside. I noticed cars in front of the high school too. I believe some had headed there for the duration of the hurricane. As I passed the *Sentinel*, I saw with astonishment Mrs. Boynton's Cadillac deVille parked out in front next to Mayor Winsome's new Ford Voyager, and another car I didn't recognize. I changed my mind about going to Usher's, pulled in beside them and went into the office.

A conclave. Boynton, Winsome, and Prynne sat around Mrs. Boynton's office, drinking Cokes. Piles of papers, an adding machine, and legal documents all around made clear they were talking business.

"Hi y'all!" I called out, banging the door hard behind me, against the wind, and walking into Mrs. Boynton's office. "How's the real estate deal goin'?"

Three angry faces glared up at me.

"I don't believe I invited you to attend this meeting," Mrs. Boynton said.

"Hold on there, Fanny," Winsome said. "Maybe John knows what's become of Rod Usher."

"Your friend's done a bunk," Mrs. Boynton said. "Man didn't have the courage to face the music."

"Sad thing, fine old family," said Winsome.

"It's put us in an untenable legal position, John," Prynne

said. "If you know where he is, advise him to come and ne-
gotiate with us. He can't escape his situation."

"More to the point, he can't escape Aldo Marco," Mrs.
Boynton said. "If you had anything to do with his taking off
like this. . . ."

"Come in, sit down, join us, John," Winsome said. "We
could use some advice. You know Usher, you know how he
thinks."

I came in and sat down. Mrs. Boynton had boarded up the
window in her office. No light came in through the cracks, but
she had two powerful, battery-powered lanterns on her desk.

"Have a Coke, John," Winsome said.

I took one and popped the cap. "What happens if he
doesn't turn up?" I asked. "Screw up the deal?"

Prynne frowned. "Well, that depends. *We* can wait. The
deal we are offering Usher is a good one. I myself am sure he
will see sense once he gets over the death of his sister and has
time to reflect. But we have other partners in the financing
and they are firm on this deadline."

I took a swig of my coke. "I don't know where Rod is," I
said. "I'm pretty sure he won't sell, but I agree with you all
that his disappearance is worrisome. Especially in this
weather. I can't help wondering if something happened
to him. Trees are falling, buildings coming apart at the
seams . . . if he was caught out there. . . ."

"That's it, John," Winsome said eagerly. "If he's skipped
to avoid the deal, that's one thing. But what if he's out in
the storm somewhere? He's not thinking straight. If we look
for him, he's maybe going to hide from us. If *you* look for
him. . . ."

"I won't help you find him so you can bully him," I said.

"You can forget that idea. Your friend Marco has a nasty line of threats and I don't want him trying them out on Rod. And someone's trying to frighten Rod by playing ghost. Preying on his neurotic fears." At least, I hoped that was the explanation.

"I think there is a misunderstanding here," Prynne said.

"How's that?"

"None of your business . . ." Boynton began, but I interrupted her.

"You want my help. But I can tell you right now that you're not going to get it unless you level with me. I need to know what you are up to. You're going to have to open up."

Boynton's face had been getting redder and redder as I spoke. "Why you . . ."

"He's right, Fanny," Prynne said, giving her a look. "I think we should fill John in. He will never help us unless he is sure we mean his friend no harm, that our business is legal, and that we, not Marco, are in control here, right John?"

I nodded. I was suspicious. What lie were they going to come up with now?

The three of them looked at each other. Mrs. Boynton cleared her throat and fingered her pearl choker. The diamond clasp flashed in the lamplight. "Well," she said. "Well . . . uh . . . we . . . uh . . ."

"Let me tell it, Fanny," Winsome said. "See here, John, this is a business deal. You have to have your wits about you in business, especially when you have Yankees involved. About six months ago now, a real estate syndicate up North started nosing around town. O' course I heard about it."

"And I heard about it," Mrs. Boynton said.

"I also," Prynne chimed in.

"They wanted to get the Usher place," the mayor said, "For some big resort complex. So we got the idea of buying up the surrounding land. We did that. Now of course, our piece will be worth a great deal more than we paid for it if Usher sells to the New Yorkers. Nothing wrong with that, surely?"

"Or maybe you'll be left real overextended if he doesn't," I said.

Prynne moved restlessly in his chair. "There are always risks in business dealings," he said. "You may think we have been a bit overdiscreet. . ."

"Sneaky and underhanded, more like it," I said angrily.

"That's your prerogative, to see it that way," Prynne said, sitting stiffly up in his chair. "But I can assure you there is nothing illegal in what we have done. Nor unethical."

"Oh yeah? What about getting Usher's books, revealing his financial statements to those whose interests are adverse to his?"

The three looked at one another, and Prynne's ears turned pink.

"Do you know what Usher is hiding?" Mrs. Boynton asked, her voice more gentle than I had ever heard it.

I hesitated, then shook my head.

"One thing I swear to you, John," Mrs. Boynton said, sincerity in her voice. "We have nothing to do with the so-called ghosts around the Sanatorium. Rod Usher has major business problems, and he has taken some ingenious ways to deal with them. I am sure his business troubles are not helping his mental state. Our deal will be best for Rod Usher, trust me on this. Find your friend and tell him to sign with us."

I wanted to believe her. But too much remained unexplained, too much still secret. "Why should I trust you? You've got yourself in tight with Aldo Marco. He doesn't give a damn for Crowley Creek or what happens to Rod. As long as he's part of the deal, you can count me out. I won't help you find Rod."

"I gave you your job back, John," Mrs. Boynton said. She was almost pleading now.

"Yes, you did," I said. "But we're talking about Rod Usher and my conditions are the same as they've been from the start. I help my friend. I do what's best for him."

We were all silent.

"Just find him, John." Mayor Winsome said. "We need to find him before Marco's deadline expires. I'm afraid for him, if he crosses Marco."

Again, no one spoke. In the silence we could hear the wind, its deep bass roar, trembling and vibrating in our ears. We realized that we had been shouting to hear one another over its sound, which had been so constant over the last day that we had grown used to it.

"I heard tell this is the peak," Winsome said. "Eye is supposed to pass over tonight or tomorrow morning. We got to be sure Rod Usher is okay."

He was right. "I'll do what I can," I said, getting up.

"Find your friend," Mrs. Boynton said. "I'm afraid for him. Last time I saw him, he looked as if the devil was after him, know what I mean?"

"I know what you mean," I said, and turned and left the room. Just before opening the door I looked back at them. All three stared after me in silence. They looked frightened.

\* \* \*

I got in the Bronco, intending to drive on to Usher House. But for some reason, I turned back and drove home instead.

I found Edith upstairs in her office. "How you doing?" I said, collapsing in a chair and looking at her. She wore a heavy, black turtleneck sweater and baggy jeans. Her face looked pale.

"I wish this hurricane would pass over," she said. "With the phones not working, I can't call my boys. I haven't talked to them in two days. I hope they are okay."

"Hey, Edith, the hurricane is here, not in Roanoke, surely they're okay."

"They're with their father," Edith said. "How do I know they are all right?"

I looked at her. "What's worrying you, Edith?"

She stared down at her hands, lying on the desk. She spoke very softly. "He has a terrible temper, John. He can't take being crossed. Too long looking after the boys brings out the worst in him. . . ."

I got up and walked over to her, put my hand on her shoulder. "Edith, are you saying he beats your boys?"

She stood up suddenly and walked to the window. Although boarded up, it trembled in the storm, vibrating in rhythm with the wind's fury. "He can be so vicious, John," she said, her back to me. "I don't like it, not talking to them . . . I know he's unhappy right now, and when he's unhappy, he takes it out on others."

I didn't know what to say.

"Not like you, John Charles. You take it out on yourself."

Her words sank into me. I walked over to her and reached out for her. At the same time, she turned. I put my arms around her, and she rested her head against my shoulder. I could feel tears seeping into my shirt. "Oh Edith," I said.

We stood there, I holding her, as she cried gently. The wind howled. Powerful feelings of tenderness, admiration, and desire surged up in me, but I could think of nothing to say. I wanted to tell her how good it felt to hold her, but I was afraid to, afraid to say anything that might break the spell.

She raised her head and looked at me. Her eyes glistened, full of tears. "I'm sorry, John Charles," she said very softly.

"Don't be sorry, Edith," I said. "I've wanted to hold you so often."

"I wanted you to, too," she said, a little smile quivering at the corner of her mouth.

"You did?" I said, astonished.

"But it isn't right, John Charles, you know it's not."

"Why not?"

She shook her head, and slowly pulled away from me. I could feel the warmth moving out of my heart as the distance widened between us. She walked back to her chair and sat down, and I sat down in mine. "Why not, Edith? Why isn't it right?"

"Oh John, please . . . I can't talk about it. Let's talk about something else. Tell me what's going on. About Usher House, about Rod, about what you've found. And about those Poe papers you gave me."

How beautiful she looked. That sweet voice of hers, like a balm. Of course, she was hurting, bruised so badly by her marriage breakup, probably the last thing she wanted was to get involved with someone. And she was still married, she had kids to worry about, and I so much younger, she probably felt silly even taking me seriously. And then, my drinking, likely it frightened her, and I couldn't blame her.

Only the lowest form of man would take advantage of a woman in such circumstances, press her when she felt worried and unsettled.

"John? Bring me up to date."

Her eyes implored me to accept the situation, to change the subject.

"Okay. For starters, I just came back from meeting with Mrs. Boynton, Prynne, and Winsome. They admitted that they are assembling the property around Usher's. They admitted they are working with Marco, but his deal is separate from theirs."

"Do you believe them?"

"As far as it goes, but I think it goes farther."

"I do too. I think they're involved in the money laundry. I think Marco has paid them off—maybe the mayor has agreed to give him some kind of zoning variance. The mayor just bought a new van."

"Yes, I saw that."

"John, I couldn't make head or tail of that Edgar Allan Poe writing you gave me. What was he talking about?"

"Well, on the face of it, I'd say, about having an affair with a married woman. Apparently, he got involved with two different women at the same time after his wife, Cissy, died. He may have been sleeping with one while courting the other, and he felt bad about it."

"Amazing. I sure didn't get that."

"You'd probably have to know his biography, the dates and all."

"So it doesn't have anything to do with the Usher business?"

"Right."

"You don't sound convinced."

"I'm not."

"What then? What's the connection?"

"I don't know!" I said. "But I'm sure it's connected somehow. I do know one thing, though. The answers are at Usher's. I feel real strongly that we should get over there, Edith."

"Go out in this weather?"

"I know, it's crazy. And dangerous. But I've got the Bronco filled with sandbags and I'm going. I'm going to find some of these 'walking dead.' I think it's pretty obvious someone's using the stories about ghosts at Ushers."

"But why?"

"That's the question all right. From what Aldo Marco and Mrs. Boynton have said, I get the idea it has something to do with Usher's business problems. Both of them hinted that Rod is behind it."

"But Rod seems frightened by them."

I stood up. "I'm going over there. I think there's a good chance Rod could be in that house somewhere. With all the tunnels and hidden passageways, he could hide out there for weeks."

Edith shook her head. "I just can't see why he'd do that. You think he's hiding from Marco? Is he that cowardly?"

"I don't know, Edith. He's not well. When you're weak, ill, sad . . . you're not likely to be at your bravest."

"I want to go with you, John."

I was tempted. It would be easier to search the house with a helper. Otherwise, my quarry could just play cat and mouse with me, as they'd done up to now. But it would be crazy for Edith to risk going out in the storm.

"I can't let you do that, Edith."

"No, I'm going. I've made up my mind." She gave me a fierce look.

"Edith . . ."

"Now John, don't start getting all protective. I'm grown up and I know my mind. If you're going, I'm going."

She had a point. And why else had I come back to the house, if not to get Edith? "Okay. But let's go over what you've found out, first, then get something to eat. Maybe pack stuff. With the hurricane peaking, we may get stuck over there.

"Agreed." We smiled at one another. I wanted to take her into my arms, hold her close, but I restrained myself.

Edith and I did not leave for Usher House until late that evening. Another tree came down on the driveway, blocking the way out. An old, gnarled peach tree, it had been planted by my grandfather, Crowley Poe, and it was one of two trees that had grown together over the years, their branches interwoven so closely that the family called them "the lovers." We used to pretend that the bigger one was the male and the more delicate, slender tree, the female. Although we had many other fruit trees, we always got the richest and most bountiful harvest from these two. My mother had made peach preserves from their fruit, and even today the taste of peach preserves always reminds me of her in the kitchen, her hair pulled back, steam escaping from the big, black, graniteware sterilizer on top of the stove, and the smell of peaches cooking. I don't think of my mother much. Years passed before I could even admit to myself that she had taken her own life.

She never really recovered from the death of my little brother, but also, she had a delicacy of temperament that made her unsuited to tragedy and to trouble—unable to bear it. Sadly, her death came as no surprise to any of us.

The storm appeared to have ripped the "female" peach tree right out of the soil, now so soaked with rain that it had let go of the deep roots. When it fell, the female had taken many branches of the male with her because a goodly number of the branches had grown entwined. So now the male tree, denuded almost half of itself, whipped about in the storm as if tormented by its loss. Its roots had been loosened, and we all feared that at any minute it too might be uprooted and flung upon us by the wind.

The peach tree lay across the driveway, a mass of waving branches and suckers. Edith, Marilyn, the Slacks, and I set to work chopping and hauling. The wind tore at us, the rain soaked us, and every swing of the axe seemed to be impeded by the wind, which seemed to be trying to protect the ancient tree from final destruction.

It took a long time to chop the tree up enough to get it off the driveway. Often, when we would load the branches into the wheelbarrow, the wind would get up under them and they would rise up out of the barrow, as if of their own volition, and take off across the lawn. An eerie sight.

Once finished, Edith and I decided to have an early dinner before setting out for Usher House. Marilyn, who had helped with the tree, joined us. The Slacks had their own apartment in the tenant buildings behind the garage and they headed back there.

We heated up some soup over the Coleman stove. Marilyn came into the kitchen just as I got ready to serve up, wearing one of my flannel shirts. She had obviously spent some time on her hair and had recovered her usual cheerfulness. "Thought that damn tree was going to take my head right off," she said. "The way those branches whipped about, it looked like the action of that lion tamer at the circus, the one with all the whips he used to lash around."

I found some bread in the breadbox. It felt stale, but I gave everyone a piece. Marilyn spread butter and honey on hers and took a big bite.

"The storm can't go on much longer, now," I said. "The eye of the hurricane is supposed to pass over tonight."

"You're lucky your house is so high and so well built," Edith said. "It would be a tragedy if something happened to this old place. It's part of our history."

I didn't say anything. Truth to tell, there was too much history in the house. Old families have this weight of the past, much of it steeped in terrible secrets. If the tempest blew it away and we could have a fresh start, wouldn't that be better?

"It's holdin' up great so far," Marilyn said. "I went around and checked the leaks. The buckets are doin' okay, and you don't seem to have sprung any new ones. You're going to need a major roof repair when this is all over, though."

"How's your beauty shop?" I asked, sitting down with my soup and digging in.

"Lots of damage. I sure hope insurance's going to cover it. Maybe I'll come out ahead. Maybe they'll put in a new ceiling and redo the wiring and the heating. Every cloud has a silver lining they say. You hear anything from your boys, Edith?"

"Not a word. There's no way to, with the telephones not

working. I hope they're not worried about me. Surely Robert would have told them our house is far enough away from Crowley Creek, and high."

"I can't believe y'all are going out in this," Marilyn said. "It's crazy. Whatever's on your mind, can't it wait till to-morrow?"

"Not really," Edith said, brightening up. "We're going to take the Bronco."

"Does it have a cell phone?" Marilyn wanted to know.

"No," I said. "But I'm real worried about Rod. "I just feel like I have to go over there." Now that the subject had been raised, I suddenly needed to go. I swallowed the rest of my soup and got up, looking around the kitchen to see if we needed anything besides the supplies already collected. I looked at Edith, who still sat there calmly eating her soup. Hurry up, Edith I thought. Hurry up, time is running out. Now why did I think that? What difference did it make when we left? But, as if she had heard my thoughts, Edith looked at me, put down her spoon, and stood up.

"I'm ready," she said.

"I'll do these dishes and pray for you," Marilyn said, only half kidding.

She gave Edith a big hug and kiss and we went out into the wind.


The headlights cast a narrow beam of light, and it seemed as if we drove through a long, low tunnel. Blackness whirled around us. Branches, sometimes whole trees, debris, parts of roofs, splintered siding, roof tiles, flew by and from time to time I swerved to avoid them, throwing Edith against her seat belt. She clutched the door handle, her face bright and intent. The rain seemed lighter, finer, as if the heavens had exhausted themselves after soaking the earth, but the wind blew as fiercely as ever. Twice we had to drive off the road, around a fallen tree. We saw few other cars on the road. Two large pickups passed us, carrying sandbags.

Usher House looked dark. The small windows along the front had not been boarded up. Inset, with tiny leaded panes, they were unlikely to be broken by the storm. Dim lights flickered within, perhaps driven by generator power.

We parked in front of the Sanatorium entrance. In the darkness, we could just make out the inky waters of the tarn lapping against the side of the house. I thought I should check the fissure, but first I wanted to go inside and look for Rod. I opened the car door for Edith and put my arm around her waist to support her against the wind. She leaned against me and we struggled up to the front door, opened it, and went in.

The reception area looked dim, lit by a single, tall candelabrum. Surprisingly, the old man sat calmly at the desk, writing in a large ledger. The thick walls shut out the sound of the storm and the reception area seemed almost immune from the tempest raging outside.

He looked up when we came in, watching as I leaned all my weight against the heavy door and pressed it shut against the wind. He stared at me for a minute, then recognized me. "Mr. Poe! You okay?"

"Yes. . . ." We approached the desk. "How is everything here? The building holding up?"

"Could be worse," he said. "They're saying this is the

storm of the century. We got a big crack in the side of the house, and the lake is overflowed, right up to that side of the building. You seen it?"

"I did. Is water coming in?"

"Some . . . not a great deal. They built well in those days. Wall is a foot thick in that wing, crack don't go all the way through, leastways, not yet. Don't want that lake water in here, that's bad water. Dead water."

"Any sign of Dr. Usher?"

"Nope. . . . Dr. Giron is real worried. We all are. But he could have driven to Richmond and not been able to call."

"Doesn't the Sanatorium have a cell phone?"

"I wouldn't know about that," the old man said. He carefully capped his fountain pen and laid it aside. "I just know this phone here is dead. If we have an emergency with the patients, Dr. Giron says we're on our own."

"This is Mrs. Dunn," I said. "She and I want to look for Dr. Usher here in the building."

"Help yourself."

"We'd like to look in the inside corridors, the ones you took me through the first time I came here. Could you open that door for us?"

Slowly, the old man shook his head. "That time, Dr. Usher told me to take you by the inside way. He didn't want his sister to know he had called you—hated to worry her. I never let anyone in those passages without his permission."

Edith and I looked at each other. On the way over, we had agreed that the first possibility we needed to explore was whether Rod had hidden somewhere in the building. We could both imagine how his fear of the ghosts might drive him to do that. "Surely the staff here has looked throughout the house and you know he is not here?"

"That's right."

"But have you looked in the interior passages?"

"Like I said, no one goes in there without Dr. Usher's permission."

Edith leaned over to me. "Did you hear that? He didn't really answer you. We don't know who had permission."

She was right. "Who had Dr. Usher's permission?"

The old man's face grew stubborn. "I can't say."

Damn the old man. I wanted to push him aside, find the release to the door, open it. I would have too, if he hadn't been so old and feeble. He had a kind of dignity that kept me on my side of the desk, simmering.

"We're real worried about Dr. Usher," Edith said, gently.

A look of concern replaced the old man's stubborn expression.

"We fear his mind is disturbed . . . we fear he might do himself harm," Edith went on in the same, soothing tone. You could hear her sincerity and the old man looked at her, his rheumy eyes fixed on her face. "John Charles, here, is Dr. Usher's oldest, dearest friend. He's the one Dr. Usher called when he was in trouble. Dr. Usher trusted John in those passageways once. Surely, he would be the one Dr. Usher would trust now, if he was in trouble . . . confused, or maybe hurt, ill, somewhere there, waiting for help. . . ."

Uncertainty appeared in the old man's face. "I don't rightly know . . ."

"Dr. Usher needs his friend . . . right now . . . John feels it, that's why he's here."

"He called to you from his heart, did he?" the old man said to me.

I didn't know what to say. I didn't believe in such things, but at the same time, I had this terrible feeling of urgency. "I have to get in there," I said, barely controlling my impatience. *"I just have to."*

"The Lord has his ways," the old man said, making up his mind. He slid his hand under the desk and the panel behind him opened up. Before he could change his mind, Edith and I had called out our thank-you's and entered the corridor. We heard the heavy door slide to behind.

Edith gasped and clutched my hand. We found ourselves in a blackness so profound and oppressive that it seemed as if we had been entombed deep under the earth. No sound, no vibration, no air. Obviously, the generator power did not extend to these inner hallways. I snapped on my powerful flashlight. Its beam cast a narrow, low tunnel of light. All that I had seen here before was, for the moment, invisible outside the narrow beam. The brass gas sconces on the walls, the other corridors branching off, the beams and posts in partial decay, could not be seen. Only this pathway into the darkness. Slowly, we began to walk forward.

Edith held tightly to my hand. Her own felt moist, and I could hear her breath coming in short gasps. But as we progressed, her confidence increased, her grip loosened, and her breathing returned to normal.

No one else could have been walking in that corridor without light. And we saw no other light. No one else could have been walking there without making a sound—our own breathing, our own steps, our own sighs echoed in our ears. And we heard no other sounds. My senses heightened, I felt as I often had when hunting, as if my hearing, my sense of smell, my sight had become preternaturally sensitive. My skin prickled at the slightest movement of air. Every part of my being had become alert—listening, watching, sensing, waiting for the presence of another person. My memory for space, too, now seemed extraordinarily acute. I knew exactly where we were. Suddenly I remembered every step of my previous journeys. A map of those passageways appeared in my mind's eye, as if imprinted on my brain. As if each traverse of Usher House had been building that map and now I knew, not only where I had been before, but where passageways must be and must branch, in an inevitable architectural logic.

Slowly, I led Edith through the maze of corridors. She trusted me and never questioned my choices or my direction. First we walked the long corridor to Usher's studio, opened the door and looked inside. Candles burned low in the candelabra, in the wall sconces. No sign of Usher. Then we passed through the other corridors, many of which led outside, ending in trapdoors. Each of these doorways opened outward like a hatch, some into the outside storm and one, to my surprise, into the gardener's shack I had earlier discovered. All had been heavily insulated with thick, padded felt, which explained why my tapping in the gardener's hut had not provoked a hollow sound. Few could be opened from the outside. One turned out to be locked from the other side, so we could not see where it emerged.

All this took a great deal of time. In the darkness, lit only by my flashlight, time seemed elastic. At certain moments it seemed we had been walking forever. At other times, it seemed that only seconds earlier the reception door had swung shut behind us. At one point the batteries of my flashlight flickered, dimmed, and then died. I had brought replacements, however, and we continued our search.

The time came when we had explored all the passageways and realized that we were alone. If "those who walked," the "ghosts," had ever used the passages, they did not walk there now. Perhaps they hid in the room beyond the locked door. Impossible to know.

"We've seen it all now," I said to Edith. I spoke in a whisper. We had been whispering ever since we entered the maze.

"Let's check Roderick's studio one more time," she said.

We retraced our steps and reentered the studio. As soon as we opened the door I sensed his presence. A second later, I saw him. He lay on the sofa, his eyes closed, his lute clutched to his chest. Almost all the candles had guttered out, filling the room with the acrid smell of hot, melting wax. Only the tapers in the giant, two-branched, silver candelabrum he had placed on the table by his sofa still burned. They cast a lurid glow on his pale face and we could see that he slept. As we approached, his eyes twitched and slowly opened. For a moment he stared at us, bewildered. Then consciousness returned, he sat up slowly, letting the lute slide to the floor. "John Charles!" he said, his voice feeble and distant.

"Hello, Rod," I said, approaching more closely. How pale he looked! How thin. Like a wraith of his former self. "I am so glad, so glad to see you," I said. "I feared . . . I feared you were . . ."

He stared at me, then beyond me, at Edith. I recovered myself a little, "Oh, Rod, this is Edith Dunn."

"Edith . . ." he said, his voice fading off.

"Where were you Rod?" I said. "We looked for you everywhere. All of us worried so about you."

"It is dawn of the seventh day," he said.

Edith and I looked at one another. Then I remembered. It was on the "seventh day" that, in Edgar Allan Poe's story, Madeline Usher returned from the dead.

"I had to come back, here, so she could find me. I tried to find her, but I failed."

I looked at my watch. He was right about one thing, morning had come. The small windows in this salon had not been boarded up. I raised my eyes and saw, to my astonishment, pale blue sky. Thin, weak rays of sunlight now penetrated the dim room. I realized that the roar of the wind that we had been hearing for the past three days had ceased.

Edith's eyes followed my gaze. "It's the eye of the hurricane," she said. "It won't be long now."

"It won't be long now," Rod repeated after her. He stood up and looked at the door. "Soon we will hear it: the terrible clamorous grating of the iron door opening upon the copper vault, the beating of her footsteps upon the stair, the pounding of her heart, her terrible dying moan. And exactly as your ancestor wrote, I will open the door and there before us, her bloodstained corpse!"

"Rod!" I said, going right up to him and staring him down. "I swear to you! You will not hear that! You will not see that!"

He started, sank down on the sofa. For a moment, we all listened, as if expecting the very sounds he had described. But we heard nothing, only the eerie silence of no wind, no rain, no hurricane.

"Where have you been these last few days, Dr. Usher?" Edith said, her voice warm, concerned. "You look ill. Would you like me to call your doctor?" She went over to the table and poured some water from the silver pitcher and handed it to him. He drank it down thirstily, then handed her back the empty glass. She poured him another, and he drank it down as well. "Shall I call Dr. Giron?" Edith said, in that same kind voice.

"No! I will be fine, just give me a moment. . . . So tired . . . hungry . . . thirsty . . . such a long journey." He picked up his lute, clutched it to his breast, and leaned back against the sofa cushions. He plucked a string. The sound vibrated in the room, then faded away.

"Where did you go on your long journey?" Edith said softly.

"I went to the other place," Rod said, looking at her with that wild look of his, an expression that seemed to compound terror and a mad kind of certainty. "I saw her there. I asked her forgiveness. But she could not grant it. She is too restless, doomed to wander, she must die again to be released, and for that we must be patient, wait."

"What is that other place, Rod?" Edith asked, sounding to me like a mother comforting a child.

He must have heard the same thing in her voice, because when he replied, he spoke as a child to its mother. "The place you go when you are naughty. I was naughty. I let her die. She was naughty. She left me when I asked her to stay. How can I be good when there's only half of me left? She took the other half." A tear rolled down his cheek.

He picked up his lute, plucked a chord, and began to sing:

> Sometimes I feel like a motherless child.
> Sometimes I feel like a motherless child.
> A long way from home.
> True believer, a long way from home.

"Rod!" I said, but I felt helpless. It appeared that he had now become completely irrational. Wherever he had been in the last few days, it seemed to have taken him over the edge.

He plucked another chord, minor and discordant, and sang:

> There is a tree in Paradise
> And the Pilgrims call it the Tree of Life.
> All my trials, Lord, soon be over.
> All my sorrows, Lord, soon be over.
> Too late, my brother, too late, but never mind
> All my sorrows, Lord, soon be over.

At the words "my brother" he gave me a look so full of grief and fear that I felt overwhelmed. Whatever ailed Roderick Usher was beyond my power to help.

Suddenly, we all heard a high, keening noise. Rod sat up, his eyes bright, staring. The noise deepened into a roar. The sunlight vanished and out the windows I could see huge black-furled clouds race across the sky. Wind and rain struck the building with such force we could all feel it shudder around us. We heard a shrieking sound, like an enormous iron door dragged across stone paving, and then a resounding, shuddering crash, as if the earth had split open. Roderick froze, staring at the door, but Edith and I, feeling the house move under us, leaped to our feet and rushed out of the room.

The House of Usher shook upon its foundations.

# THIRTEEN

The grand ballroom was in chaos. Women screamed, men shouted as rain poured through the gaping, jagged fissure in the wall. The black-and-white marble floor had cracked too, revealing beneath it the foul water of the tarn that had penetrated underneath, undermining the structure. Outside in the darkness, the wind howled with a maniacal fury.

Behind us, Usher stood, staring, transfixed. Then his eyes cleared. "The other wing is sound!" he shouted to me above the din. "Follow me and I will lead you to safety!"

I ran halfway up the stairs, took a deep breath and bellowed above the din: "Attention people! Don't panic! Dr. Usher will lead you to a safe place! Follow him!" The room quieted, although people now stood ankle-deep in water. Women lifted their babies, men grabbed their toddlers onto their shoulders. "Form a line, keep calm," I shouted.

Order returned as people collected their wits. Usher opened a door and walked rapidly down a corridor, the townsfolk following. Edith gathered up some small children, I did the same, and waiting until the last person had left, I shut the door to the ballroom. The building shuddered violently in the wind. Loud cracking reports resonated; we could feel the house breaking apart around us.

Usher led the townsfolk toward the Sanatorium wing. We trooped, half running, through the reception area and out a doorway on the other side. We came to a tall, double mahogany door. Usher drew a large old-fashioned brass key from his pocket and opened the door. Inside, we found ourselves in a huge, decrepit room. Cowering at the far end stood the most pathetic group of old folks I have ever seen. Some slumped weakly in wheelchairs, some leaned on walkers, some lay on cots. Their clothes shabby, rags in some cases. A few wrapped in bloody bandages. I recognized with a shock the little, old fellow I had seen hiding in the garden, the one with the wispy beard and the glasses, Alastair Mason. "It's the ghosts!" I said to Edith. Rod stood right behind me. "Yes," he said, "God forgive me. It's the poor folks we hide here. But I had to bring you here; it is the only room large enough and safe enough."

Edith confronted him. "You pretend they're dead so you can take on more patients! You hide them from the state."

Rod didn't deny it. "We take all the money they have and then we make them 'die,' poor pathetic creatures," he said. "But it's better than their alternatives. They have enough food, minimal medical care." For a moment, he seemed completely lucid. Then the mad look appeared again in his eyes.

"But I didn't do enough! The curse, the curse promised by my ancestors was not forestalled. The evil is too deep. It runs in my blood, it ran in Madeleine's."

Another shrieking, rending noise, another cracking boom. "The house is going!" I shouted to Edith, who stared at Rod, shocked. "We must get everyone out of here before it comes down on us."

I raced out of the room, down the corridor to the visitors' room of the Sanatorium. I figured I would find the other patients there. Sure enough, the Sanatorium patients had been gathered together, along with the doctors and nurses. As soon as I came in, Dr. Giron hurried over to me. "Thank God you're here," he said. "I've called for help on my cellular phone, but we must evacuate right away, help can't reach us in time. The cellars are flooding with the polluted waters of the lake. The building can't last much longer. It is breaking open. Please . . ."

"Bring the patients to the front door of the Sanatorium," I said. "Bring the weakest and most ill first. I'll organize the townspeople and their cars. We'll take everyone to the high school. They'll be safe there."

"Yes! Yes! At once," he said. Turning away from me, he began ordering the nurses around.

I ran back to the room where Rod kept the "ghosts" locked in. Quickly I told Edith the plan and with her help, set to work.

The next hour passed in a blur. What we proposed to do was dangerous. At least a hundred people needed to be ferried through the storm to safety. Many now ill, weak and some were confused. Among the townspeople we had babies and toddlers, mothers terrified of being separated from their children. Some men would only help their own families. In times of crisis, some rise to their best; some sink to their worst. But Edith, I, and to give him credit, Dr. Giron, managed to persuade, threaten, bully, or cajole the people with cars to take others. Finally we had them all organized. We assembled a long convoy with my Bronco at the front and another 4×4 at the rear.

In the frenzy I lost sight of Rod. The noise was deafening. While the Sanatorium wing (the oldest part of the house) had stayed dry, the rest, closer to the tarn and with larger windows, was awash, and the water kept rising. Very soon this wing too would break apart and flood.

Folks acted crazy. Some didn't want to leave their possessions; they wanted to go back to the ballroom for their tape decks, CD players, knapsacks. Others at first refused to drive through the storm, not wanting to put their vehicles at risk. Meanwhile, all around us the tempest raged and the house cracked and buckled. Trying to load the people into the cars felt like herding cats. People would dart out to get something they had forgotten, head toward the house, lose their nerve when they heard another enormous, shuddering crack, and run back to the convoy. Meanwhile the tarn spread like a malignant spirit, rising against the side of the house, lapping under the convoy of cars and trucks. "Get in, get in your cars and stay in!" I shouted.

Finally, the last count, we had everybody, or almost everybody. But where was Rod? Edith came running up to tell me that we had to set off. People were in the cars, ready to go. "But no sign of Rod!" I shouted at her, above the wind.

"He's gone to get his Cherokee!" she shouted back.

At that moment, around the side of the house, came a white Jeep Cherokee, the top badly bashed in, Rod at the wheel, his eyes staring, blank.

"God, look at him! He's completely out of it!"

"We don't have time for this, John!" Edith shouted. "If we don't drive off now lots of these cars won't make it. The water's rising too fast!"

"You take my Bronco!" I called out, tossing her the keys. "I've got to go with Rod!"

She didn't question me. She ran to the Bronco, jumped in, and set off. I waved the cars after her, and the convoy slowly began driving away, away from Usher House.

Rod drove up, leaned over, and opened the passenger-side door for me. I jumped in. "John!" Rod said. "Thank God. You will protect me. Your goodness will protect me. So now we can rescue Madeleine. There is no time to spare."


Rod would say no more. He drove carefully up a sloping lane, away from Usher House. He parked on a barren rise, looking back down over the house and the surrounding landscape. Beyond the house I could see the convoy of cars driving away, with my red Bronco in the lead. So far so good. The cars gained the highway and drove toward town as we watched. Rain lashed them, wind buffeted them, flood waters sheeted away from their wheels, but they drove onward. Soon they breasted the farthest hill and disappeared over the horizon.

Our position was very exposed. The tempest beat upon

the roof of the Cherokee. Water worked its way into the joints and soon covered the floor of the car. Despite the fact that the backseat and cargo area had been filled with sandbags, the car shook and trembled in the wind.

"What are we doing here, Rod?" I said to my friend. Looking at him, my heart filled with pity. He had aged so much during his disappearance that he now looked like an old man. His flesh had melted away and his skin hung around his neck in loose folds. His eyes pouched and sunken in, his hair lank and colorless.

"We are waiting for Madeleine," he said. He spoke so softly that I could barely hear him. "She will tell you, she will explain about the ghosts. It was her idea. No . . . no . . . Roderick Usher," he said, as if scolding himself, "tell the truth . . . it was *your* idea."

"What idea?"

"My ancestor, Roderick Usher, he laid a vow upon his descendants to use this land, this house, for good. I had to have twenty percent of my patients charity cases. But the state cares not for good or evil; you know that John. The state cares for law and order, is that not right?"

What was he talking about? I couldn't follow him.

He went on. "But what are law and order when good and evil are at stake? Good and evil soak into the soil, they penetrate the waters, they rise up into the soul of man and shape our fate." He looked at me, waiting for my response.

"Right." I said, not wanting to make things worse by questioning him.

"Yes. Right. I wanted to do right. Yet the Sanatorium had taken all our resources, the house absorbed our funds endlessly as we sought to keep it sound. We needed more patients, so we took the money from the poor ones and hid them. At night, they walked about, and people saw them and thought them ghosts. And so they were—dead yet not dead. Meanwhile, we had the right number of poor to keep faith with the will, yet we could take on richer ones to sustain the House. It was not lawful, but it was *right*. You see?"

"I see . . ." I said.

"Aldo Marco saw, too. He saw our books, he saw the numbers that revealed the 'ghost patients.' He threatened me. We had more patients than the law allowed. The inspectors would come from the state and close the Sanatorium. You would have fought back, John. But I could not do so. I had to wait for Madeleine."

I shook my head, filled with foreboding.

"We can't stay here, Rod," I said. "This is crazy, sitting in a car, on a hill, in a hurricane. We must go somewhere safe."

"We are waiting for Madeleine," he said. He gave me a look so filled with sadness and entreaty that I felt helpless. What had driven my friend to this state? I didn't believe for a moment that financial problems or the threats of Aldo Marco could have caused it.

He trembled, he opened his mouth to speak, but nothing came out. He wanted to say something more, but he had not the strength of will to do so.

"Did Madeleine accept the 'ghost patient' idea?"

"Madeleine hated it. But she could deny me nothing. I could deny her nothing." He paused. Took a deep breath. Stared out the window into the storm. "Madeleine and I were born almost in the same instant, twins in soul, twins in heart. We should have been one person. Neither of us could bear it, that separation . . . man and woman, two halves of one soul; we were drawn together."

*Incest.* The word rose up into my mind as he spoke. This was the secret I had tried so hard not to see, yet had felt all along. I had hidden from my own knowledge, just as my ancestor Edgar Allan Poe had hidden from his. I had recognized his self-deception in all his writings, yet had been unable to admit it to myself because I would have had to ask what he was hiding, and I was afraid of the answer. The knowledge Edgar Allan refused to face fueled the horror, dread, and moral loathing in his story. Now I knew the terrible secret that had destroyed the House of Usher, the sin that the first Roderick Usher feared would send him to damnation. Now I understood the painting of his son, so full of images of stains on the soul. Now I understood so much I had refused to face. I looked at my old friend; feelings of disgust, pity, and horror welling up inside me. He read reproach, shock, disgust, in my eyes.

"She wanted to escape me!" he cried, "but I could not bear it! When the offer came for her to go to the Mayo Clinic, she wanted to sell the house, close the Sanatorium, leave me, start a new life. But then, the curse would rise up and destroy us, for we would have broken faith with our ancestors."

"The first Roderick and Madeline?"

"They too found themselves bound together in love and sin. Their love child was our ancestor. The first Madeline died from childbirth, cursed by the fruit of their love. Her brother's grief destroyed his mind—and mine. This sin is deep in our blood. Such a love as ours is older than we are."

Now I grew angry. "It's wrong what you did! Talking about ancestors doesn't make it right. And it doesn't sound like love when you kept your sister near you when she wanted to leave. Sounds more like selfishness."

He paled. "No! Don't say that!" He put his hand on the door, started to open it.

"Rod! What are you doing? You can't go out there!"

"Take that back! Take it back! I am not selfish." He gave me a sly look. "She didn't *really* want to leave. Getting sick, weak, she knew that she needed me. And I, I too sickened as she withdrew from me. I cannot live without her. She is my other half. Don't you see?"

I did see. I was horrified. I had to get the man to help. He had gone beyond reason, beyond anything I could do. "What are we doing here, Rod?" I asked again.

"We are waiting for Madeleine," he said, confidence in his voice. But then a worried look crossed his face. "But how will she know where to come? She will expect to see me in the salon! Why did you make me leave the house? John! We must go back. I must wait in the salon. The other Madeline went there when she rose from the dead, and covered in blood, rendered justice from her brother. Madeleine will look for me there."

He reached forward to turn the starter.

I grabbed his hand. "We're not going back to that house," I said.

"She's inside me, John," he said. "I hear her. She wants me to go back to the house. She must walk, she must take her revenge. I must die. And you, you knew, you always knew. From the first. You knew that Madeleine and I were born to be lovers in soul and in flesh. Your friendship blessed us. Your goodness gave us forgiveness."

*"What?"*

"But now, I see it. You have withdrawn your blessing. Madeleine drew away, but she could not live apart from me, as I could not from her, and so she died. Now you too will die."

His eyes were brilliant, staring, his body rigid with tension. I leaned over to grab the key, but he moved too fast for me. He started up the Jeep and drove toward Usher House. I pulled at his arm but it felt like a steel rod, held tense by his madness.

In the headlights of the Cherokee, the wind and rain created a strange effect, as if glowing clouds of vapor swirled around, gathered together and raced with us toward the House of Usher. "See that?" Usher said, pointing to the shapes visible in the lights. "See that? Just as my ancestor saw on *his* last night. And *your* ancestor stood there with him, when Madeline arrived, just as you shall do. You must. Or she will not come."

We drove toward Usher House. As we approached, I saw that it had suffered serious damage. The entire wing where the fissure had opened up had sunk partly underwater. The Sanatorium wing, the older side, still stood, but it now appeared tilted off center, as if the hurricane had forced it off its foundations. From the tarn an eerie white light glowed, and a phosphorescent exhalation swirled above, twisting vaporous tendrils partly enshrouding the crumbling newer wing.

"See!" Roderick said, pointing at it. "Exactly as your ancestor pictured it in his story!"

We drove through the flooded parking lot, water rising up around the axles. Rod ignored it. Water now filled the bottom of the Cherokee, black water, smelling of decay.

"Rod! Get hold of yourself," I shouted above the wind. "This is crazy. Insane."

He paid no attention. He stopped the car, reached in his pocket, and took out a rope. Before I realized what had happened he had knotted a slip noose, put it over my neck, looped it through the tubular padded-frame support above the door, and pulled it so tight that the slightest motion would choke me. "Don't move," he said, jumping out of the Jeep and racing around to my side of the car.

Ignoring his command, I held my body rigid so as not to tighten the noose and reached carefully up with my fingers to loosen the rope. But just as I got my fingers under it, he jerked open the door on my side, untied the rope and pulled. I fell sideways out of the Jeep. The rope slackened and I stood up and lunged at him. I got him in an armlock. We struggled. We stood in water over our ankles. We lost our footing and both of us fell, the rope jerking tight against my neck. For a moment I lost consciousness. When I came to, he was leaning over me, his pale face mad, his mouth open, his eyes glittering. But he loosened the rope. "John! Oh God, John, not yet . . . no, not yet. . . ." I stood up, disoriented, gasping for breath, unable to believe what was happening. I put my hand to my neck. The skin had been rubbed raw; the rope hung loose.

Now he drew a hypodermic from his jacket pocket and pressed it up against my neck. "Don't worry, John," he said soothingly. "It is not your time. Just do as I say, and all will pass off as it is written. Remember, your ancestor survived the 'Fall of the House of Usher.' Mine didn't." He smiled—a mad, meaningless smile.

"What's in that needle?" I said, my voice harsh.

"It's an overdose of insulin, John, I'm sorry to say. Fatal. Just do as I tell you and it won't be needed. I am your friend. You *were* my friend. And Madeleine trusted you. That is to your eternal credit."

"There was no overdose of insulin in the old story," I said.

"Good try, John. I like that." He opened the front door of the Sanatorium and we walked in together, he holding the needle against my neck. I considered breaking away, grabbing his arm. But he had made clear he did not want to kill me. He could have done so when the noose tightened on my neck and I lost consciousness. So why risk a sudden movement that might cause him to press in the plunger on the syringe? He had so obviously gone around the bend. A better moment would surely come.

My heart beat loudly in my chest. I could feel it thumping, louder in my ears than the roaring of the wind, the rattling of the windows in their casements, the wrenching booms of the old house breaking apart.

Rod marched me into his studio. He pushed me gently down on the sofa, pulled the noose taut around my neck and tied the other end of the rope around the leg of the sofa so that my slightest move would tauten the noose and strangle me. I could feel the rough hemp chafe. He sat next to me, the needle of the hypo poking through my jeans, pricking my thigh.

"Don't try to loosen the rope, John. All I want you to do is sit here with me until she comes."

Now close to him, I could feel him shivering. His face glistened with sweat and a strange, acrid smell emanated from him. He had passed into the grip of some terrible fear that completely deranged him. Perhaps I could calm him. But first I would have to get hold of myself. My feelings roiled about in such a turmoil of fear, disgust, guilt, and shock that I couldn't think straight. And I had to think straight. Had to.

I wanted to tell him the house was going . . . that sitting here we risked having the whole ancient stone pile fall in on us. But that would only increase his panic and the conflict that tormented him. What in *hell* was he waiting for? If I knew that, I might get an idea what to do!

"I am your friend, Rod," I said. "You called me to help. So why . . ."

"But of course I did! Did not your ancestor witness the original fall of the House of Usher? If Madeleine is to come back, you must be by my side, just as Edgar Allan stayed beside the first Roderick Usher."

"But that's a *story!*"

He leaned closer to me and spoke into my ear. "No," he whispered. "That's what I've come to see . . . the old story is full of the deepest truths. That is why it has endured. That's why it has moved generations. That's why we must let it guide and save us now!"

My poor, poor friend. Had he not seen the fatalism and guilt that my obsessed ancestor had embodied in the old story? How wrong to be guided by something so dark and perverse. Did he not see that there can be no salvation in hiding the truth? Only in facing up to it. Something my ancestor, no, my ancestors, had never succeeded in doing.

I turned to my friend. I looked into those mad, terrified eyes. "You have told me part of the truth. Now you must tell me the rest."

"I didn't tell; we tell no one, that is our promise," he said, speaking in that strange, childlike voice he had used twice before. He looked at me, then tilted his head. "But was Madeleine thinking of telling you, John? That last time when she picked the daisies? Did she tell you she wanted to leave me?"

"*You* told me, Rod," I said, staring at him sternly. "You told me on the hill that you and Madeleine were lovers. That she wanted to leave you and have a life of her own and you wanted to stop her."

"I did *not* tell!" He jumped up suddenly, pulled another length of twine out of his pocket, grabbed my hands and tied them behind my back. "Watch what you say, John," he muttered as he knotted the rope. As the slightest move tightened the noose, I could not stop him, but I tensed and held my hands as far apart as possible while he tied, hoping to create some slack.

We heard another enormous boom. In the far wall of the room, in the dimness, a crack slowly opened. Rod stared at it. "Oh God, oh God, Madeleine . . ." he rushed to the doors, opened them, and ran from the room.

Now, alone, I could feel the house shuddering, hear the wind and storm raging. Water blew in through the opening in the wall. Sitting as upright and still as possible, I flexed my hands and tried to loosen the bonds that held me. The rough hemp rope burned into my flesh as I twisted. I could feel the flesh tear and bleed, but I was making progress.

A deafening crash. The double doors to the salon burst open. Madeleine stood in the doorway. She wore her long cloak. Her pale face, ravaged and old, stared at me from the shadows of the hood.

Looking back at her, I continued to twist my hands out of the rope. Skin shredded, ripped away. The pain increased, but the blood had made my hands slippery and I was almost free.

"I have come to tell you the truth," she said, in that same eerie whisper I had heard before.

"Come closer," I said calmly. "I can't hear you." My calmness was assumed. My heart thumped loudly in my chest and sweat ran down my back. I felt suddenly chilled to the bone.

She hesitated.

"I can't hear you above the storm. Come closer," I said.

She glided toward me. Now, even in the dim light, I could see her face. Surely that was Madeleine!

"You are surprised," she whispered. "Now you see. I am not dead. I am here to say the truth. To punish Roderick Usher for my death. He murdered me! He was my lover, my life, my death! I was his lover, his life, his death! I walk this house so that he will suffer the fear, the anguish that I suffered, suspecting my beloved was poisoning me to death . . . and doing nothing. I did nothing to stop him . . . for he was me and I was him. . . ."

As she spoke, I loosened my hands and freed them from the rope.

"Look! The window!" I said.

She turned. I forced my fingers under the noose, wrenched it free, leaped up from the sofa, grabbed her, flung her to the sofa and pulled the cloak away. It took every ounce of my force, my will, my courage to do it. My body moved with dreamlike slowness and she resisted. She was very strong.

I stared down at the creature on the sofa, seeing a face cataleptic with shock, skin blanched with fear. For a moment I could not understand what I saw. The face . . . was it Rod? . . . was it Madeleine? Both stared up at me, the face shifting from the expression of one to the other. One instant Madeleine looked up at me, the next moment it was Rod.

"Rod!" Suddenly, I understood.

He put his ravaged face in his hands and began to weep. Then he looked up at me, his eyes cleared, and I looked deep into that tormented soul. Pity welled up in me. "Help me, John," he said in the old voice I remembered so well. "I hear your words. You say: *tell the truth*. I told you the truth. You did not want to hear it, but now, now you can help me."

"More truth, Rod," I said. "I must have it all. You must face it all."

He shuddered, looked at me pleadingly, as if hoping I would back off.

"It is the only way," I said.

He took a deep breath and his eyes sank deeper into their sockets. His fists bunched tight, and the tendons stood out in his neck. "I . . . I . . . I killed her, John. I tried to be my own nemesis, but I failed. I tried to keep her alive after death—I became her so that I could punish me for my sin, but I failed. I call you to witness my truth and save the House of Usher."

His terrible words transfixed us both. They vibrated

above the clamor of the storm. Then, with a wrenching, shrieking sound, the fissure broke open. A gust of wind full of the glowing fumes from the tarn poured into the room. The floor beneath us split open, tilted, and the house flung us into the whirlwind.

# FOURTEEN

*Cold. The smell of death and decay. Blackness. Lassitude. Let go, sink into it, let it happen. Pain, a pounding pain in my skull . . . don't move . . . then the pain will go away; sink down down into the black waters. . . . Water! That's what it is, I'm drowning!*

With an enormous effort I kicked off one water-filled boot, then the other, and reached out paddling with my ravaged hands, kicked, rose to the surface. I spit out a mouthful of the evil black water. Coughed. Vomited up more. Retching, I struggled out of the water.

I found myself on the edge of the tarn. For a moment, I sat there, coughing up water and vomit, shuddering, my head pounding, fiery pain in my hands and around my neck. I could hear the house boom and crash as it crumbled into the tarn. I didn't look at it. Slowly, my thoughts came into focus. Rod! Where was he? I looked around. There! Crawling out of the tarn, shivering and coughing. He emerged completely and collapsed against a tree.

I could hear him coughing, sobbing. Poor damned soul. Wait a minute. He doesn't deserve your pity. He killed his sister. He means to kill you, I told myself. Leave him. Get the hell out of here. If anybody deserves to die, he does. It would be a blessing to just let him die here.

How dark it was. I looked around me. I saw his Jeep Cherokee, half submerged in the rising waters of the tarn. Get it out, that was the first thing.

I staggered through the water to the Jeep and tried to open the door. The water pressure held it shut. The driver's window was open and the water had not yet reached it. I put my hands on the window. Blood ran down the window. I saw the skin on my hands torn, peeling away from the ligaments. How had that happened? I could barely remember. But luckily, the worst damage had been done to the back of my hands. I tightened my grip and hoisted myself up, then fell headfirst into the Jeep.

The key was in the ignition. Would it start? I turned the key. Amazing. She turned over. Died, but she *had* turned over. Don't flood it, John, I told myself. Ironic thought, flood. It seemed the *world* was flooded. Gently, I tried again. This time the engine spluttered, coughed. Died. Sounding better. Once more.

"*John!*" What was that? Rod calling or just the wind? Who cares? Give her a minute, then, gently . . . gently . . . here she goes. . . . *Way to go!* Nothing more lovely than the sound of an engine coming to life.

I put her into four-wheel drive and slowly drove up onto higher ground.

*"John!"*

To hell with him. Let him die here. He didn't deserve to live. I drove over toward him. Don't help him, a voice inside me said. He slept with his sister, murdered her slowly with poison, watched her die. He kept those poor, old, sick people like dogs. But I continued to drive carefully toward him, around the flooded-out tarn. How very dark it was, how loud the wind.

*"John Charles. . . ."* He lay, propped against a tree, too weak to stand. But I didn't trust his apparent weakness. Don't they say madmen have inhuman strength and cunning? He'd sure proved the truth of that saying.

I found I'd stuck the rope he'd tied me within my pocket and it was still there. My stockinged feet squished through the mud. How cold it was. Rain poured down my face; I could hardly see. I wiped my eyes with my bloody hands. Approaching, I grabbed his arms roughly and tied them behind his back.

"John!" He protested.

"Shut up, you son of a bitch."

I dragged him to the Jeep and with all my strength hoisted him in.

"You're . . . you're covered with blood . . ." he said, his voice faint.

"Shut up."

He shut up. I went around to the driver's side. For a moment I stood there, taking in the situation. Above me, there was a lurid flash of light. The roar of the wind seemed to lessen. Now I saw the clouds, where before the sky had been a roiling mass of inky blackness hidden by sheets of rain. I could hear the hideous cracking and booming as the stone house continued to crash in on itself.

I got into the driver's seat, backed away, and then turned the Jeep carefully; the water was still high and the ground beneath it sodden and treacherous.

I drove slowly out of the water and onto the laneway. Then I stopped and we both turned and looked back through the driver's window.

The clouds broke apart. The moon cast a fierce radiance over the scene, but my window was smeared with blood, so that everything was colored by the bloody hue. The wind, now coming in sudden, whirling gusts, buffeted the collapsing house. The ancient edifice shuddered, cracked; the stone walls tumbled into the flood waters. Nothing remained of the newer wing but rubble. Beyond the crumbling house, the clouds darkened the sky, then parted, and a huge, evil-looking moon cast a blood-red radiance upon the ruins. In its light, I could see debris whirling in the cyclone. Suddenly, there was an enormous sucking, grating sound, so loud that I clapped my hands over my ears. Then the broken walls of the old wing slid silently into the waters and the deep, dank tarn closed over the remains of the House of Usher.

The storm had begun to let up. As I drove toward town I could see that the water level had gone down on the road; the rain fell with less ferocity, and the clouds, now broken, raced away toward the west, allowing the moon to shine through and relieving the darkness in which we had been living for the last three days. Beside me, Rod was mumbling to himself. Occasionally I could distinguish a word or a fragment of a sentence. He spoke in two voices. Sometimes I heard the whisper of Madeleine's voice, other times his own mad intonation.

I passed Crowley Estates, where Marilyn lived. The small houses of the subdivision lay in shambles. Most had lost their roofs. Some had blown off their foundations. Uprooted trees and power lines were strewn about.

The town of Crowley Creek had fared better. Because it was high above the creek, it had missed the brunt of the flood water. The boarded-up buildings, constructed solidly in the last century, looked relatively intact. A few people could be seen walking about, almost aimlessly, taking count of the damage.

At the high school there was an air of relief. Everyone realized that the worst was over. Folks were gathering up their possessions and making plans to go back to their homes—those who still had them. The mayor was bustling about, listening to horror stories and promising to do his best with the state and county authorities. I found Edith and took her aside.

For a moment, we both just looked at each other. Seeing that she was safe, I felt the tight constricting band fastened around my chest loosen, and I breathed freely for the first time since she had driven away into the storm at the head of the convoy.

"That must have been some drive," I said to her, everything forgotten—for the moment—but the fact that she was safe.

She reached up with a finger and touched my face. "John," she said softly, "do you know you are soaked to the skin and covered with blood?" She led me to a chair, found a cloth, and gently wiped my face. "Your face is okay," she said. I couldn't stop looking at her, at her eyes, her face, her shining brown hair, her tender expression. The sight of her soothed my heart. "But your neck . . . what happened?"

When I didn't reply, she carefully wiped my neck and then put some salve on the painful ring where the rope had rubbed it raw. I held up my hands and she gasped, stared for a second, then ran for Dr. Giron.

He bustled over with a medical kit and his usual prissy expression, but when he saw my hands, he too looked taken aback. "Good God man. The backs of your hands and wrists are shredded! You've lost a lot of blood. What in God's name caused this. Did something fall on them?" As he spoke he gently cleaned the skin as best as he could. "You may need plastic surgery. I've never seen anything like this. You must be in great pain."

"He's very pale, doctor," Edith said.

Dr. Giron grumbled when I refused a shot for pain. "You need to get out of those wet clothes as soon as possible. I understand people are going home now. Edith should drive you home at once. As soon as you are dry, you need to get to a proper hospital and have those hands attended to. You hear? Don't be a martyr, man. Time is of the essence with injuries like that."

He went off muttering. How could I tell him I had absorbed so much pain in my heart that what I felt in my hands didn't matter? Sure it hurt, but it was as if I were separated from the hurt by what had happened between me and my old friend. What Rod had told me had shocked me so deeply I could hardly take in the physical pain.

"Let's go, John," Edith said. "You need to get home and

change. You don't even have any boots on. Then we'll go the MCV hospital in Richmond."

"Edith, Rod Usher is in the car outside. He's tied up."

"Tied up? What do you mean?"

"Edith . . . it's a long story. But . . . Rod poisoned Madeleine . . . slowly. Now I think he wants to die too. I don't know what to do."

"John," Edith said. "My God . . ." she looked at me for a long time and seemed to see everything I was feeling. "Well!" she stood up straighter. "First thing, we get you home, looked after, dried off . . ."

"And a whiskey, definitely a whiskey" I said.

"Yes. Then we decide what to do. Is Rod tied up enough so I can drive his Jeep?"

"Yes."

"And can you drive your Bronco? With your hands like that?"

"Yes."

"I wish you didn't have to, but I think it's best. You need to tell me everything so we can decide what to do, and you're in no condition to do that now."

We walked outside together. The pain from my hands began to penetrate into my consciousness. The bandages Dr. Giron had wrapped around them were beginning to turn red. I could feel weakness and exhaustion growing. We needed to get a move on.

Outside, the rain had nearly stopped. A low, sullen, gray cloud mass now hung over the town. It must have been close to dawn. A fine drizzle fell. I pointed out Rod's Jeep Cherokee to Edith and walked over to it. I opened the door on Rod's side. He stared at me with blank eyes. "We're going to Crowley House, Rod," I said. "Edith is going to drive you. Everything will be all right."

"Madeleine is coming too," he said.

Edith shook her head, got into the driver's seat and started it up.

"I'll follow you, I said. "That way I can keep an eye on him. Don't trust him. He's not himself."

"I can see that," Edith said dryly.

"Whatever you do, don't untie him."

"You got it." She put the car in gear and drove slowly off down Central Avenue.

I followed. I could see that she was staring straight ahead and that Rod was slumped against the window. I wondered if he would talk to Edith. Would he tell her about him and Madeleine? Would he say that I had given their incest my blessing? It had been terrible hearing him say that. I dreaded to think he might repeat it to Edith.

Once at Crowley House I found some dry clothes for Rod, which I gave to Edith to help him into. I also managed to change myself, which wasn't easy, considering the state of my hands. I added a new layer of wrappings to the ones Dr. Giron had put on, which were now pretty well soaked through with blood. I was growing weaker and knew I needed treatment. But the nearest real hospital was a forty-five minute drive. Probably the town clinic could not deal with my hands any better than Dr. Giron had. With all the storm damage, many people hurt, medical attention would be hard to get in town. And without power, their means would be limited. But Richmond had missed the brunt of the storm. We had to get to the hospital there.

When I came down into the kitchen, Rod was sitting at

the table wearing my dry clothes and drinking a Coke through a straw. His hands remained tied behind his back. "I told her to untie me," he said to me as soon as I came in. "When she changed my clothes she kept one hand tied to the chair. Then she retied them like this. It's not right, John Charles."

Edith ignored him. "John," she said. "This is what I suggest. I drive you to Richmond for medical treatment. We take him with us and try to find him some help." She gave me a meaningful look. I understood. We both walked out into the hall.

"He's completely bats, John. Nothing he says makes any sense."

"It makes a terrible sense, Edith. Terrible. He murdered his sister."

"Well, he'll never stand trial in the state he's in. He confessed to you?"

"Yes."

"John, we need to take him in."

"I don't know if I can do that."

"If he confessed . . . there's hope, don't you think?"

How my hands hurt. The pain radiated up my arms. I was exhausted. It was hard to think straight. But Edith was right.

With heavy hearts, we walked Rod to the car, tied him into the backseat, and set off for Richmond.

# FIFTEEN

Now I sit here in my father's library reflecting on all these events a month after the second fall of the House of Usher. Before me on my father's desk is the casket. It is open. I have been replacing the papers I loaned to Edith and those I hid in the secret drawer. I am going to put this casket away and not take it out again. My ancestor delved into dark matters better left alone. No reason for me to do the same.

Outside, it is bright and cold. Frost sparkles on the grass and on the branches of the trees, which look almost as if they have grown a skin of crystal. But many of the most beautiful trees are missing. The hurricane felled almost half, some over two centuries old.

As I pick up the casket I see how well my hands are recovering. The skin on the backs is new and pink. The grafts have taken well and should heal with only a few scars. I flex my fingers. They move stiffly and the skin feels tight. The doctors warned me of that effect and said it would pass away.

The house is in better shape than before the hurricane. I had the roof repaired, put in new windows where I needed to and did some structural work. I know now that I am never going to sell it, so I might as well keep it up. As long as the underlying structure is kept sound, it should be good for another century at least.

I know it looks as if I am in good shape too. The short story I wrote about the fall of the House of Usher won the Pacific Prize for fiction. Mrs. Boynton was impressed. Speaking of Mrs. Boynton, she and her buddies lost big on their investments around the House of Usher. That goes for Aldo Marco too. With Rod institutionalized, his property is so tied up legally, it looks as if it will be years before it can be sold to anyone. Since they tried to take advantage of his illness, it seems only fitting.

As for Rod, I can't say I've come to terms with what happened. Why did he call me in the first place? Did his right hand truly not know what his left hand was doing? Or did he see me as someone who was so accepting that I just went along with everything, and so, by my support, gave him permission? It's a terrible thought. Thinking of that now, I get up, go over to the sideboard, and pour myself a good measure of Blanton's single barrel bourbon. A few sips and it seems to matter less.

Rod sure acted surprised when Edith and I took him to the Virginia Psychiatric Institute and had him committed. After we did that, we told the state police the whole story and they went to interview him. They even disinterred Madeleine and did an autopsy. But it all came to nothing. The physical evidence was not conclusive, and in any case, Rod is too mad to be tried.

What is wrong with him? That's what Edith and I talk about often. The psychiatrists don't even have a name for his condition. He doesn't conform to the standard "multiple personality" syndrome, or to schizophrenia, or to anything at all for that matter. I don't think they have a description in their "shrink" book for "man who gives in to evil" disease, or "too much family pride goeth before a fall" disease, or even "loving your sister too much" disease, for that matter. And they sure don't have a cure for any of them either.

Actually, I don't think Rod wants to be cured. He wants to wallow in the death of Madeleine because that is what makes him feel most alive.

What could I have done differently? Would any action of mine have saved Madeleine? Surely there must have been something . . . something . . .

I remember how she looked at me that day I came to Usher's, the day she picked the daisies and seemed so ill. I remember that she said she wanted to talk to me and Rod sent her away. Did he fear she would tell me of their incestuous relationship? Did that fear drive him over the edge? Because she died the next day, so he must have given her the final large dose of digoxin soon after I saw her.

I can't help wondering what he thought of when he wandered about Usher House pretending to be his sister, his twin. Perhaps it eased his pain to take on her persona and believe he was seeking to punish himself. Perhaps he really believed that he became her in those moments, and so transcended her death. I cannot imagine what it must be like to be the lover of your own twin.

Another glass of Blanton's seems called for.

Marilyn is still mad at me. She wants me to stop drinking. Well, Mrs. Boynton does too, for that matter. I feel bad about Marilyn, she's one terrific woman. As for Mrs. Boynton . . . I don't give a damn.

Edith and I are good friends. I admire her very much and she seems to like me too. I'd like there to be more between us, but she doesn't want to talk about it. So I guess we'll just have to wait and see how that turns out.

As for the House of Usher, it is gone. It sank into rubble under the tarn. The tarn itself is so polluted, and the pollutants spread through the old tunnels and into the soil so that in the end the entire property had to be condemned. It will be a long time before it is clean again.

# NOTE TO THE READER

John Charles Poe is a fictional creation. I have taken the liberty of grafting him onto my family tree, inventing for the purpose Laura Crowley. In fact, the best evidence is that Edgar Allan Poe had no direct descendants.

The town of Crowley Creek is also fictional. It has been dropped somewhere in a sixty-mile radius south or southeast or southwest of Richmond, and combines many of the best (and some of the worst) qualities of the small towns in that region. It is obvious, then, that the characters who inhabit Crowley Creek and the novel are also inventions.

The casket papers, on the other hand, are, in part, the work of Edgar Allan Poe. They consist of fragments of his writings, culled from Edgar Allan Poe's journals, letters, and essays. These fragments have been woven together with my own ideas about what he might have written had he in fact produced a trove of secret papers. In truth, he was too busy to do so. As he said himself in the one of the "papers" used in this novel, "I must sell all the works of my pen to make a living." Poe always lived on the edge of poverty, frequently hand to mouth. His life was extremely difficult and the lack of money surely contributed to both the early demise of his wife and his own untimely end.

As for the events in this novel, they are based on Poe's story, "The Fall of the House of Usher." I have taken the events, images, and mysterious subtext of the original story and retold them for our time.

Interested readers might be amused to revisit the original story and see how its events reappear: phrases, images, sounds, and context from Edgar Allan Poe's masterpiece have been threaded into this "sequel."

The continuing interest in my ancestor's work shows that one intriguing way to enter into the battle between good and evil, life and death, sanity and madness, is in the pages of fiction. In 1839 his aim was to entertain, to provoke, and to deepen his reader's perceptions of the reality on the edge of the world of the everyday.

I have tried to be a worthy student of the master.

—Robert Poe,
Virginia Beach, 1996

For a complimentary copy of the Robert Poe newsletter, please write to:

The Robert Poe Newsletter
c/o Forge Books
175 Fifth Avenue
14th Floor
New York, NY 10010

# Available by mail from

**TOR FORGE**

## 1812 • David Nevin
The War of 1812 would either make America a global power sweeping to the Pacific or break it into small pieces bound to mighty England. Only the courage of James Madison, Andrew Jackson, and their wives could determine the nation's fate.

## PRIDE OF LIONS • Morgan Llywelyn
*Pride of Lions*, the sequel to the immensely popular *Lion of Ireland*, is a stunningly realistic novel of the dreams and bloodshed, passion and treachery, of eleventh-century Ireland and its lusty people.

## WALTZING IN RAGTIME • Eileen Charbonneau
The daughter of a lumber baron is struggling to make it as a journalist in turn-of-the-century San Francisco when she meets ranger Matthew Hart, whose passion for nature challenges her deepest held beliefs.

## BUFFALO SOLDIERS • Tom Willard
Former slaves had proven they could fight valiantly for their freedom, but in the West they were to fight for the freedom and security of the white settlers who often despised them.

## THIN MOON AND COLD MIST • Kathleen O'Neal Gear
Serving in the trenches as a Civil War Confederate spy, a woman of the West makes her way alone towards the promise of the untamed Colorado frontier—until her new life has room for love.

## SPIRIT OF THE EAGLE • Vella Munn
Luash, a young woman of the Modoc tribe, tries to stop the Secretary of War from destroying her people.

## THE OVERLAND TRAIL • Wendi Lee
Based on the authentic diaries of the women who crossed the country in the late 1840s. America, a widowed pioneer, and Dancing Feather, a young Paiute, set out to recover America's kidnapped infant daughter—and to forge a bridge between their two worlds.